# Secret Keeper

# Secret Keeper

*Secret Keeper Trilogy*
*Book 1*

Melanie Joye

Historical Romance by
Melanie Joye
from

*Wisteria Publications*

**Wisteria Publications**
507-4 Briar Hill Heights
New Tecumseth, ON
L9R 1Z7


**Secret Keeper**
ISBN: 978-1-988763-22-4
Copyright © 2019 by Melanie Joye

Published in Canada 2019

Layout and Cover Art by Taria van Weesenbeek
Back Cover Photo Credit: Melanie Climenhage

Please contact the author at jamn2@rogers.com for any questions or comments.

*Do not move an ancient boundary stone or encroach on the fields of the fatherless*

*Proverbs 23:10 - NIV*

## Keeper Trilogy

# Acknowledgements

*I want to thank my editor Kaarina Brooks and my readers: Sara, Nancy, Raili and Cathy.*

# Secret Keeper

## *Keeper Trilogy Book One*

| **MacEwen Keep** | **Campbell Keep** | **Rose Keep** |
|---|---|---|
| | Angus Campbell | |
| Fallon MacEwen | Annella Campbell | Justus De Ros |
| Lochlan MacEwen | Iain Campbell | |
| Brianna MacEwen | | |
| | | Caol De Ros |
| | | Bonnie of Rose |
| | | Davyd De Ros |

## Prologue

**AD—1575**, somewhere in the Scottish Highlands

Annella lay entangled with Lochlan on the velvety moss. Hidden. Their marriage was consummated. Nothing could come between them.

What had awakened her? She smiled at her husband. He still lay deep in sleep exhausted from their loving. She trailed a finger across his cheek and down the side of his tanned face. Something deep within her leapt for joy.

Married!

The tumbled down kirk had been the perfect place for them to exchange their vows. Ancestors before her had been baptized, married and buried in that holy place. The memories and spirits that lingered there were their witnesses. Before God, and the unseen world of those who had lived long ago, they had knelt at the crumbled stone altar facing each other.

"In life and in death, I pledge my life, my love, my heart to you. I am yours." Lochlan's voice had been clear and firm as he had looked into her dark eyes. And then, it was her turn. She smiled. His beautiful face always elicited that response from her. He did not like her describing him as beautiful but his eyes, the colour of sea foam or mayhap a silver moon, drew her in to unending places always yearning to learn about him.

"In life and in death, I pledge my life, my love, my heart to you. I am yours," she said. Her voice trembled.

Lochlan had torn a thin strip of wool from his plaid. He took her hand. "In the name of the Father." He wrapped the strip around their joined hands once.

"In the name of the Son." She wrapped the strip around their joined hands.

"In the name of the Holy Ghost," they chorused and wrapped it a final time together. "Amen".

An infusion of warmth had encompassed her from a spot deep in her heart. She was Lochlan MacEwen's wife, no longer Annella Campbell but Annella MacEwen. Her spirit danced and twirled in celebration.

For a moment, they had stared at each other, slow grins forming. Then, without speaking, they had reached out and embraced. When his lips met hers in their first husband and wife kiss, the sun had escaped the clouds and scattered dancing rays to caress their embrace, acknowledging the union. Even the purple thistles seemed to bow solemnly to this sacred event.

Lochlan had taken her hand and led her to their secret place. Here, surrounded by age old stones and moss, they stood before each other. Lochlan reached for her and slipped a gold band on her finger, a symbol to represent the unbreaking bond of their union. He tugged the ribband from the end of her coiled braid and ran his fingers through her tresses. He pulled her to him, opening the laces of her gown, exploring hesitantly. Then boldly. New discoveries.

They lay, naked, curled in each other's arms. Exhausted. Married.

Annella snapped her head up and looked at the barren rocks around her. Why had the ground shaken? She remained as still as the blackened crags that rose up to hide them. Listening, waiting. Lochlan slept. He was known to sleep through much. His older brother Fallon always jested that lightning could strike and the castle could fall and still Lochlan would sleep.

The vibrations travelled through her body, louder, more forceful. The ground shook again. No, it rumbled. Closer. Harder. Was the ground opening up, angry because of their clandestine marriage? Surely not. This was their special place, camouflaged and protected by rocks and layers of stones. Lochlan and she had happened upon this covert spot months ago as they were exploring together. Hopes and dreams had come to life here. Surely, they were safe from danger and enemies.

Again the warning tremor. Horses! Riders! And there were many! She knew immediately that they were her father's men. She'd been gone too long, too many hours. This had been her special day, planned carefully and secretly with Lochan, but she should have known they would come. It seemed someone was always watching her, monitoring her every move.

The pounding of thunderous hooves vibrated up her arms. Annella looked at Lochlan. Should she awaken him? Should they run? Would her father's men find them? Her Da, Angus Campbell, always demanded his orders to be followed. On many occasions, she had witnessed members of her clan trembling before him, their Laird, when he was angered.

Annella sensed danger. The riders would soon be upon them. What of Lochlan? What if they were found? She couldn't risk endangering him.

Voices yelled, bellowed, rumbled together. She closed her eyes tight, drawing in an angry breath. She recognized a voice—Ruadh, the Campbell's lead warrior. Danger was close and moving closer. Quickly, Annella dressed and braided her hair. Without thought, she snatched the wedding strip, that thin piece of plaid, from the ground and tied it to the tip of her coiled hair. She scrambled through the rocks, looking back to Lochlan one last time. She took in her husband's face, his body and breathed in his spirit. Turning away, she took the danger with her.

Annella peeked over the edge of a boulder. The Campbell men rested upon their horses. Some of them drank from a flask. Ruadh stood with two warriors pointing in various directions. No! They were planning to divide the group and search the area.

Annella scrambled around a large rock and through the adjoining copse of trees. To confuse them, she approached the group from the opposite direction from where her husband lay. She was only a running step away from the edge of the wood when her braid tangled in a low branch. She fumbled quickly with the snag. They were coming! She panicked and all but ripped her hair from the branch and ran out into the meadow. Breathing deeply, she slowed and walked toward them. Ruadh turned and approached, holding the reins of her mare in his hands. Obviously Ruadh had anticipated finding her since her mare had been brought along to return her home.

Staring ahead, erect and silent, Annella rode on her mare toward the Campbell Keep. She secreted away the golden band into the folds of her garment. Lochlan was safe. She would send a message to him later to explain. But for now, all that remained of the afternoon's union was her sleeping husband and a strip of plaid tangled in a tree branch waving in the wind.

*Chapter One*

**1600 AD**—25 years later

Braeson wandered through the long wooden barn studying the ponies that sheltered there. He reached out his hand and touched a dark roan on its nose. The Seiltainn stilled and stared at him. He should have brought along some treats.

A rustling noise behind him drew Braeson's attention. Frowning, he turned his head sharply looking to the ponies on the opposite side of the long walkway that snaked through the middle of the low shed. A human form hurled itself at him. Reds and golds twirled. Hair? Hands and nails scratched at his face. Girl? Woman? He crashed to the hard dirt floor, lying on his back to ward off the punches. Fists flung at him. A knee ground into his gut keeping him pinned. Raising his arms over his face, he realized he must do more to protect himself, for the creature was not stopping and neither was she losing strength. He reached below her bruising knee and grabbed a slender ankle, flinging her from him. Screeching, she landed on her back, legs and skirts swirling. He leapt to his feet.

A woman-fiend raised herself from the ground growling at him, glaring. Braeson wondered at her colouring, at eyes that were the same shade as her hair, deep copper with golden specks. Heat radiated from her as she surged toward him again, like a snapping flame from a fire. This time he was ready and, sneering, he caught her around the waist pulling the she-demon against him. A low guttural sound emanated from her as she raised her scorn-filled face to him. A sprinkle of freckles travelled across the bridge of her nose and a few were painted beneath her burnished copper eyes.

A smile pushed through his sneer. He was winning this struggle as he pinned her hands behind her back and . . . he gasped at the sheer pain that surged across the side of his head. His breath escaped him as he stared, amazed. The she-fiend had whacked him behind his left ear with a blunt object. Had she a third hand for he had been certain that he held both securely?

Dizziness overtook him as he stumbled to the dirt floor. Confusion spun as the shadowy grays of the barn dimmed to pewter . . . charcoal. Darkness embraced him.

Braeson stirred, raising a hand to his head. Mumbled voices floated in the distance. Were they coming closer?

"Here Caol. Tis here." A woman's disdainful voice slithered into his awakening consciousness. Feet shuffled and stopped beside him. Opening his eyes, Braeson swam back from the darkness, to pewter and finally the grays of the shed returned.

The she-fiend stood over him, sneering, with hands on her hips "I hit him here, Caol."

"Chit!" Braeson growled rubbing the side of his head. Wet. "You are a chit!" he roared at the she-demon. "Reckless chit." He held out his hand, staring at the blood.

"I'm no chit" she snarled and then frowned. "What's a chit?"

"You!" Braeson shouted, wincing. He closed his eyes to ward off the pain. What object did she use to inflict such agony? He scanned the area close to him but could not identify the weapon.

"Thief!" she sneered and raised herself higher, glaring down her straight nose, her copper eyes burning holes through him. "Reiver, you'll not take the ponies."

Another stepped into his view. Braeson breathed a sigh of relief. This person was a friend. "Caol, do you know this she-demon?" he growled through his clenched teeth.

Caol knelt on one knee, studying him. His grin grew as he spoke. "She clobbered you good, English."

"He was stealing the ponies, Caol. I smacked him upside his noggin."

The she-demon had the audacity to smirk.

"This thief fell." She smacked her hands together. "Hard!"

Braeson frowned at his friend's grinning face. His head pounded. Damned demon.

"Her fists are fast. But faster yet is her sling," Caol replied with a hint of contained humour in his voice. Braeson noticed that his friend also rubbed the side of his head, as if remembering a past experience.

Braeson eyed the she-demon who still stood, arms akimbo, glaring at him. He wondered how long he had lain on the dirt floor. He rubbed his head again. The pain was ebbing and it appeared the bleeding had stopped. He took a deep breath. Her attack could have been fatal had she hit him harder. He shook his head to nudge away the thought of Braemoore losing two Masters within a year.

"Take him to the dungeon, Caol?" the she-demon questioned. "Let him stew for a time."

"What have you done?" boomed another voice from not too far away.

"Tis a thief, Lochlan. A reiver. Trying to steal some ponies." She lifted her chin higher and glared at Braeson. Her copper eyes accusing, condemning. "I smacked him on the head. Caol is taking him to the dungeon."

A man squatted beside Braeson, his gaze intent. Braeson noticed the startled look that crossed the man's face as he took in his appearance, his coat and clothes. The man placed a hand on the floor as if to steady himself. "A reiver?" he whispered. His pale grey eyes studied Braeson for a moment longer. "Tis a long way to come and steal?"

"Lochlan, tis Braeson, the Earl of Braemoore from north England," explained Caol. "You recall he was to visit Rose Castle in hopes of purchasing ponies?" Caol looked at Braeson with a tinge of amusement in his eyes. He extended his hand toward Lochlan, who still squatted beside Braeson staring at him with a peculiar wide-eyed gape. "Braeson, tis Lochlan MacEwen."

Braeson took note of a serious calm that descended on Caol as his friend rose and turned to the she-demon.

"Tis Bonnie of Rose." Caol gave the young woman a warning scowl. "An apology will be made before the day's end."

The man, Lochlan MacEwen, rose. "Caol, I trust you'll take the Earl to Lady Brianna. And you," he turned to Bonnie of Rose. "You saucy lass, to the fields with you. There are sheep to be herded to the lower pasture and you will help."

"But, Lochlan," argued the she-demon. "He is a reiver. You'll not trust him."

"He is a guest of this castle," bellowed Lochlan. "I've not known you to be a fool before . . . Silkie." A tenderness emanated from the man's voice when the endearment was spoken.

"But, Lochlan—" she began.

The man took the chit by the elbow and led her toward the shed door. "He is a guest," boomed Lochlan. "Egads. You are shaming your Laird, Justus De Ros!"

"But Lochlan, he must be a thief. He is English!" declared the she-demon.

"There are good English! You saucy lass!" retorted Lochlan, tugging her through the door and out of Braeson's view.

Her final words floated back to him. "Name one, Lochlan," she challenged. "Who is one good English?"

Braeson, Fourth Earl of Braemoore, closed his eyes and took a deep breath. He and Caol had arrived at the castle about an hour past. Already he had been hit over the head, knocked out, threatened with the dungeon and declared a *no good English.*

Braeson heard snickering and then a snort. Opening his eyes, he saw Caol doubled over, grasping his belly and howling with laughter.

"Welcome to Rose Castle, Braeson," sputtered Caol.

# Chapter Two

Bonnie crept along the wall of the bailey toward the kitchen door. If she could just sneak away to her chamber unseen, she could care for her sore feet.

Lochlan had refused to allow her to ride her mare, Daisy, to fetch the sheep. Instead, he had told her to walk which would provide her a chance to calm down and think about her foolish action. The walk to and from the field had been too long and too arduous.

Bonnie placed her hand against the door, pushing it open inch by inch. Stepping into the kitchen, she stopped and took a deep breath. Cook stood across the room, his back to Bonnie, working at a table. She edged around the kitchen and sidled into the corridor, her hopes rising that she'd reach her room unseen. Brianna, Justus De Ros' wife, met her at the bottom of the stairs.

"Bonnie," Lady Brianna uttered on a sigh. The Lady's eyebrows were arched and she didn't smile.

"You will return to the kitchen and prepare a healing poultice for the Earl's wound." Lady Brianna said little else, as she took Bonnie firmly by the elbow and escorted her back to the kitchen.

The Lady stood over her as Bonnie perched on a high stool before the mortar and pestle board grinding together the dried fern and ivy leaves. She poured the powder into a wooden bowl and mixed it with mutton tallow. Soon, it formed into a firm poultice. She placed it in a small pewter container which she slipped into the folds of her gown. Bonnie turned to Brianna. She was unsure as to how she would present the healing substance to the Earl but by the look on Brianna's face she could not tarry with her decision.

"Bonnie," Brianna shook her head. "I am without words." She shook her head again and paused for a moment staring at Bonnie. "Come along, lass." Linking her arm with Bonnie's, Brianna led her in silence up the stairs and into Bonnie's chamber. A tub of warm water had been readied and Nell, a castle maid, was waiting.

Brianna sighed deeply. "Bonnie, I have raised you as a lady and a lady you will be this eve. You will scrub yourself clean and dress in your green gown. You will prepare your hair and be on your best behaviour at the dinner when we welcome our guest!" Another deep sigh. "You will offer the poultice and apologize to our guest."

Bonnie noticed that Brianna emphasized the last word, guest. "I thought—" she began.

"You thought wrong, lass," replied Brianna. "You will apologize."

"But, I thought—"

"De Ros demands that you apologize," continued Brianna.

"But—"

"I must agree with him. You have not shown our guest our Scottish hospitality," Brianna's eyebrows rose higher.

"But, no English deserves our hospi—"

"Enough!" Brianna stated, her terse tone signaling the end of the conversation. "Prepare yourself, lass." She walked to the chamber door, then paused and turned back. "Bonnie."

Swallowing, Bonnie stared into Brianna's grim grey eyes, hesitant to reply. What more did the Lady have to say? "Aye, Brianna."

"You will dance with the Earl tonight as well." And with that, Brianna closed the door behind her.

Bonnie's groan began low in her chest and rose into a loud growled bellow. She was certain she heard Brianna chuckle as she walked along the hallway. She spun around to find Nell peering at her.

"Come lass. Let us get to work. Let us ready for this

eve." Nell drew her to the tub of water and began to unlace her gown.

Bonnie's head ached as she sat in the warm water allowing Nell to lather her hair with soap. Closing her eyes, she thought again of her absurd day. Her feet still burned from the laborious walk, herding the sheep to the glen below the castle. She really had believed that Earl English was a reiver. Lochlan had not given her a chance to explain.

*His clothes alone were not of a reiver,* he had roared. *Reivers do not dress in English garb.* Bonnie shook her head to chase away the memory of Lochlan's anger. Twas common for one Scottish clan to steal from another. Mayhap the reiver had dressed in disguise to not implicate another clan. She had been so certain that the stranger in the pony shed had been a thief. Bonnie rubbed her eyes, unsure if the moisture in them was from the tub water or her tears.

Bonnie donned her green gown. She swayed her hips before the chamber mirror and was pleased to see the gown's hem swirl around her ankles. She and Brianna had stitched the gown over the winter to welcome these early spring days. She sat on the chair in front of her chamber desk as Nell brushed her hair into a shine. The maid twisted the coppery tresses into a side braid that fell over the front of her shoulder. Then, she wove a splash of wood violets into the braid that complimented the jewelled spring green of the gown.

"Tis good, tis good. Fresh and lovely," Nell exclaimed. The maid smiled and then winked as she tucked the small pewter container into Bonnie's hand. "All will be well, lass. All will be well, this eve."


Bonnie stood in the archway of the great room, peering into the dark night. Her heart beat too fast for her task was not complete. She was unsure how to present her apology and the healing poultice to Earl English. She smiled into the dark. Earl English, she had named him, even though others called him Braeson. She wrinkled her nose and wondered about his strange moniker. Braeson. Son of Brae? For certain, twas odd.

She took a single step through the archway and then another and another until she had faded into the garden away from the celebration. The sounds of the breeze mingled with the lively flute that cascaded across the yard from the great room. De Ros and his people were still celebrating the arrival of Caol's friend, the Earl of Braemoore. Voices floated into the garden and she heard the stamping and clapping of dancers.

Before taking her seat at the Laird's table, Bonnie had greeted the family. The look in De Ros' eyes made it clear as to what he expected. Lochlan sat with his men across the room but she felt his glare without even having to seek out his steely gray eyes. Caol, the Laird's son, silently mocked her, looking at her with veiled amusement. Bonnie had chosen a seat far down the long wooden table to avoid any further interaction with Earl English.

Later, Bonnie had danced in various groups and formations and several times had found herself partnering and exchanging dance steps with Earl English. All evening long, she truly had been the lady that Brianna had demanded. Finally, she had snuck away to this garden to contemplate her apology.

Bonnie patted a small fold in her gown where the pewter container with its healing ointment nestled. There was no way to avoid it. She must get on with it.

A rustle to her right caused her to turn quickly and peer into the darkness. Her heart beat even faster and she drew a deep breath. She would not be afraid and she would not respond. Isn't that how she had walked into, nay, flown into Earl English this morn? She had been working in a far corner of the pony shed, when she heard a similar sound, a slight rustle. Peeking around the corner, she had seen the stranger. Fear had overcome her and . . . Bonnie shook her head. Twas a chaotic start to a verra tiring day.

There it was again. The sound. This time a scraping, as if something was crawling along the garden wall.

Her fear pushed her backward step by step away from the darkness and toward the celebration. She would find Earl English and apologize.

Her hand flew to her mouth as a man stepped before her.

"Donal!" Relief flooded over her to see her dear friend, standing silently and gazing at her. Yet as she stared back, she felt her ire rise. "Have I been assigned a guard, Donal?" Bonnie demanded. Had Donal, a lead guard at Rose Castle, been sent to keep an eye on her? De Ros and Brianna and even Lochlan knew that she would apologize—eventually. And, she would apologize well! She just had to determine how to do that. She took a deep breath, the chill of the night air filling her nose and lungs.

"Nay Bonnie," Donal held the torch he carried a bit higher, studying her. "I come as a friend. I saw you step out and followed." He shrugged and then smiled.

Bonnie narrowed her eyes at her friend's too innocent expression. "Does the whole castle know of my encounter with Earl English?" Bonnie raised her fingers to her lips. She had not meant for anyone to hear of her moniker for the Rose Castle guest.

Donal shook his head, laughter in his eyes. "Only the castle's lead guards have been told of a strange and ludicrous tale from this morn." The vague humour in his eyes sobered to troubled unease. "Tis a serious concern, aye?" He frowned, looking intently at her. "What were you thinking Bonnie, clobbering him? The Earl of Braemoore comes as an invited guest to our Laird De Ros' home."

Bonnie took a step away from Donal, crossing her arms. "Twas a reiver, I thought."

"Tis near impossible to penetrate unknown into Rose lands and the castle." Again, Donal stepped beside her. "You know it could not be a thief in the pony shed." He turned his head toward her. "Bonnie?" His voice seemed too dark and too serious. "You appeared frightened as I stepped into this garden, just now."

She lifted her shoulders, then dropped them. Should she share her fear? "Twas a stirring. There." Bonnie pointed toward the spot from where the strange noises had come. It was in the opposite direction from where Donal had appeared. She looked at her friend, whose eyes flickered to the location and then back to her. A fearful chill skittered up her back as she followed Donal to the spot. Staying close to him, Bonnie watched as he lifted the torch high, waving it in various directions.

Donal looked at her as if to speak and then turned again to stare into the darkness. All was still now.

"Lass, too many strange events are happening around you." He raised a hand to count. "A broken board on the walking bridge, a stray arrow in the forest beyond the glen. We could not determine the owner of the arrow. Twas unmarked. But we have determined that you are not safe." Taking a deep breath, Donal turned bit by bit toward her. "I would have a solution to this problem." He paused. "Let us wed."

Bonnie was sure her eyes popped from her head as she stared back at Donal. She had wandered into the garden to think about her apology, not to be confronted by an absurd and unexpected marriage proposal. Yet the chill caused by Donal's words rose higher up her back. It floated around her, leaving her without words to retaliate, to oppose Donal's suggestion.

"I wonder how many other strange happenings have occurred that you have not spoken of." Donal's brows lifted as if he knew the answer to his question. "If you married you would be safe. A wife stays close to her husband's family. A wife does not wander far, now that her attentions are with her home. You would be always in close proximity to me and to my parents." He paused and then rushed on with his argument. "They love you dear. An eye on you at all times. Safety would be yours. I know we are like sister and brother, but . . ."

Bonnie was unsure when she started shaking her head—back and forth, back and forth. Slowly at first but then faster until finally she stopped in awe of

Donal's words. In awe of his willing sacrifice. "You would marry me to keep me safe? A marriage between friends without a deep wife and husband love?"

"Aye, Bonnie. These strange events are causing De Ros and the guards great concern for your well-being. Twas fear that drove you to attack the Earl." He touched her arm as if to waylay her. "Nay, do not turn away from the truth, Bonnie." Donal raised his hands and then let them fall to his sides. "In the past, you ran from the incidents, the arrow, the crumbling bridge—"

She lifted her head, feigning courage even though it was fast dwindling away. "I walked alone to the back field today and returned unharmed. All went well." She looked down to her feet, choosing not to mention how they still ached from the trek. Yet it was when she raised her head and saw Donal look past her, that her suspicions rose. "Tell me true. Was I assigned a guard? Today, to the field and back? And now, this eve?" She crossed her arms. "And De Ros and even Lochlan have encouraged your proposal. To settle me, get me out of the way so I stop hitting the guests and averting stray arrows and ruining walking bridges —"

"Shh, lass. Tis true that guards are keeping an eye on you." He paused. "And, tis the reason I followed you to this garden." When he nudged her arm with his own, she knew it was his attempt to lessen her growing hysteria. "But twas my own idea to propose. To offer you my protection."

This conversation had to come to an end. The entire day seemed ludicrous. "Donal," she began. "I canna marry you. Your sacrifice is too great. For certain."

"Bonnie," Donal said. "We must consider ways, solutions, to protect you." Donal rubbed his hand over the top of his head and took a deep breath." Marrying is a good way to protect you . . . Silkie."

"Do not use that word," she hissed. She shook her head. Silkie! She had grown up with Donal and he knew she hated that nekename and its association with her lost family and lineage. Yet he pushed on seemingly refusing to be waylaid by her protest to that word. He was too serious. Too brooding. Too, too right.

"Tis a reasonable idea. A solution to a verra grave situation," Donal retorted.

Again the chill floated around her. Fear of what she knew to be true. She did not know why she was stumbling into misfortunes of late. Marriage would offer her added protection and might be a reasonable solution. Yet she could not marry Donal. She loved him only as a dear friend. A brother. The dear man believed it was his duty to offer her marriage and his protection. Donal's sacrifice would be too great. Too great indeed. And, it had not gone unnoticed how he had taken deep breaths each time he spoke the word marriage to her, as if he had to find the courage to ask. To ask without feeling husband and wife love. Now it was her turn to find the courage to end this peculiar conversation.

"Donal," she began. "Lady Brianna says that I will choose my own husband. I cannot be tied to a loveless betrothal because strange events are happening around me. We cannot allow these misadventures to push us into another catastrophe." She sighed. "Though I am verra honoured that you would offer . . . my dear friend."

Bonnie wondered if Donal was relieved at her refusal in the way a slow smile curved his lips. But when he spoke his eyes narrowed and his voice was again dark and serious.

"So be it, Silkie. But, tis a dire situation." Shaking his head, Donal scanned the garden a final time. He placed the burning torch into a wall scone and turned to her. "All is well, here, in this garden," he said and walked away into the night.

Bonnie stomped to the wooden bench alongside the garden wall. She knew Donal was going to find Flora. Donal had asked for Bonnie's hand out of duty but she knew his heart was set on Flora. Never would she allow Donal to sacrifice his happiness, his deep feelings for Flora, in order to protect her. He was a dear friend and a loyal clansman.

She slumped onto the wooden bench and shook her head, peering into the black night and pulling her shawl closer to ward off the cool air. She simply hated the word Silkie, the nekename that had become hers. She counted three times this day that it had been whispered, first by Lochlan and then by Donal.

Her ire rose and she sat straighter to ward off her desire to scream into the darkness. The burning sensation in her feet seemed to be screaming quite loudly enough already. She peered down at her feet to ensure they were not on fire and at the same time swiped a small stone from the ground. She rubbed it in her hand. Today, she had been yelled at, scolded, glared at and silently mocked, not to mention her feet had been blistered, all because of him—Earl English.

She rubbed the stone more vigorously, her pique rising even higher, and then without thought, flung it down the garden pathway.

"Bloody hell!" echoed from the darkness.

"Oh!" Bonnie leapt to her feet just as Earl English and Caol stepped into the torch-light of the garden. She was shocked and amazed for there Earl English stood, frozen on the pathway, holding his hand to his head and staring at her. How could she have timed the stone toss so perfectly to skelp Earl English in the middle of his forehead?

"Bonnie," gasped Caol. He looked at her and then at

the Earl. It seemed that even Caol, who never lacked for words, did not know what to say. "Bonnie lass," he began again. "We've been looking for you. Silkie."

She was as speechless as the Earl who, like she, turned to Caol staring at him, expectantly, waiting for him to continue to speak, to undo the awkwardness of this situation.

"Bonnie," Caol began again for a third time. "De Ros told me that you wished to speak with the Earl." He looked at his friend and then at her as if he would continue. Instead, Caol bowed slightly and walked away leaving her alone with silent Earl English who still held his hand to his forehead.

Bonnie heard Caol snickering, muttering that hated moniker that was hers—Silkie. He would probably soon be grasping his belly and howling with laughter. She just hoped he wouldn't tell anyone that she'd smacked Earl English . . . again.

# Chapter Three

Braeson counted to ten in at least three languages before he turned from the dark shadow of his friend disappearing down the path. He breathed deeply, dropping his hands to his sides and stared at the chit who sat slumped on the bench muttering. She wore the she-demon face again, with her eyebrows drawn together and lips curled in a snarl. He felt his stomach tighten.

Disappointment.

Disappointment for the loss of the lovely young woman that he had discovered this eve at the celebration. Indeed, Braeson had watched Bonnie carefully if just to monitor her whereabouts at the feast. Would she attack him again if the opportunity arose? Had she pummeled him because she thought he was a thief, or was it because he was English? He still felt pressure on his head where she had walloped him.

Yet Braeson's apprehension had been replaced with admiration for the lovely young woman celebrating alongside her people, smiling, dancing and chatting. Even now, the revelry continued as the minstrel's lively strains floated into the night air.

Braeson had enjoyed the country jigs and several times had found himself partnering with the she-demon in a group formation. They had latched arms to swing in a circle and grasped hands, raising them skyward, as they captured the cadence and rhythm of the beating drums and lyres. He had turned his gaze again and again to her smiling, laughing face. Her green gown complimented the cinnamon hues of her hair and eyes, swirling lightly over her figure and accentuating the swell of her breast, the dip at her waist and her curving hips. Yet she had refused to acknowledge his presence, averting her eyes and giving her smile to another. She had curtsied politely after each dance but had turned away quickly. Braeson had found himself wanting her to look at him, to smile and laugh with him, and he wanted to see again the flash of fire in her cinnamon eyes that matched the russet hues of her hair.

Dear God, what was he thinking? Perchance the whack on his head had rattled his thoughts. Sometime during the evening the lovely dancing woman had disappeared, replaced now by this muttering she-demon who sat before him and who—bloody hell!—had just walloped him again.

Braeson touched his forehead and felt a slight dampness. She certainly knew how to draw blood. He pressed the palm of his hand against the spot hoping to quell the slight trickle. He peered at the ground looking for the weapon that had pierced him. He was sure it had been a mere stone yet only a few pebbles scattered the yard and some crumpled leaves fluttered at his feet.

Braeson slid his eyes again to the chit sitting on the wooden bench. Lady Brianna had urged Caol to accompany him to find Bonnie and he had an inkling he knew what it was about. Bonnie wished to speak to him, the Lady had explained. He'd prefer to forget the whole business but Scottish hospitality demanded that the she-demon apologize. Best get this over with.

Braeson squatted down face-level with Bonnie, and bit by bit, she pulled her eyes from the darkness and looked at him. Tears? What was this? This creature was not the she-demon he had battled, nor the lovely young woman he had danced with, but someone new. Silent tears slid down her face. A face that now reflected that of a childish maiden?

He pressed a hand to his temple, sliding it round to the back of his neck in an attempt to rub away his palpable tension. He was wearying of the many faces of this chit. "You wished to speak with me?" Braeson began.

"I am no Silkie!" She raised a fist and pounded it into her lap.

"Silkie?" Braeson frowned. What did a Silkie have to do with this apology?

"Caol called me a Silkie." She bowed her head and wiped away a tear.

"A nekename, perchance, to express love. Hmm?" Why was he trying to soothe her? Why was his head pounding again? Why could this not be finished?

"I do not like that love name. Many whisper it. Lochlan, Donal..." Her voice trailed off.

Lochlan had called her Silkie in the shed this morn, Braeson recalled. Caol too had just whispered the moniker. Both times it was expressed as a term of endearment. Ah, Donal. He had met Donal a few moments ago coming along the path. Caol and Donal had exchanged comments about a failed marriage proposal. Now he understood. Could it be that the chit was upset because Donal had not proposed? That would explain the tears. Braeson drew a deep breath. How did one comfort a childish maiden?

"Auld Maeve used to tell me stories of Silkies," he reassured her. He was no bard, but all loved stories he reckoned. Perchance it would soothe her temper. "In Auld Maeve's stories, Silkies are well-loved."

"Auld Maeve?" Bonnie raised her eyes. A glimmer of

anticipation sat at their edges. She was interested.

"Aye, my mother's maid," Braeson explained. "Auld Maeve always had a story to share."

"Let me hear these tales, of a Silkie well-loved," she challenged.

Did she just shift a bit to one side of the bench to make room for him? He narrowed his eyes, wondering if it was a covert attempt to hit him again. He scanned the area checking for hidden weapons before sitting beside her. When he turned his gaze back to her, her smile encouraged him to relax.

"Once there was a man who wandered along the ocean's shore," he began. "He came upon a creature, half human and half seal."

"A Silkie?" asked Bonnie.

Braeson was sure the freckles sprinkled across her lovely nose matched the colour of her eyes. "A Silkie," he continued. "The creature was hurt, close to death." As Bonnie leaned toward him, drawing a deep breath, eyes shining like embers in a warm fire, his disappointment faded. Returning was the strange sense of exaltation he had experienced when dancing with her. "The man pulled the creature from the seal skin and carried the beautiful woman to his home. He cared for her, poured oils onto her wounds and with time she healed."

"What happened to this man and the Silkie?"

Bonnie whispered. Her breath caressed his face. The aroma from the sweet wine served at the meal wafted around them. The golden specks in her eyes sparkled. The lovely woman he had met earlier this evening had reappeared.

"They fell in love and married. They were blessed with children and the family lived contentedly until one day a stranger knocked at their door." Braeson's voice deepened, signaling doom. "It was the Silkie's sister."

"Sister?" Bonnie repeated.

"Aye," Braeson continued. "The sister had shed her fur to come ashore in search of the Silkie. The sister had wandered far and wide, lost, until she happened upon the man's small home."

"But why?" asked Bonnie. "Why was the sister searching?"

"To tell the beautiful Silkie that their father was dying and he wanted to see her one last time."

"Oh, no!" Bonnie raised her fingertips to her mouth.

Braeson stopped, staring at her lips, full and luscious.

"Go on!" she urged.

Go on and kiss her? He actually was considering it. Fool! And when Bonnie rested her hand on his arm, he did the proper thing and placed his hand upon hers, caressing it softly.

"Go on," she repeated. "What happened?"

"The beautiful woman agreed to return to her father's sea house. The man and woman wept together through the long night for they knew that she might never find her way to that shore again."

As Bonnie frowned in confusion at this part of his tale, he wondered if she realized how lovely she was. "Remember," he cautioned. "The Silkie was washed ashore and did not come there on her own. She knew not the way. Nor did her sea sister."

"Oh my!" Bonnie muttered.

"In time the man fell asleep, exhausted from weeping. But the Silkie remained awake, watching as their tears turned magically into translucent pearls." Braeson fell silent for a moment watching her eyes turn to darkened hues. "The Silkie strung the beautiful stones together, creating two necklaces, matching and beautiful. Just before she took leave in the morn, the Silkie slipped one necklace around her husband's neck and the other around her own."

His eyes flittered to Bonnie's neck as she lifted her hand to it as if living the tale, and he battled his growing desire to kiss her lips, her neck. He breathed deeply and continued.

"'These are our tears that show the beauty of our love,' the Silkie explained. She urged her husband to wear it always." Braeson felt his heartbeat quicken as

Bonnie leaned closer, her sigh gently brushing his face.

"Neither knew how long they would be parted," Braeson continued. "They might grow old and not recognize each other. They promised to always wear the necklaces to help find their way back to one another. Then, the Silkie and her sister crawled into their fur skins and jumped into the sea," Braeson concluded.

"Tis sad," said Bonnie, her eyes brimming with tears. "Did they ever find each other again?"

"I know naught," said Braeson. "Auld Maeve would not tell me the end of the story."

"Well, tis not a loving story! Nay!" she protested. "I have listened to our bard spin a much finer story of love." Her hand curled into a fist and she thumped it onto her lap.

"Auld Maeve believes it to be a true love story," he stated.

Bonnie's eyes flashed fiery sparks and then she frowned at him.

"The story is full of hope." Braeson countered her unspoken argument.

"Hope?" She shook her head and a few cinnamon tresses fell from her side braid, curling delicately around her face. "I think not. Mayhap the pair are lost forever. Aye." She nodded agreeing with herself.

Braeson smiled. "Auld Maeve believes that you can never be lost if you are looking for love. For that is the hope of love. Surely, you will find it." Braeson moved closer to study her lovely face, watching as her eyes widened and her delicate brows arched higher. Why did he keep smiling at her?

"I would like to speak with Auld Maeve." Bonnie stared back at him.

He was certain a gentle smile teased at her lips—lovely luscious lips. He had a notion to kiss those lips. Perchance the lovely woman shared a similar thought as she, too, studied him. Did she just move closer or did he? He brushed his lips over hers and bent his head to deepen the kiss and—

"Ah!" Bonnie gasped, pulling her hand from his and jumping up. Her side of the bench rose from the ground and knocked him down onto his arse. "Oh . . . oh, my," she stuttered. Pushing her hand into her pocket, she pulled out a small pewter container and thrust it into his hand. "Salve for your wounds," she muttered and ran down the dark path, toward the music, toward the castle's great hall. Away from him.

For a time, Braeson closed his eyes and drew deep breaths. Bonnie had hit him on the head twice and landed him on his arse twice. Rising from the ground, he shook his head, rubbed his sore arse and walked the opposite way into the darkness, confused. Who was this chit, this she-demon, this lovely young woman with the warm luscious lips who was enticing him to live . . . again?

## Chapter Four

"Fire! Fire!" A guardsman repeatedly bellowed the words from atop the castle wall. The cries echoed through the glen and swirled around Bonnie. They pounded in rhythm with her mare's hooves as she cantered across the field toward the billowing smoke.

Bonnie rode astride the mare, lifting herself higher by pressing hard on the stirrups to see as far as possible. Could it be a croft that was ablaze? But whose? Mayhap a dry field or a pile of dry waste? She sat down low again pressing her head against the horse's neck. Straining to see. Straining to hurry.

"Run, sweet Daisy, run" she urged, holding tightly to the reins. Looking over her shoulder, she clicked her tongue encouraging the gray Shetland pony that was attached by a rope to Daisy's tether. The pony ploughed along, carrying on either flank a woven basket filled with rags to battle the blaze.

Bonnie held her legs firmly to Daisy's sides and

added even more pressure as she cantered around a small pond and up the hill. She held Daisy still at its brink for but a second, her eyes roaming the valley below to a clump of high bushes that hid the fire beyond.

"Fly, Daisy, fly!" Bonnie gave the horse full rein as the mare plunged down the hill. Daisy knew this path well and galloped into the vale toward the bushes. Bonnie leaned with the horse as it rounded the vegetation then came to a sudden halt as did her heart. Twas Tamhas and Aggie's cottage, Donal's parents.

As Bonnie dismounted, two boys came running, unhooked the baskets from the pony, lifted them to their shoulders and ran to the small pond a short distance from the burning structure. The freckle-faced stable boy who worked alongside Bonnie in the pony shed led Daisy and the gray to the far side of the pond away from danger.

Bonnie turned and took in the harrowing scene. At the pond, women were dipping rags and then running to the men to exchange dry, charred cloths for wet ones. Familiar voices rose above the noise. Lochlan stood close to the cottage, yelling orders as workers swung cloths to beat down the orange flames that refused to die. Water splashed over rims of buckets as they passed from hand to hand. Caol stood at the head of one line, Donal at another, heaving the water onto the remaining walls of the structure. Scorched rocks lay on the ground where walls once stood. Wooden beams that had held the thatched roof in place were charred sticks. Only two outside walls of Tamhas' and Aggie's cottage still stood.

Running to the pond's shore, Bonnie dropped her plaid shawl from her shoulders. She grabbed a rag from a basket and dunked it beneath the cold water. She flung it into a bucket and ran with it to Lochlan.

"Tis good, lass. Tis good," Lochlan said between exhausted breaths. "Braeson will take the rag and you'll return with more."

Braeson! Bonnie turned sharply to the man working alongside Lochlan. Twas Braeson working amongst her people. Helping her people. He paid little notice to her, so focused was he on the remains of what looked to be a bed still glowing with low flames. He dropped the charred rag into the bucket and Bonnie shoved her wet one into his hands. Since last night, she had determined to avoid him but here he was almost as close to her as they had been on the garden bench.

"Hurry, lass. Hurry." Lochlan's voice urged her back to the pond where she continued to dip rags and distribute them, all the while trying to avoid looking at Braeson . . . Earl English! And there he worked beside Lochlan, together swinging their rags high over their heads and then beating down onto the orange flames.

The rhythm stopped only when she pushed a wet cloth into their hands in exchange for a burnt one.

Bonnie could hardly catch her breath and twas not due to the physical exertion of running to and fro. Why was Earl English amongst her people battling the fire alongside them? Stealing away not only her breath but also her delight in working with her own people. Had she known, twould have been best to have stayed at the keep with Brianna and organize the rags there.

For certain, twas her own fault she was feeling like this. Why had she kissed Earl English? Or had he kissed her? He had captured her attention while she had danced with him last eve. Oh, she had tried to feign disinterest but every time they had touched a shiver had skittered deep within her. Later, he had lulled her toward him in the guise of a fairy story, and he had not only captured her breath but her apology with a kiss.

Bonnie shook her head and turned away from these thoughts and Earl English, scurrying to the pond where the women worked silently. All chatter had ceased. Only the grunts of human effort, the slap of linens and the beat of running feet were heard. Bit by bit, the workers slowed. Bonnie wiped her forearm over her damp, hot face. Deep sighs of exhaustion whispered around her and people took a step back from the remains to stare and rest.

"Hie the water to the ground surrounding the remains," commanded Donal as some of the older boys hurried alongside him to do his bidding. "No sparks will dare ignite the wet debris beyond. Or reach my house." He had built a small cottage next to his parents' home and did not want his new house to catch fire.

Bonnie ran to Aggie and hugged the older woman. "Are you hurt, Aggie? How did the flames start?"

Aggie turned to the crowd that was gathering to listen to her tale. "Twas after the cock crowed," she began. "Tahmas and Donal were readying the animals for plough. I be at the well pulling water and twas when I turned back, already flames rose high on the outside chimney wall." Aggie's voice trembled as she spoke. 'Tis I that cried fire." Black ash on reddened cheeks told of the woman's efforts to quell the fire.

"Outside you say, Aggie?" asked Lochlan.

"Aye," Aggie continued. "Twas never a fire at the hearth, for only when I bring in the water do I stir the day's fire."

Lochlan frowned and looked at the charred remains. He stared long and hard and then walked to where Donal stood, still directing the children with the buckets. He spoke to Donal. Bonnie wondered what words passed between the two men. She watched as Donal shook his head and pointed to the far west field where the animals stood tethered to a low bush waiting to begin the day's work.

Bonnie turned away and gathered with the group of men and women at the pond as they too washed the black of the smoke and dust from their faces and arms. Several men stood bare chested, their tunics dropped to their waists. Bonnie knelt at the edge and scooped the cool water into her cupped hands and poured it over her face. She tasted its freshness against her parched lips as it trickled down her neck and into the collar of her gown. She raised her head and her pulse quickened. Earl English stood knee deep in the water, bare chested, his English trews wet to above his knees. He was washing away the soot that clung to him, on his face, on his arms, across his chest with . . . her plaid! Her plaid! How could it be that he held her shawl? Had she not dropped it by the pond and . . . ? She scrambled to her feet, stepped into the pond to ankle deep and stared.

Oh, how Earl English was brawny—so tall and lean. Caol and Donal were brawny too but they were like brothers to her. When she looked at them she felt like a sister. Looking at Earl English, she felt a tremor pulse, low in her stomach, tight and fluttery.

Bonnie watched as Braeson dipped her shawl into the water and brushed it across his face. She admired his eyes, the colour of sea foam when the ocean is angry, fringed in dark lashes. He pulled her plaid from his face and rubbed it down his neck and over his wide, solid chest. He was brawny, as were Caol and Donal she reminded herself, but she had never wanted to kiss them like she had wanted to kiss Earl English last eve in the garden.

As Braeson had shared the Silkie tale, she had moved closer and closer fascinated to listen, admiring his face that changed with expressions of love and hope. What had made her touch Braeson's lips for that moment? Mayhap she was that Silkie in the story and had found her true love.

Rubbish, Bonnie lass! You have no pearl necklace to claim for your own. She shook herself free of such ludicrous thoughts and walked to where Earl English stood with Caol and Donal. She would claim her shawl, the rags and return to the castle. There was washing to do. Such nonsense!

"Donal! Donal!" a woman's voice called.

Bonnie and the men turned and watched as Flora ran down the hill, exhausted and out of breath. Donal ran toward her and caught her in his arms. She hugged him tightly to her and then moved away quickly, looking around shyly. The clan knew that Donal and Flora shared feelings but no hand had yet been declared. Flora touched Donal's arm and said something to him. They both turned and stared at the charred remains.

"Donal will make a fine husband," began Bonnie.

"Then why did you say no, lass?" asked Caol.

"How do you know what I said?" She glared at Caol and placed her hands on her hips.

"Donal told me that he was going to offer for your hand," replied Caol.

"Why should he offer for mine?" argued Bonnie. "Look yonder." She pointed toward Donal and Flora who now walked around the remaining cottage. "Mayhap De Ros and Lochlan asked him to offer for me."

"Tis not true lass," Caol explained. "Indeed, they encouraged him to consider Flora."

"But why would he ask for my hand?" Bonnie continued to observe the couple.

"He is concerned for your safety. Donal believes danger lurks near you." Caol pinned Bonnie with a brotherly stare. "Do not act ignorant, lass. You know your safety is a concern. He offered for your hand to protect you."

"I cannot marry a brother. Tis what he is." Bonnie shook her head and turned back to Caol. "I cannot hurt Flora," she whispered. "Nay, Donal's sacrifice would be too great."

Caol reached for Bonnie's hand. "You are a sweet friend and sister. But your safety is a growing concern.

Too many strange incidents have happened to believe you safe."

To know that Donal would sacrifice his happiness for her left her speechless. He was a childhood friend who over the years had become like a brother. Protecting her, arguing with her, bossing her. It was true that danger appeared to be following her, a falling branch when walking in the forest, footsteps behind her when riding Daisy, a broken saddle strap that had sent her tumbling. Too many to ignore.

"Who did you tell about Donal's proposal?" asked Caol.

"Not one," she replied.

"Lochlan has looked closely at the charred remains and cottage wall. He is convinced that the fire started outside the cottage," explained Caol.

Bonnie drew closer to Caol as he continued. "He discovered the location, on the far side away from anyone's view, where a small pewter pot was found. In it a fire started, charred remains left. From the pot rose the flames up one of the outside walls."

"It was started on purpose?" asked Bonnie.

"Aye," continued Caol. "Mayhap a warning."

"A warning?" She frowned as her heart skipped a beat.

"Mayhap for Donal . . . to stay away from you." Again, she and Caol looked at Donal and Flora. Their heads were close and they whispered.

"Mayhap someone in the castle who overheard the proposal and is watching," said Caol. "But who?"

Bonnie glanced quickly at Braeson, staring, questioning. Mayhap it was Earl English. Had not the English burned her home those years past? Had they not stolen her life away?

"Bonnie!" Caol's voice held a warning. "Cease! Or you'll be apologizing again."

She averted her eyes to her plaid still held in Braeson's hands. She recalled how the last apology had ended, her pulse quickened and her eyes wandered to Earl English's lips. She sniffed noisily to chase the thought away and lifted her eyes to Braeson. "I will collect my plaid and then hie to the castle."

"Mayhap the fire over-heated your addled thoughts," cautioned Caol.

She grabbed one end of the plaid and pulled. But Earl English refused to release it. He growled, ice-gray eyes narrowed, holding tight to his corner of the plaid. Not budging.

"I only want my plaid." She tugged again. She noted a gleam brightening in Earl English's eyes. A smile pushing through his sneer. She pulled even harder. It was her plaid, was it not?

With a snap, the Earl released his end and grinned as she stumbled backward from the force, and tumbled with a splash, to sit on her bottom in the shallows of the pond.

"You will cool off well," Earl English advised. He gave a slight bow, turned and walked away.

## Chapter Five

Braeson sat atop his steed and gazed out over the ponies that trotted around the field or grazed on clumps of grass. This marked his fifth day at Rose Castle and today he would make his final choice of the Shetland ponies he would purchase from Lady Brianna. He and his men along with the purchased ponies would begin the journey back to Braemoore, his home in England.

There were ponies that could be got in England or even from the continent. But Braeson recalled how Caol had described the strength of these unique northern creatures and their work ethic, so he had chosen to travel to Scotland to investigate. He was not to be disappointed and already he had made some silent decisions about which ponies he would choose. Indeed, the ponies would support the work on Braemoore and the efforts of the people who lived there and worked the land. Already Braeson could visualize the ponies pulling carts, ploughing small fields and providing transport.

Like his father, Braeson embraced the culture of the estate and the surrounding countryside. While some land owners demanded their people meet unrealistic quotas by the sweat of their hands and crude tools, Braeson's father had not. Now, neither did Braeson. Over the decades, a mutual respect between Braemoore's Masters and its people had been established. Births, deaths and celebrations had been witnessed together. New generations of families worked on the estate land and cared for it dearly. These ponies would be an addition to the tools and implements required to help Braemoore thrive. Satisfaction tilted Braeson's lips into a slight smile. These ponies were as much a gift to Braemoore's people as they were to the land and the operation of the estate.

Caol approached and steadied his horse beside Braeson. "You have made choices, aye?" he questioned.

Braeson watched as Bonnie drove a small cart, pulled by a sturdy brown pony, over the draw bridge and onto the swath of land that lay in front of the castle. He turned to his friend. "Ten I've chosen to study. From this group I'll choose the seven to purchase."

The ponies of various colours galloped around the low glen, others stood still and some cantered to various spots alone or in smaller groups, nickering as Bonnie and Angus, the pony master, shepherded them. Bonnie picked up speed and raced the brown Shetland in various directions to demonstrate the pony's ability to pull a cart. She wore a kerchief about her head yet her hair flew from beneath it, dancing golds and auburns in the sun's morning rays. As Bonnie drove the buggy, a large black galloped beside her, refusing to leave her side even as she encouraged it away.

"The black is Tokie," Caol explained. "Twas weak at birth, a twin. Twas not thriving. Bonnie spent several nights with it, coaxing it to life."

Braeson watched the woman and pony interact. The pony had certainly thrived and was the largest on the field. Its strength was apparent and its muscles rippled as it trotted alongside the cart.

"I cannot believe that Bonnie will be happy if the animal is purchased." He envisioned her frown, her cinnamon eyes shooting fireballs at him when she would learn of Tokie's departure.

"I do not think so, Braeson. Lady Brianna raises these ponies for sale," Caol explained. "Tokie interacts well with the other ponies and follows commands when Bonnie is absent. Bonnie agrees that the beast has proven worthy to be purchased."

Braeson continued to gaze at the herd. A stable boy walked amongst them. Braeson had seen the freckled-face lad in the pony shed. Angus, the pony master, pointed to a small roan and the boy tugged at the pony's mane and threw his leg over its back. He sat atop it for a short time, petting the beast and talking gently to it. The pony master gestured with his hands and the pair trotted in wide circles several times. Again Angus commanded, and the boy led the creature into a faster trot, encouraging it to canter round and round the herd and alongside Bonnie and the cart. Soon the boy and pony were galloping around the field and in and out of the herd. They galloped to the castle portcullis and abruptly stopped. The boy turned the pony and raced it back across the field, away from the castle, toward the copse of trees at the bottom of the glen and disappeared into its shadows.

"Verra strange," Caol mumbled.

The boy reappeared and dismounted. He stood and waved to Bonnie encouraging her to follow and walked with the pony into the woods, disappearing once again. Bonnie urged her pony and cart forward. Her voice floated to Braeson as she called to the boy and then jumped from the buggy and walked to the edge of the woods. She commanded Tokie to remain and then disappeared into the trees. Tokie, however, chose to follow.

Braeson held his breath. He felt his stomach tighten, disappointed that the lovely woman with the dancing tresses had vanished into the woods. Why did he long to listen to her laugh as she interacted with the ponies, commanding the cart pony and scolding Tokie? Watching the woman pulled him from his sad thoughts and challenged him to return to the present. For too long, he had wallowed in despair, mourning his father, who had passed away far too soon. He had hoped the journey to Scotland's north might distract him from the deep sorrow that gripped him. In this moment, all he knew was this chit, this she-demon, this lovely woman provoked him to feel alive again.

Braeson released his breath slowly, waiting for Bonnie to reappear. Odd that the boy had ridden the pony into the woods during a demonstration. He recalled Caol's words to Bonnie the day of the fire. Words that spoke of danger lurking near to her. *"Your safety is a growing concern. Too many strange incidents to believe you safe."*

Was this another strange occurrence, a boy and woman disappearing into the woods during a demonstration? The silence crept deeper into the glen, slithering around Braeson and pounding in his ears. Echoing. Waiting.

Without thought, Braeson galloped across the glen

unsure when his stillness broke into action. A horn from the keep tower bellowed behind him and a watchman atop the wall shouted. Braeson rode low in his saddle, leaning forward as he charged into the woods, emerging through to the other side. He halted on a wide stretch of rocky grassland, taking measure of the appalling scene before him.

Two horsemen encircled Bonnie who was struggling against a third rider that sat on a large brown speckled horse. The rider held her around the waist, lifting her slightly so that her feet dangled above the ground. Her arms and legs flailed as she fought to free herself from the villain's grasp. Her fist flew up and struck the rider's face. Braeson actually winced as did the rider. How well he knew her physical strength! Bonnie dropped to the ground, free, and ran across the expanse, changing direction as two riders charged at her. One held a whip high in the air and lashed it across her back, wrapping it around her torso.

Stabbing his spurs into his mount and wrenching his sword from its sheath, Braeson exploded into the scene. He cut the whip that encircled Bonnie. Then, bending forward, he snatched her around the waist and sat her on his lap. He urged his horse on as it raced through the thin woods and toward the glen and the castle.

"Nay, Bonnie. Do not struggle. It is I, Braeson." He

felt her body stiffen and then still. She turned her face toward him for a moment. A welt travelled across a cheek bone, swelling from what seemed to be a lash from a whip. Blood seeped through the sleeve of her blouse and her skirt was ripped along one side. She coiled her body into a ball, pulled her legs against her chest and wrapped her arms around her legs. She tucked her head down and remained still, except for the whimpers that emanated from her, low keening, like a hurt animal caught in a hunter's trap.

Guards joined them, racing alongside and following through the gate into the courtyard. In one fluid sweep, Braeson dismounted and, holding Bonnie in his arms, he turned toward the castle entrance.

"Shh, my sweet." He rocked her gently as he ascended the steps, toward Lady Brianna who was rushing forward followed by the castle steward. The Lady halted and quickly took in Bonnie's injuries.

"Call for Alice," she commanded. "She is to bring her herbs and healing ointments."

John, the steward, stepped forward taking Bonnie from Braeson's arms and carried her into the castle entrance. Brianna rushed after them, instructing a castle maid to prepare a bath.

Braeson remained at the castle entrance, watching as Bonnie disappeared up the main wooden staircase, around a corner and out of sight. He yearned to follow her and . . . what? To hold her again? Braeson looked down at his hands. Empty. He felt a deep searing-void inside himself. That void, that dark abyss of grief, had begun to grow again the moment John had taken Bonnie from him.

## Chapter Six

Braeson leaned against the wooden frame at the entrance to the almost deserted great room. He stared at the closed door to the Laird's library where loud voices permeated through it. From time to time, a serving girl entered to fill Braeson's cup with ale and then skittered away.

The voices had been thundering since shortly after Braeson had carried Bonnie up the stairs to the entrance of the Keep. Guards had been entering and exiting the library, sullen and quiet, yet focused on their tasks.

Caol had been the first to enter his father's library. Voices had roared and then had quieted. After what had seemed like a very long time, the door opened and Donal exited with the freckled-faced stable boy whose face was red and streaked with tears. He squirmed under Donal's strong arm and received a shaking as he walked, head down now, across the great hall and out the entrance. Thereafter, the pattern of voices rising and quieting beyond the library door had even caused the servants to disappear, muttering about remembered tasks to complete.

Caol and Donal had both been smattered in blood. A servant girl had whispered to Braeson that the three riders had been cut down and fast buried in an unknown location. Braeson looked at his own clothes that carried traces of Bonnie's blood. How severe were her wounds? The castle was too gloomy, a stark difference from the usually lively environment that Braeson had observed in his short time at Rose Castle.

Clearly, the stable boy had been part of a scheme to entrap Bonnie. Would she live? The void in Braeson seemed to widen at that thought. Surely she could not die. Yet the whip that had entangled her had found its mark a few times prior to his rescue. Her torn skirt had revealed lacerations across her thigh. A red hand print had stained her calf. What did they want with her? There was so much he did not know about this red—no golden, perchance copper haired lass. In a matter of a few day, she had challenged, flirted with, and angered him, yet more than once had enticed him to turn his head toward her. Was that not what he had been doing just a short time ago, as he had watched her with the ponies? Turning his eyes to her? He had watched her more than the ponies. By God! They were the very purpose for his journey to Scotland, and he'd all but forgotten it in his growing fascination with the lovely, young woman. He rubbed his hands over his face.

"My Lord."

Braeson raised his head in surprise. Lady Brianna stood before him, hands clasped. He bowed to her and then extended his hand toward a bench.

"Tis not easy having two Lairds in one castle. Aye?" stated the Lady.

Braeson settled beside her on the bench as Lady Brianna frowned toward the closed door. He also frowned. Of what riddles did this Lady speak?

"De Ros and Lochlan both are Lairds, Masters of their Keeps," began Brianna.

Braeson glanced toward the library, confused. Lochlan a Laird? He had thought him a lead guardsman at Rose Castle. Lochan's leadership at the fire and his reprimand of Bonnie the day of Braeson's arrival had suggested this role.

Lady Brianna leaned in closer to Braeson, speaking softly. "Seventeen years past, Lochlan asked for refuge here at Rose Castle." She turned her head and scanned the room as if a secret was hiding within its walls. "The MacEwen Keep—where Lochlan is Laird—was attacked, the tower burned to the ground. Several lost their lives that night."

"Attacked?" questioned Braeson. He had believed that Lochlan lived here at Rose Castle. "Did Lochlan not stay to rebuild, to fight, to defend the MacEwen lands?" Braeson strove to convey his question without judgement. Had this Master abandoned his lands and people?

Lady Brianna's chin rose. "Aye! Lochlan and his people worked together to rebuild and continued to thrive." The Lady looked down to her clasped hands and then lifted misted eyes to Braeson. "Much was lost that eve when the castle burned. It lies heavy on Lochlan's thoughts. Each year since, in early winter, he finds refuge here at Rose Keep and returns to his MacEwen lands in the early spring."

Braeson nodded, encouraging Lady Brianna to continue.

"After the attack, during the journey to Rose Castle, Lochlan found a young girl. The bairn was unknown to the MacEwen clan." Brianna paused and looked into Braeson's eyes. "Bonnie."

"Bonnie?" Braeson whispered.

"An old woman, Ina, had a small cottage far beyond the castle gates, in the MacEwen lower lands." Brianna's face softened as she became the storyteller. "On the eve of the attack, Ina's cottage was also set ablaze. When Lochlan came upon it, he found Ina wounded from the flames and a red haired bairn—

about three years old—sitting by her." The Lady smiled. "Aye. Bonnie."

"Was the child hidden?" he questioned. The Lady's story conveyed a tale of secrets and hidden meaning.

"Aye. She had been hidden away on the MacEwen land. Ina had kept the child's existence a secret, explaining to Lochlan that the girl had been found at her doorstep three years prior—a babe, newly born, without name or history, wrapped in a seal skin blanket." The Lady lifted her brows and her lips formed a gentle smile. "It was Ina who bestowed our dear Silkie the name, Bonnie . . ."

"Ah!" Braeson imagined Bonnie's face. Indeed, an appropriate moniker for the lovely young woman.

"And Ina chose to hide the bairn. She believed a dark omen was connected to the babe." The Lady's eyes flitted around the room again and then returned to his face. He leaned closer expecting her to explain Ina's choice to hide the child but Lady Brianna shook her head slightly and finished. "Ina did not recover from her wounds. With her final breath, she encouraged Lochlan to take Bonnie far away and keep her safe."

"But, why was the bairn hidden?" he questioned, demanded. His voice was louder now, more urgent.

Lady Brianna shook her head once and then Braeson watched as a veil dropped over the Lady's eyes. There would be no more answers. No more stories about Bonnie.

In the years that Braeson had known Caol, his friend had never shared this story of Bonnie. Caol had spoken of a girl named Bonnie often in the same stories with a man named Lochlan. Yet Caol, never at a loss for words, had many a family story to share—a bard always ready to spin a tale. But not once had he shared this amazing account of a bairn who had been abandoned at an old woman's threshold.

Secrets surrounded the auburn-haired woman. The Lady sat silently beside him, studying his face carefully. What could he say to fill the awkward silence? "Bonnie. I thought she was, perchance, Lochlan's daughter."

"Nay, Bonnie has been raised here at Rose Castle." Lady Brianna swept her arm toward the great room. "Here is her family. But Lochlan loves her as if she were his own child." Brianna's face softened again remembering. "When Lochlan brought Bonnie to Rose Keep, Caol, from De Ros' first marriage, became her brother. De Ros became her father." Lady Brianna smiled. "I, her mother."

"Might I ask, why this location?" Braeson asked. "Rose lands?

"Bonnie was not the only person Lochlan brought to Rose Castle that day." Anger flashed in her eyes before she allowed a smile to tug at her mouth. "All those years past, Lochlan intended to bring only me to Rose Keep. He believed I could not be safe remaining on MacEwen land. In my fear, I fled with him willingly. But, Lochlan had a plan unbeknownst to me." She drew a deep breath and her eyes flitted to a spot somewhere beyond Braeson's shoulder as if remembering the long ago experience.

The Lady was clever. In her attempt to divert him from Bonnie's secrets she was sharing another chapter of the harrowing tale.

She slid her eyes to him. "Lochlan gave me to De Ros as his wife." A bewildered shadow crossed her face and she lifted a hand to wave it away. "But how I came to be Justus De Ros' wife is another story, for another time." Brianna turned again to Braeson. "Lochlan is my brother."

"Ah". Braeson closed his eyes and then opened them staring into Lady Brianna's face. Why had he not noticed before? Her stunningly beautiful . . . "The eyes," he whispered.

"Aye, a child of a MacEwen always takes on the MacEwen eyes." Lady Brianna gazed at Braeson's face, her eyebrows raised. She reached out and laid her hand gently over Braeson's. "Tis the MacEwen mark."

Braeson studied the Lady's eyes, fringed delicately with black lashes. They were the colour of ocean gray—the colour of sea foam that sat upon the ocean waves in a storm. The same eyes as Lochlan MacEwen's. How had he not noticed? Perchance the auburn-haired woman had stolen his attention.

"Ina's belief in Bonnie's omen, tis true." said Lady Brianna. "Two Lairds sit in the room railing at each other to determine what is to become of our daughter, our sister, our friend." She stared at him as if he held a secret answer.

"And Bonnie, how does she fare?" Braeson's heart beat too fast. He held his breath.

Brianna smiled and once again patted his hand. "She will recover and quickly. When you found her, the strangers had just begun to attack her. A hot bath, ointments, loving hands and a good cry have been our sweet lass' remedies. She is asleep." Brianna stood. "But you, my Lord, must clean up. I have a suspicion that soon you will speak to De Ros and Lochlan. They will want to know your part in all of this."

Part? His part in Bonnie's rescue had been minimal.

When they stood, the Lady slipped her hand through his arm and raised smiling eyes to him. "We have prepared a bath for you and your man has laid out clean clothes. Come. I believe all will be well."

As Lady Brianna looked at him with her piercing seafoam eyes, her smile slipped away to a thoughtful expression. She nodded once at him as if making a silent decision. Then, she signaled a maid to escort him to his rooms.

Braeson wondered if he should follow the maid or collect his men and run. The Lady was too clever and too secretive. What storm had he journeyed into coming to Rose Castle?

# Chapter Seven

Bonnie sat on a wooden box close to Tokie. The single lantern cast a soft yet dreary glow in the pony shed.

"Tokie, Tokie, Tokie," Bonnie whispered to the black pony as she stared into its soft, dark eyes and petted its muzzle. "What is going to happen to your Silkie?" She kissed the pony again and again. "Tokie, Tokie, Tokie," she whispered.

Bonnie had awakened from her long sleep when Angus knocked on her bed chamber door and muttered urgently to Lady Brianna. It seemed that during the attack, Louie, the stable boy, had attempted to escape from Rose lands on Tokie's back. But Tokie had refused to obey him. The wee beast had run in circles bucking the boy from atop it. When Caol had snatched the boy, the pony had galloped back to the castle gate, was led into its stall and had refused to settle. Only when two guards had escorted Bonnie to the pony shed, and she had been allowed to sit with the pony, had Tokie calmed.

She wished that she could settle herself too. Her hands shook, her chest felt tight and her stomach was in a knot. She hugged the animal and murmured her distraught words against its neck. "I do not know what is to become of your Silkie." Oh, how she hated that word, yet in her confusion and fear she felt like the lost Silkie in Braeson's fairy tale, unknowing what would come next in her life.

"The pony will stay with you."

Bonnie was sure her heart slammed against her ribs. She had not heard him enter the shed. Now he stood inside the stall door. Bonnie raised her eyes to Braeson and then dropped them quickly. Had he heard what she had named herself, or did he pretend to misinterpret her muffled words?

"This is what is going to become of the beast," he concluded.

She lifted her eyes to Braeson as he drew nearer. Then, he crouched beside her and petted the pony. She was glad the guards had only lit one lantern. She pulled her plaid closer around her face and allowed her unbound hair to fall forward. The welt on her face would heal, Alice had reassured her, but she felt the stretch of the skin below her eye and span across a swollen cheek.

"Tokie will make a good worker when he is full grown," Bonnie said softly. "He will come to obey well if he is shown kindness."

"Tokie has not been chosen." Braeson turned to her. "The pony has proven its devotion to you. He will stay."

Bonnie closed her eyes and placed her forehead against Tokie's muzzle. She wondered why those men had wanted her. Were they the same men who had stolen Ina from her years ago? She was sure the fire on the MacEwen lands had been connected to her. She had been three but she remembered sitting beside Ina throughout the early morn, surrounded by simmering coals and burnt ashes. Frightened.

Bits of memories of that time floated round her. It was in the late morn that riders approached the burnt remains of the little cottage that she had known as home. She had scrambled behind Ina and stared at the man who neared. He was tall and big. His hair was black, like the nighttime, and his eyes seemed almost white in the morning's mist.

She remembered Ina whispering to the man. "The bairn, take her far away. Hide her. Keep her safe." Then Ina had reached into the folds of her charred robes and given the man a package.

When the man had told Bonnie that Ina was dead she had curled into a ball, closing her eyes, stealing away from the pain of Ina's loss. The man, Lochlan, had wrapped her seal skin blanket around her, picked her up and carried her into a small woods where a group of riders sat silently upon their horses. Lochlan placed her upon the lap of a young woman.

Bonnie had ridden for days, held and soothed by the young woman, whom the man had called Brianna, to a new home—Rose Castle.

Twas seventeen years past. Bonnie had been given a family here. But now her enemies had found her. Who they were she did not know. She had heard De Ros whisper once to Brianna that he suspected the English. Mayhap the Campbells too.

"Yet it is not Tokie that you spoke of, just now, aye?" questioned Braeson.

Bonnie looked up, her plaid falling away from her face. She was startled to see Braeson peering closely at her. His heavily lashed eyes narrowed as he studied her face. So he had heard her speak of herself as Silkie—that shameful nekename.

The well of emotion within her intensified and threatened to overflow. Braeson's presence brought back the horror of her earlier experience this day and mingled with long ago memories of sitting beside Ina. The dear woman had held on to life long enough to see her safe. Twas an incredible sacrifice of love.

Where would Bonnie escape to now? Where was her home? She remained silent. There were no words for the fear that had wrapped itself around her. Mayhap this Silkie would never find her home. She rubbed her hand against her breast that ached with such a deep sadness. Her throat tightened, preventing her from replying. She remembered the fairy stories that Lady Brianna had told her when she was a wee lass. *Silkies never stay too long in one place.*

"Bonnie," he whispered. "What did they do?"

As she lifted her hand to shield her face from his scrutiny, Braeson pulled it away and gently held it.

"Lady Brianna reassured me that you will heal. But—" Braeson closed his eyes.

She heard him draw in his breath as if he too were reliving the morning's nightmare.

He looked at her, his eyes searching her face. Her hand warmed at the spot where he gently rubbed his thumb. "If only I would not have waited so long, wondering . . . you would not have suffered." Braeson gingerly ran his finger alongside the welt on her face.

Bonnie remembered the feel of Braeson's arms around her and how he had held her gently, whispering words of comfort as they raced toward the castle. How could his arms be a safe place when he was English? Had it not been the English who had taken Ina from her all those years ago? And now, just this morn, they had attempted to take her again.

"Who were those men?" Braeson questioned.

Bonnie withdrew her hand and edged away from Braeson. Her heart thumped and yet she was not sure if it beat faster from fear, or from Braeson's touch. On her hand, on her face. Or was it his eyes, the colour of seafoam, and the way he looked at her as if he might have some answers to her troubles.

She shook her head. "I do not know but they have found me again. They came for me before and chased me from my home. Lochlan hied me away from the MacEwen lands. De Ros and Brianna took me in as their own." She felt her face flush and tears sting her eyes. "I am neither MacEwen nor De Ros."

The shed door opened and Bonnie quickly turned her head and wiped her tears. A guard appeared and bowed to Braeson. "The Laird is wishing to speak with you, my Lord."

Braeson turned back to Bonnie. He reached into his dark cape and withdrew the pewter container that she had given to him only a few evenings past. He lifted her hand gently and kissed it.

"Auld Maeve told me that Silkies always find their way home." He smiled and placed the container in her hand and then strode from Tokie's stall and out of the shed.

Bonnie opened the container, dipped her finger into the ointment and gently rubbed it on her bruised face. She would like to meet Auld Maeve and talk to her about Silkies. Mayhap Maeve could show her the way home.

Yet such foolish and fanciful thoughts could not be considered. Angrily, she swiped the few tears away. Nay. She was not a Silkie. She loathed that ugly word that always poked at her lost heritage. She was a woman, a lost woman for certain, who was no longer safe at Rose Castle.

This time, she jabbed her fingers into the poultice and smeared it along a laceration on her arm. She would have to flee from this place she called home. But, she needed help to ward off these enemies who meant to destroy her. Her hand fisted. Who? Who could possibly help her?

# Chapter Eight

"The lad will return to his clan only when all has been resolved," explained Justus de Ros, Laird of Rose Castle, who sat behind a wooden table in the library.

The room was a large, entombed cave. As Braeson had approached the castle, upon his arrival at Rose Keep, he had noted it sat high on a rock cliff peering far out to the North Sea. When Braeson had been escorted through the library doorway, he had been surprised to follow the guard down several stone steps before he actually entered the room. He understood now why the loud voices had penetrated into the great room. The stone cavern was an echo chamber. Scanning the room, he had wondered if it were possible that it had been chiselled out of the cliff stone by ancestors' long dead, or if the oddly shaped cave was a natural structure

The ceiling was high and several candles hung from large wooden cross beams that extended the length and width of the room. In one wall was a massive stone fireplace with its fire burning low, leaving the space cool and damp. Books lined several wooden shelves to the side of the fireplace. Weapons hung on the wall behind the Laird's table. A large tapestry covered a wall at the far end of the room. Yet it was the wood carvings that decorated the space and hung or sat in various spots that Braeson found most noticeable. Carvings of animals and ships, plants and fruits of various sizes. A thumbnail sized grape sat beside a hand sized wooden cradle, a babe, delicately carved, lay inside.

"He will be sure to receive a severe punishment when he is forced to look his Da in the face and confess his crimes," De Ros growled. He lifted an undistinguishable wooden carving and tossed it into the fire. The blaze snapped and rose higher.

Braeson turned and looked at the other men who sat at the table with De Ros. Caol sat to his father's right, silent and watchful.

"You will sit." De Ros pointed to the empty chair beside the MacEwen Laird.

Braeson nodded his agreement and settled. "Who is the lad?" he questioned.

"He is the second son of a clan to the far northwest. Sent to us just recently to learn a trade and to live amongst us. Just for a time." De Ros pounded his fist on the table causing the candles to flicker. "He will learn about loyalty the hard way when he returns to his clan."

During their journey from north England to Rose Castle, Caol had explained to Braeson the intricacies and peculiarities of clan interactions. The lad's behaviour had now jeopardized relations between the two clans.

"Twill be a long day in hell before this keep accepts another from any clan to foster," De Ros stated.

"The hour grows late," stated Lochlan glaring at De Ros. "Time will take care of the lad. We must take control of this night! Dusk is creeping closer as we speak."

A hush fell over the room. Only a log crackled in the fireplace. The three men turned to Braeson expectantly as if he held answers to the day's trauma.

"Caol explains that you excel in languages," De Ros stated.

What connection did languages have to this day's events? "It was a study area in which I excelled," Braeson acknowledged. He had been an Oxford student and had received permission from the English court years ago to attend the Université de Paris for his final years of study to immerse himself completely in European languages and culture. His Queen saw him as a potential participant in negotiations between

England and other realms. *A diplomat and a translator,* the sovereign court's letter of permission had read.

Lochlan slid two parchments across the table to Braeson. "Years ago, a fire burned the MacEwen castle. A parchment was knifed to a tree close to the cottage where Bonnie lived." Lochlan pushed the yellowed parchment, discovered years past, toward Braeson. "This noon when we searched the attack area, another parchment was secured to a tree."

Braeson picked up the two missives and scanned the few words and symbols scribed on each. Code, he thought. He could not decipher what it meant but it was a coded script likely placed to confuse and threaten the finder.

"The words are cyphered. Written in a covert language." Braeson pointed to one of the parchments. "This symbol means *treasure.* I suspect of Norse origin."

Both Lochann and De Ros gasped.

"Are you certain?" demanded De Ros. "Are there no indicators of French or English?

"The script, the symbols appear to be of a Norse tradition." Braeson continued.

"I had thought them—believed them to be of English origin," whispered De Ros, staring at the parchments, shaking his head.

"English?" Braeson questioned. He took note of the

glance exchanged between the two Lairds, an unspoken message. Then De Ros lowered his veiled eyes. Neither man moved. Even his friend, Caol stared at the men, frowning.

Lochlan turned to Braeson with a slight smile in his eyes erasing any tension that the question had created. "Tis another story," Lochlan said. "A question for another time."

Braeson felt his ire rise. Anger grew in his gut. He was English. Were they suspicious of him? Did these men surmise that he had a role in Bonnie's attempted abduction? For now, Braeson would allow his anger and his own suspicions to simmer.

De Ros' next statement redirected the discussion. "The lad reported that a dozen men travel together, hidden deep in the crags, unnoticed." He tapped his hand on the table and nodded. "Three were killed this afternoon. Nine live." De Ros looked up as if a plan were unfolding. "We must remove Bonnie from the keep. It is too dangerous to have her remain with us," he explained. "A guard reported that a cottage was set afire early this eve. It stood at the north east border of Rose land." The Laird rubbed a hand across his forehead. "It is a warning, a sign. Evil lurks amongst us."

Lochlan nodded. "Aye, Bonnie must travel south away from any association with the De Ros or the

MacEwen lands." He tapped his fist on the table. "Tis difficult, but she must go to ensure safety, not only for herself but for us, her clans."

The suspicion that Braeson had detected a moment ago crept into his stomach. Why did these three men look at him as if he held the remedy to Bonnie's problem?

Again, Lochlan and De Ros exchanged a glance. Caol also moved forward looking at Braeson as if measuring his worth.

"We would like to offer Bonnie's hand to you in marriage," stated De Ros.

Bloody hell! Damnation!

Braeson was sure his dinner meal was slowly crawling up from his stomach ready to spew across the room. That she-demon, childish maiden, teary-eyed Silkie would never be his responsibility.

Lochlan reached into the fold of his plaid and drew out a small cloth bundle. From it he pulled a necklace and tossed it onto the table before Braeson. "Her dowry, passed to me by an old woman, Ina." he stated. "The treasure was bundled in Bonnie's blanket the eve the woman found the babe at her door."

Braeson stared at the necklace. A three-strand rope of shimmering, luminescent pearls lay before him. He stood, holding the necklace high and touched the pearls gingerly. Turning his head, he met Lochlan's scrutinizing gaze.

"Bonnie is not a pony to be sold to the highest bidder!" Braeson growled. "This day has been full of treachery. I will not be a part of it." He hurled the pearls at the stone fireplace. "You have a young woman in need of protection and I will not steal her treasure, her birthright, from her."

"Tis good to see your Scottish blood reflecting such honour," retorted Lochlan, his lips lifting into a slight smile.

"Tis not the Scottish blood that you see, but English," countered Braeson. "Apart from my mother, Annella Campbell and her servants, I've witnessed little honour demonstrated by any Scot."

A long ago picture emerged, now just a shadow in his memory, of when Braeson was a boy of eight. He had been excited to meet Angus Campbell, his Scottish grandfather. Angus Campbell, along with his young son, had journeyed from his home in Scotland to northern England. He had come to meet Braeson, his grandson, and see again his daughter, Lady Annella.

Within hours of his grandfather's arrival, Braeson remembered standing in stunned silence, as Angus Campbell had attacked his daughter, Annella. Servants had run to get Braeson's father. It had taken several servants to pull Braeson's father off of Angus Campbell in order to prevent the old man's death. His

Scottish grandfather and his young son—whose name Braeson had long forgotten—had been expelled from Braemoore never to visit again.

"If you think because I am English that I am a part of the threat that surrounds Bonnie, you are deceived." Braeson walked toward the door, then stopped and turned back to the men. "My business is complete. Please convey to Lady Brianna my gratitude for her hospitality." He bowed to them and placed a foot on the bottom step. "My men and I will depart at first light."

"It is our Scottish honour that is offering Bonnie's hand to you in marriage," thundered De Ros.

Braeson shook with anger and took a deep breath. Would these men not stop this nonsense? A rustling behind Braeson caused him to turn.

Caol stood a short distance from him. His friend's typically humorous face was now etched with exhaustion. Concern lingered in his tired eyes. "We attempt to shield our Bonnie from danger," Caol said. "You do not stand accused. Rather you stand as my friend. It is your help we seek. You whom we trust."

Caol's quiet, desperate words broke through Braeson's tension, diffusing some of his anger. He gave a slight nod to Caol to acknowledge this understanding between friends. "I will not rob Bonnie of the protection she requires." Braeson turned back to the two men still at the table, still watching, obviously measuring his words. "Removing her from this region for a time, until the situation can be resolved, will be suitable. My mother, Lady Annella, lives at our northern residence in England—Braemoore. It is well guarded and Bonnie will be welcomed."

"We cannot send a maid from the Highlands with a group of men," Lochlan protested. "Tis not proper for a maid to be unchaperoned."

"She may bring a servant to accompany her." Braeson stated. "That will fulfill requirements for a chaperon."

"Nay, my Lord. She must flee from Scotland wed, or not at all," continued Lochlan. "She will be hidden away as a married woman, almost as if she were disguised. Her enemies recognize her only as a young woman, a maid. They will not be hunting for a married woman." Lochlan paused, his steely eyes softened and a melancholic tone drifted across his final words. "It must all appear authentic. True."

Braeson bristled. He should have continued up the stairway and not looked back. He stared at them, incredulous to their reasoning and their certainty that marriage was the only solution to Bonnie's troubles. Would Bonnie be forced into a marriage for protection? Had he not made a reasonable offer of his home in northern England?

Braeson walked across the room to the fireplace

where the pearl necklace had caught onto a metal hook protruding from the mantel. It swayed in the heat, glimmering as it danced in an erratic pattern.

He gripped the mantel and peered into the fire. When his Scottish grandfather, Angus Campbell, had struck his mother, she had hit her head on the wooden mantel of the fireplace as she had fallen to the ground. Braeson had thought her dead. She lay still, unconscious for two days—he remembered counting the sun ups and sun downs. His father had sat by his mother's bed refusing food or sleep. He had spoken to Braeson only once. It had been at the end of the second day. *If she leaves us, the void will be too wide and too deep to endure,* his father had whispered.

Braeson recalled the void he had felt when he had passed Bonnie into the arms of the castle steward after the attack. It had lessened when he saw her in the pony shed and then had reappeared as he walked away from her to this meeting. He had forgotten about it for a time in his anger at these men—Lochlan, De Ros, even Caol—and their insinuations that he was dishonourable. But now, as he stared at the fire and at the dancing necklace, he felt the void flourish again into a low gut pain. His father spoke to him from beyond the grave—t*oo wide and too deep.*

Braeson struck the mantel with his fist and then pushed away from it. Turning to the three silent men, he whispered, "It is a night for clandestine activity. Bid the priest. We will wed immediately and leave thereafter. Prepare."

$$Chapter\ Nine$$

Bonnie struggled against the hands that pulled and tugged at her. She slapped them away from her shoulders, her head. They had found her again and were calling her name. Bonnie! How did they know her name? Whispering her name. Before they had been loud and brash. *You whore. Shut your mouth.* One of them had slapped her hard on her face and she had fought. They could not fool her now. She summoned her strength and bellowed.

Bonnie's eyes snapped open as a hand clamped down tight over her mouth. She stared into the familiar eyes of Lady Brianna—warm and soft. Nay! Eyes tinged in fear, dark gray, the colour of the ocean waves when a storm is rolling in.

"Bonnie lass."

Brianna lifted her hand and caressed Bonnie's cheek, her hair. She studied her face and smiled. "You must have fallen asleep after this eve's meal." She grasped Bonnie's hand and fell silent.

Bonnie felt her heart steady and she rubbed her eyes. "I thought I had been caught again and I had to get away—"

"Tis only a dream, lass." Brianna squeezed her hand and sat on the side of the bed. "You are safe and we mean to keep you thus."

Bonnie tossed the cover from her and sat beside Brianna. She studied their clasped hands for a time, savouring the comfort. "How, Brianna? They have found me."

"There are many plans at work this eve, lass, and we must make haste to prepare." Brianna rose, pulling Bonnie to stand too.

A heaviness descended on Bonnie's shoulders. Brianna's quiet tone was too calm, too whispered. "Plans?"

Brianna turned as Alice, her maid, entered through the secret panel in the chamber wall. Alice held one of Bonnie's travelling garments.

"De Ros and Lochlan have found a safe house for you," Brianna began. "They are determined that you leave as soon as possible. The moon is hidden tonight. You will travel with darkness as your cloak."

"But where? How?" Bonnie's heart pumped harder. It seemed as if light fingers were crawling up her back, frightening her.

Brianna placed a gentle hand on Bonnie's lips. "We must whisper," she explained. "To ensure safety, De Ros and Lochlan have shared the plans with only a few."

Now Bonnie understood the use of the secret passageway this eve. Alice held a wealth of secrets that she would die with before she wagged her tongue. That explained Alice's presence in the chamber. As Bonnie had eaten her dinner and then slept, decisions and plans had been made inside the castle walls. Secrets. She looked from Brianna to Alice.

"You must change into this garment and ready yourself for several days journey." Brianna nodded toward Alice and the maid stepped forward and began to untie the laces on Bonnie's gown. "You and your companions will journey by night and sleep by day."

"Companions?" asked Bonnie. She watched Brianna closely, sure that the Lady had chosen the word to shroud the truth behind this secretive journey. "Who are my companions, Brianna?"

Brianna stilled for a moment, then turned from the garments she was organizing and looked at Bonnie, now dressed only in her chemise. "You will travel from the Highlands with the Earl of Braemoore and his men."

"Earl English!" Bonnie stood with her hands on her hips facing Brianna. "Nay! How can Lochlan and De

Ros throw me to the English when it is the English who seek to harm me?"

"You will whisper, lass," Brianna instructed. She took Bonnie by the hand and led her to a soft chair in front of the fireplace. "Sit." Brianna sat in the other chair. "Much has been discussed and much has been discovered today," Brianna whispered. "There is nothing to fear from the Earl or his men. The Earl has agreed to provide you with protection. You will remain at his residence in England until this matter has been resolved."

"His residence? England?" Bonnie jumped up. "Please, Brianna, do not let the Lairds do this. I had determined that I must run away. Send me to a clan. I will hide as a maid in their kitchen."

Brianna's mouth lifted with a hint of a smile. She shook her head. "Nay. The danger must be taken far away from Scotland. Too much is at risk. Another cottage was set afire late this afternoon."

Bonnie held her hand to her heart, taking a deep breath in hopes of chasing away her rising hysteria.

"No one was hurt," the Lady explained. "But it, too, is a harbinger. A warning." She took the fresh gown from Alice and lifted it over Bonnie's head.

Bonnie lifted her arms into the gown and savoured the comfort found in this simple act that she and Brianna had performed over the years—a mother helping her daughter. The gown fell neatly over her form. Its hem tickled the tops of her feet as Alice began to lace it. Tears stung at Bonnie's eyes. She did not want to leave this castle. The only home she could remember. Yet others were in danger too. And all because of her.

Alice coaxed Bonnie to the chair in front of her chamber desk and began to brush her hair.

Brianna squatted beside Bonnie. "Few know of the plan. You will leave this eve with the Lairds and Caol. Some of De Ros' men and Lochlan's men will also travel with you to the edge of Rose territory."

"But—"

Brianna placed a finger against Bonnie's lips and frowned. "De Ros has already sent missives to the Lairds of the territories through which you will travel. All will go well, with their permission."

"But has De Ros told them I am with the Earl? They will know!"

"Nay. Only that a group of men are travelling who have purchased ponies," explained Brianna. "The ponies will be sent later in order that your group can travel at a faster pace."

How could the Lairds send her away? Nay, give her away . . . and to Earl English. Now anger mixed with Bonnie's rising hysteria.

"Cease, Alice!" Bonnie commanded. "My hair is quite

brushed." Bonnie's scalp was tingling from Alice's efforts, her panic and anger growing as she took in Brianna's words.

"Tis important to look lovely, lass," Alice replied. "It must shine and sparkle on this eve." A secretive glance passed between the Lady and Alice.

Bonnie swatted the brush from the maid's hand, and jumped up, moving away from Alice, from Brianna. "Twill be covered by my hood and without a moon the shine will be hidden." She pulled her plaid shawl from the bed and wrapped it tight around her shoulders. Why could she not quite catch her breath?

"You look fresh and ready," said Brianna, standing. "Come. Alice will gather additional clothing and send them to be readied." She held out her hand." De Ros and Lochlan would like a word with you and the Earl in the library."

Again, a secret glance passed between Brianna and her maid.

"How long am I to stay with the Earl?" Bonnie questioned, tears threatening to fall.

"That is for you and the Earl to discuss." Brianna stood before Bonnie, looking into her eyes.

Bonnie frowned and shook her head. "Why? Surely De Ros and Lochlan will instruct him on matters and send a missive as to when I can return."

Brianna remained silent for a time and Bonnie

sensed that a final piece of the secret was about to be revealed.

"The Lairds have placed this matter into the Earl's hands. They have negotiated that you will remain under the Earl's protection for an indefinite period of time until he chooses to allow you to return."

"Allow?" Bonnie's voice rose above a whisper. Her stomach clenched and invisible fingers rose higher to take her breath from her. "Until he chooses?" She closed her eyes and a tear trickled down her face. She drew a deep breath before she opened them again. "What exactly have the Lairds negotiated?"

Brianna took Bonnie's hand and whispered softly. "You will wed tonight and be the Earl's bride."

Bonnie stared at Brianna. Disbelief. She shook her head and tried to speak but could only sputter. She stumbled toward the secret chamber door, prepared to tell her Lairds exactly what she thought of their negotiations. Wed? Bride of the Earl? Her protest welled up from her centre. Just as she began to laugh hysterically, a hand clamped over her mouth, another gripped her arm, swinging her around. She looked into the pale grey eyes of Lochlan MacEwen.

"Tis a night of sacrifices, lass," whispered Lochlan. "Already Donal and three guards prepare to ride from the safety of Rose Castle, travelling West to MacEwen lands to draw out and waylay these enemies." He raised his eyebrows and slowly lowered his hand watching her carefully. "They sacrifice for you and the clan. Giving up their own safety for the well-being of others."

"But you have said that I could choose my husband," retorted Bonnie. She pulled back from Lochlan and glared at Brianna. "You forsake your promise."

Lochlan tugged gently on her arm, directing her attention to him. "My promise has always been to protect you. Much has been forsaken and much already sacrificed."

"But—"

"I remember a bawling bairn, sitting beside a dying woman who was brutally beaten and burnt, defending her own," Lochlan whispered. "What will your sacrifice be to ensure safety for the clan while this problem is resolved?"

Lochlan released her and stepped back. He spoke a final time, his voice firm without negotiation. "You will marry the Earl and hie away tonight." He extended his hand toward the secret passageway.

Bonnie took a deep breath, and walked into the darkness of the tunnel.

## Chapter Ten

Braeson walked beside Donal through a shadowy tunnel beneath Rose Keep. Upon Braeson's agreement to marry Bonnie, and stating his final word, "Prepare", Donal had stepped into the room from behind the tapestry of the castle library. Cunning lot!

Since then, Donal had been his companion guiding him through a secret passageway toward the Rose stables in order that Braeson might inform his men. Braeson smirked into the gray shadows of the tunnel. He had taken his lead guardsman, Jack, aside to explain the intricate details of the unexpected midnight departure. The expression on the older guardsman's face, when Braeson enlightened him about his imminent marriage, had been nothing short of astonishment. Jack was not one to hold his tongue, yet the guardsman had remained speechless. His face had grown red in stark contrast to his white beard. Braeson was unsure if Jack was attempting to hold in his laughter or his anger. Had Braeson not slapped him on the back, the guardsman might have exploded. Braeson snorted as he imagined Jack's funeral and his marriage all in one night, here, at Rose Castle. Indeed, it would be a story that any bard would treasure. He must have snorted a second time because Donal peered at him strangely as if to speak, yet remained silent.

Braeson rubbed the smirk from his face in an attempt to regain his wits as he followed Donal up a hidden, rickety wooden staircase inside the walls of the Keep. Bloody Hell! Had he lost his mind? Had he just thrown away all of the sense his father had tried to instill in him? He had actually agreed to marry that woman. Was she really Bonnie of Rose or a she-demon of hell?

What would his father have said? If only Braeson could send a missive to the afterlife and have it returned with his father's reply. Braeson's stomach tightened at the thought of his father and he closed his eyes briefly as he stepped into the hall at the top of the stairway. Since his father's death a year past, the sorrow had failed to subside.

Donal continued along a narrow corridor and stopped before a panel in the wall. Opening it, he revealed Braeson's chamber. "I will remain at this post, my Lord. Once you have prepared and gathered your belongings, I will escort you to the library." Donal stepped aside and bowed slightly as Braeson entered his chamber.

The panel closing behind Braeson made him feel a prisoner. He had a growing suspicion that this marriage might be much like a prison. He rubbed his neck. Perchance a noose. A life sentence.

Braeson's father had always encouraged him to marry and had enjoyed his own marriage. He had believed love came after marriage and had encouraged Braeson to choose a woman who would honour him and his family's name. Did that describe the woman he had just agreed to marry?

"Egads!" Had he just mumbled the word aloud? He was even beginning to sound like these people!

Braeson moved about the room collecting his belongings. Bonnie would require a Braemoore cape to cover her in her travels. He examined his own, a finely-cured, brown leather cloak. He brushed the dust from it. He spotted a second one lying on the chair by the wall. He chuckled, realizing that Jack had recovered enough to direct the Braemoore men to prepare. Obviously Jack had already been in this chamber and packed most items, in readiness for the journey. Braeson shoved a few remaining items into his satchel. He sat on the bed and rubbed his hands over his face. Where had his sanity gone? He had actually negotiated with these people to take their problem home with him. He and Bonnie would be married within minutes, and leave within the hour.

Her people were strangers to whom he owed nothing. Nothing, except payment for the seven ponies he had purchased. Yet he acknowledged that he had liked these strangers long before he had even met them. He and Caol had become acquaintances at the Université de Paris. After exchanging a few stories about their families, Caol had discovered Braeson's mother was Scottish. That was when their friendship had grown into loyalty and trustworthiness.

*At least you're half-Scot, Braeson.* Isn't that what Caol had said to him? Yet for some reason which he did not understand, upon meeting Caol's people, his sense of familiarity with them went far beyond that of new acquaintances. It was as if they had provided him an almost familial place within their clans. It was one more mystery he had encountered upon meeting these people. Hadn't Auld Maeve whispered that there were mysteries about these people—secrets and clandestine activities—that kept the greatest of the Scottish clans alive and thriving?

The family that surrounded his soon-to-be wife were good people. Braeson's father had included that word—good—in the description of a fine wife. A good honourable woman. Did that description direct one to marry a woman that he'd only met a handful of days ago? And what a meeting that had been. Bonnie had almost landed him in the afterlife with his father.

Braeson shook his head in an effort to straighten his thoughts. He did like the family, or was it families? He had not met a family before where two men and one woman were raising a child as their own. To whom did Bonnie belong? Who were her people? How could he confront the mysteries that surrounded this red haired she-demon? Or was her hair red and gold? He was still unsure. Earlier in the pony shed, the late afternoon sun rays that had edged their way in through the roof slats had painted it a deep auburn. Yet even in the shadows there had been a hint of golden strands. And her eyes had matched the changing hues of her hair as the shadows in the barn waxed and waned.

The pearl necklace would look stunning around Bonnie's neck, gently caressing her skin. Her skin was a golden colour as if it had been kissed by the sun. It mixed well with the many hues of her cinnamon eyes and hair. Her beauty would outshine the exquisiteness of the necklace but what a stunning exhibit the necklace was. Three strands of intricately threaded pearls—each pearl, like a snowflake, owning its own unique shape. He recalled how the colours had shimmered in the light of the fireplace—pink, blue and green—ebbing and flowing.

Braeson had recognized the necklace immediately when it had rattled in front of him on the wooden table in the library. He could not resist touching it, admiring it. He wondered if De Ros and Lochlan realized that the pearl rope was only one half of a complete necklace. It would be a perfect fit to its other half that was secreted away at his home in Braemoore. Surely, it was happenstance that Bonnie possessed one half of the pearl necklace and he the other. He chuckled. Oh, how Auld Maeve would smile at this real-life story. "See!" she would declare. "The Silkie and her man have found each other."

Braeson closed his eyes and shook his head. He had long stopped believing in Silkies and tales whispered to him by Auld Maeve. In all decency, he could not accept the necklace that had been tossed to him by Lochlan. He would not be bribed over such a delicate yet treacherous matter. It was not honourable. The necklace was Bonnie's birthright. When he had left the library, he had also left the necklace still dangling in the fireplace heat.

*It was not honourable.* He scanned the room searching for his father. It was as if his dead sire stood there, speaking these very words to him. How many times had his father spoken to him about honour? Braeson would honour Bonnie with his protection and she would honour his family's name. Braeson laughed aloud. She would? Hadn't she mumbled against the English several times this past week?

He continued to chuckle over the ridiculous notion of his soon-to-be-wife honouring his name, even as Donal, his prison guard, stepped into the room from the secret stairwell.

"All is ready, my Lord?" Donal raised his eyebrows as if to question why the Earl of Braemoore was laughing alone.

Braeson rose, collected his satchel and cloaks and followed the guard through the secret entrance and down the passageway to the library.

Just before they entered the room, Donal turned to Braeson. "I would advise that you maintain your humour as you journey to England with our Bonnie, my Lord."

Braeson stared back at Donal. Surely it was not too late to pull out of this arrangement and run.

*It is your word that makes you honourable, my son.* His father's words again resounded from the dead.

As Donal flipped the tapestry aside, Braeson took a moment to place the cloaks on a chair, then he turned, looking into the library. The first face he saw was that of the she-demon, auburn eyes glaring and her lovely mouth scowling . . . at him.

Bonnie was unable to stop trembling as she stood

before the priest. A loud thrumming intensified in her head as her heart pounded too loudly and too fast. She felt like a spectator rather than a participant at her marriage ceremony. She watched, as if standing outside of herself, as the young woman named Bonnie repeated the words the priest instructed, held hands with a stranger and nodded in agreement. Her Lairds, De Ros and Lochlan, were positioned on either side of Brianna, who stood stoically, yet tears shimmered at her eyes.

Bonnie had started shivering the moment she entered the passage to the library. The trembling bespoke of myriad emotions from the day's treachery. Attempted kidnapping to maid snatching. She did not believe for a moment that Lochlan and De Ros had negotiated this marriage for her in good faith. Nay! Earl English, like all the English, was a master manipulator. Somehow he had convinced her Lairds that this was the solution to the danger faced by Bonnie. Whisk her away to England.

"Bonnie?"

Why the Earl desired her as his wife she did not know. But when this ceremony was complete she would be legally his. His property.

"Bonnie?"

Someone was calling her name.

"Lass?"

Someone shook her shoulder gently and she raised her head and looked at the priest.

"Do you have a symbol of this betrothal?" the priest questioned, looking from her to Braeson.

She raised her head higher, staring at the Earl, his eyes—beautiful, pale gray with a hint of something unrecognizable, as if a gray fog blocked her from seeing into his soul, his empty soul.

"I do," Braeson answered. He pulled a gold chain from inside his dark coat. A small golden ring hung from it. Braeson unwound it from the chain and handed it to the priest.

The priest made the sign of the cross over it. "This ring represents the unbreaking bond of this union." He handed it back to the Earl.

Earl English took her hand and slid the ring onto her finger. Bonnie frowned and peered at the band carefully. It was a flat gold band engraved with intertwined ivy leaves. She looked at the Earl staring into his beautiful soulless eyes again. What secrets did he hold?

"Join hands for the final blessing," the priest directed. Again he made the sign of the cross, this time over their joined hands. "What God has joined, let it not be forsaken." He nodded at Braeson.

Bonnie sneered as the Earl raised her ringed hand to his lips and kissed it softly. She noticed Caol, who stood on the far side of Earl English. Exhaustion edged his eyes, worry his brow. Where was Caol's usual smile? She wondered what role Caol had in the negotiation of this marriage. She felt her eyes mist and turned away only to be enfolded into Brianna's embrace.

"Out of darkness come many treasures, lass," the older woman whispered. "Look for them."

Bonnie felt a strong hand at her elbow and turned to see the Earl bow his head to Brianna in farewell.

"Come Bonnie, we must begin our journey." He looked around. "Caol has just left and is to remain at least an hour ahead of us."

Braeson seemed to have his plan well organized, Bonnie thought. Cunning man that he was.

He directed her toward the secret passage where Lochlan had just disappeared. They stood alone behind the tapestry.

"Wait," he directed. He began to pull at the plaid shawl she had wrapped around her shoulders.

"No!" she stepped away from him and wrapped her plaid more snuggly around herself. "Tis mine."

The Earl's hand snaked out and grabbed her wrist pulling her close. "The plaid is to be left behind. You will be too easily identified. Wear this dark cape." He nodded toward a garment that lay on the chair inside the tunnel.

Bonnie stared at the foreign cape. She had sacrificed much today. She gripped her wool shawl, her plaid, and felt the softness of the fabric. How many times had she worn it and felt its familiar protection. Smelled its aroma—the smell of this castle, her home. She loved this plaid that represented who she was, the De Ros weave, with the MacEwen emblem embroidered at each corner.

*I am neither MacEwen nor De Ros.* The words wrapped themselves around her in a blanket of sorrow as she closed her eyes and took a deep breath. Trembling, she shed the plaid from her shoulders and allowed it to drop to the ground. She reached for the dark cape and pulled it around her. It fell to her ankles and would make an excellent cover throughout the night. She glared at the Earl as he stepped closer and whispered for only her to hear.

"It is a dangerous night, Bonnie." He flicked the cape's hood up over her head allowing his hands to remain on either side. "But all will be well." His lips brushed gently over hers. "Follow me," he commanded and walked deeper into the secret tunnel.

Bonnie pushed the tapestry aside to peek a final time into the library. Only De Ros and Brianna remained in the room, standing close, whispering. Just as she turned away and stepped toward the tunnel, her foot snagged on her plaid that lay on the floor. Her eyes lingered on it for a moment and then she followed the light that Earl English's torch offered.

Twas a night of secrets and mysteries. How could it be that the MacEwen's emblem of intertwined ivy leaves on her plaid was also engraved on her wedding ring?

## Chapter Eleven

Braeson snapped his head up. A slight noise, a minute rustle—and he locked eyes with a she-cat. It was heavy with milk, slinking into the camp, hissing, its tail raised and readying to leap. Braeson reached for a knife tucked at the back of his waist. Turning his head slightly, he took note of where his men were positioned. They, too, held weapons. Young Williem had his bow pulled. Braeson's wolfhound stood ready to charge, fangs bared.

The pebbles fell over the scene like gentle raindrops followed by a stone that skidded across Braeson's right ear and struck the wild cat. It lay motionless.

"Bloody hell!" roared Braeson. He touched his ear. Wet. Blood smeared his finger. He drew a deep breath and shook his head. He had an inkling about who had thrown the stone as it was not a strategy any of his men would employ to down a cat. The wolfhound charged and grabbed the feline by its scruff and shook it. Damned mongrel! Braeson did not want blood spewed and see more wild beasts come in for a meal.

"Drop it," commanded Braeson. They had to break camp and move into the night. "Oliver, bury the cat," he directed. Was the cat still alive? Did its eyes just open and then roll back?

"You will not bury the cat!"

Braeson and his men turned in surprise toward the commanding voice. Those were the first words the she-demon had uttered since this journey had begun two nights past.

Bonnie scrambled off the rock overhang with speed and agility that impressed Braeson, disgruntled though he was. As she ran toward the cat, he stepped into her path and for a moment placed his hands at her waist, steadying her as she bumped into him.

"You'll not approach it," Braeson said between gritted teeth. "It could be diseased, coming into the camp in such a brazen manner."

"Tis not dead, only addled a wee bit." Bonnie attempted to swerve round Braeson but he grabbed her arm and held her in place. "I came upon her lair while I washed in the stream."

He held her arm fast as she attempted to move past him a second time and took note of the grimace that passed over her face. The pressure of his hand must have touched a wound from the whip when her assailants had attacked. He again placed his hands at her waist and held her still.

Braeson turned back to the motionless cat and then looked again at Bonnie through narrowed eyes, studying her. She was a tall woman but still had to stand on tip toe to see the dead cat over his shoulder. This was the closest he had been to the she-demon since they had stood side by side stating their marriage vows. He scanned her face. The bruises from the brutal attack were shading to purple and yellow. A speckled crimson contusion sat like a rainbow above her left eye.

"You speak," he said.

She lifted her eyes from the cat to him, glaring, and then dropped them to his chest.

"The men who have pledged fealty to me, and thus would lay down their lives for you, my wife." Braeson paused when Bonnie's eyes again snapped up to his. "You place their lives in danger."

"Nay," she pushed at his chest to escape his hold.

"Aye," he continued. He tightened his grip by sliding his hands from her waist to her back and clasping them together. This drew her up against his chest. Her hands were entrapped between their bodies.

"Release me," Bonnie whispered.

"I cannot," he stated. "We are here for you. To bring you to safety. Yet you run from my men." He nodded toward two of his guards who were scrambling down the rocks that Bonnie had just descended. The fearful and puzzled looks on their faces indicated that she had outrun them when they were supposed to be guarding her. Braeson touched his ear. "You throw stones at us."

"The rock, twas for the cat, to down it for its own good." Bonnie pushed free enough to hold high a leather sling in her hand. "The cat tis only addled for a short time," she explained. "Only to keep it safe for its babes so that your men do not kill it."

The she-demon stared at him with pleading eyes. She was more concerned for a wild cat and its babes then her own safety? He surmised that she knew little of the plan to get her safely to England and to his home.

"A lad from De Ros' troop brought a missive earlier this day," Braeson explained. "The troop battled three men who refused to provide information as to why you are in harm's way."

She stared at him, frowning. "The lad is a long way from Rose Keep. Why did you not wake me?" Her eyes blazed with angry sparks and she pushed again at his chest to disengage herself from his hold. "I might have sent a wee message to Brianna."

"He did not ride from the Rose Keep but rather was returning from their ride south."

Confusion grew in Bonnie's face, in her eyes, on her

wrinkled brow. She squinted and her lips puckered into a pout. "South?" she questioned. "Why would De Ros' men be returning from the south?"

"Many men ride for you. De Ros and his guards are a day's ride ahead. He journeyed first to ensure us a safe crossing through clan lands."

"But De Ros remained in his library with Brianna," she stated. "How could he be ahead of us?"

"He remained behind for a short time to comfort Brianna. She found no joy in releasing you to my protection." He allowed the words to float in the air between them for a time. "It is only to assure your safety that Lady Brianna agreed to free you. Are you not a daughter to her?"

Tears hovered in Bonnie's eyes threatening to spill. "I thought De Ros . . . I did not know." She shook her head several times as if trying to clear her thoughts.

"The missive ensured me that De Ros did join his men and his troop. They did confront three men who refused to reveal any information about you. Rather these enemies chose to fight. They are now in hell." He could not resist wiping a tear from the corner of her eye. "De Ros' troop has begun their return journey. Lochlan and his men are a day behind us. Caol and his men ride in the shadows in hopes of waylaying the enemy. All will travel with us to the border of Rose lands. All for your safe journey to your new home."

Her eyes held only sorrow now. Perchance she was beginning to understand.

"When De Ros' clansmen heard of your departure, many stepped forward to escort you. Many have stepped in harm's way for your protection."

Her tense body sagged against him. "They should not have done it. There are wives and bairns that need them."

Braeson had watched as straws were drawn to determine who would remain to guard Rose lands. Some had attempted to argue with De Ros as to who should ride to protect *their* Silkie. Orders were given. Places assigned to those left to guard the castle. Blessings were sent for their Silkie.

Now she was *his* Silkie.

"Many stand in harm's way this day. Those who have journeyed and those who have remained." Braeson leaned his head closer to her for only she would hear. "All for *our* Silkie."

Her eyes flashed slightly as they travelled back to him, her cheeks reddening. He smiled. He had hoped his final words, that moniker that she hated, would draw Bonnie from her sullenness and bring a spark again to her face. She needed that energy to move forward. Her face was inches from his and she could not avoid looking into his eyes.

"You will remain always in the presence of me or

one of my men." The shadows between them made her eyes a smoky umber. He recalled the first time he had met her and her fiery introduction.

"And the cat will live?"

Her breath fluttered around him, smelling sweetly of mint and wintergreen which she must have used for her evening ablutions.

Braeson looked over his shoulder grudgingly at the cat. A shallow hole had been dug and the men were moving to lift the cat into it. He returned his gaze to her anxious eyes. "I think not. My men are preparing to bury it."

Her body gave a jolt and she struggled against him, but he held her firmly to himself. Waiting for her acknowledgement, of her acceptance of his terms.

"Aye, tis my word you desire." She stilled and lifted her eyes again. "I will remain and not run again."

"And no more stones." He touched his ear and felt the stickiness there.

"Aye," she agreed.

Braeson released her and spun around. "Leave the cat." He directed his words to his men. "My Lady says it is only addled."

His Lady ran toward the sleeping cat.

"Jack! Oliver!" Braeson spoke through gritted teeth.

Two men stepped into Bonnie's path and barred her way. She placed her hands on her hips, as though attempting to stare the men into submission.

"Come. All is ready," Braeson stated as he scanned the camp site. During his conversation with Bonnie, his men had readied the camp for departure. "Let us travel into the night."

Jack motioned with his arm to where the horses stood waiting to carry their cargo onward. "Come Mistress," Jack encouraged. "The Master waits."

Bonnie looked at the cat a final time and then walked to her horse. Braeson stepped around it, placed his hands at her waist and assisted her onto the gray mare.

"All will be well," Braeson said. Yet he was not sure if he believed that himself.

She looked down at him, lifting her eyebrows high as if to question his words. Then she reached into a fold of her cape and shoved the container of salve into his hand. "Let us hope so, Master."

Was that mockery or sincerity in his wife's voice? His father's words spoke to him from beyond the grave. *A good and honourable woman.*

*Aye, let us hope so. Let us hope so.*

## Chapter Twelve

The vague streak of brightening sky lay narrow along the eastern horizon. If she turned on her horse far enough to the east, Bonnie could imagine the Rose Keep—home. A slow rustling would soon begin there. Cook in the kitchen. Men at the shore readying boats.

Bonnie knew Lady Brianna loved to rise early and watch the dawn creep in. Were they now both watching the same hesitant streak of brightening sky? Bonnie closed her eyes to ward off the sorrow that drifted around her.

Braeson had stated that it was Brianna who had grudgingly agreed to release Bonnie to his protection. Was it truly for Bonnie's protection, or had De Ros' clan finally tired of shielding her from the threats invading their lands? Bonnie had come to see them all as family. Brianna was her mother, Caol her brother, De Ros like a father. Even Lochlan, the MacEwen Laird, was committed to her well-being, spending the winter months at the Rose Keep and returning to the MacEwen lands in early spring when the last of the snow was melting.

After her wedding ceremony, when Bonnie had walked through the secret tunnel and into the shadowed meadow hidden by the sentinel walls of the courtyard, it had been Lochlan who had stood solitary beside her horse, holding its reins, waiting. It was he who had helped her atop her horse and had ridden with her throughout the night. A single line of guardsmen silently journeying south toward a foreign land under the darkness of night. After many hours, the first sign of dawn had wavered in the eastern skies and those around her, both the MacEwen and Braemoore men, had set up camp. A low fire had burned and Bonnie sat by it, accepting the gruel offered. Lochlan had spread her seal blanket around her shoulders and she had slept. When she had awakened, only Braeson and his men were with her at the camp. Lochlan and his troop had vanished.

*They are a day's ride behind us*, Braeson had reassured her.

A bird's short song beckoned her back to the present as Bonnie scowled into the early dawn. She need not ask where Lochlan had gone. He had released her to strangers just like Brianna, De Ros and, aye, even Caol had done.

She swallowed the rising lump in her throat and closed her eyes to ward off the threatening tears. Could Earl English be lying? She had not seen any lad bring a missive to their camp yestereve. Mayhap Braeson had tricked her people somehow to release her to him. Had they unwittingly sent her into harm's way? Mayhap she was surrounded by the men who had assaulted her days ago? The knot in her stomach tightened. Fear. She knew its grip well. It slithered from her belly, grasping her throat, stealing her breath and her courage to survive.

She watched as Braeson and Jack led their entourage off the trail, onto a path that climbed a hill where a copse of trees stood. Here they would camp for the day, hidden from view, yet able to keep watch over the surrounding area.

The bird spoke again—an unfamiliar trill.

Much like Lady Brianna, Bonnie too had always risen at dawn, hurrying to the shed to bid the ponies a good day. As she had prepared their feed and mucked out their stalls, she had listened to the birds bid welcome to the new day. The strange bird that sang now was one that did not roost near Rose Castle. They had travelled a far distance west, along the foothills of the Roinn a' Mhonaidh range, and she suspected the wild life would be different from that with which she was familiar.

"Come." Braeson directed. He stood beside her horse, a slight smile tipped the corners of his mouth. "You are tired. Your horse has stopped. One of the men will take it on to our camp."

Bonnie stared at Braeson. In her musings, she had not realized the mare had stalled. The reins lay loose in her hands.

She swayed with exhaustion, as Braeson helped her from the horse.

"Come. A stream lies beyond the camp. You can wash there."

Unlike the two previous night rides, now each time the troop stopped, Braeson was at her side to guide her to a resting spot. She suspected that last night's tussle with the wild cat, the thrown pebbles and stone and the panicked guards gave him cause to guard her himself.

Braeson led her through a short trail, shadowed by a wall of rock on either side, into a plateau with patches of tall grass that crept below her skirt and tickled her knees above her boots. She stopped and watched as Braeson continued to the edge of a meandering stream. He knelt beside it, removing his belt and sword and placing them at the stream's edge. He scrubbed his hands and then splashed water onto his face and hair.

"Come," he said turning to look back at her. "Soon

Jack will have the gruel ready and then rest can have us for a time."

Bonnie watched as Braeson walked to the edge of the cliff and looked down, scanning the surrounding area. He stretched and lifted his face to the hidden sun that was attempting to burn through the clouds. The bird sang its strange song again and then quieted.

The fading shadows revealed a small covey of grouse feeding below a tall pine perched on the far edge of the rock cliff. Bonnie reached into the folds of her skirt and found her collection of small stones. Placing one into her leather sling, she scooped a handful of dirt and threw it toward the covey. She flung the sling to the right then hurtled the stone toward a grouse that rose high into the air. The bird fell to the ground as the covey scattered and disappeared into the tree above. Braeson turned toward her as the bird thumped to the ground.

"Tis a meal," Bonnie explained.

Braeson frowned at her. Again. He seemed to scowl a lot. "How did you come to throw a sling?" he questioned.

"Brianna insisted that I learn some protection." She looked in the direction of the Rose Keep. A mountain barred the view. Even the streak of light in the eastern sky had faded. A familiar lump caught in her throat. "De Ros and Lochlan allowed me to throw a knife and sling."

Braeson's frown deepened and his eyes were two small slits. "Do pebbles and dirt also protect you?"

"Tis protection for others," she explained. "I pummelled Caol once with a stone. Twas not meant to happen." Bonnie attempted to not smirk as she recalled Caol running to the keep, blood trickling from his head. "He would die . . . so Caol thought!"

Braeson threw back his head and laughed.

Bonnie stared at his transformation. His smile revealed straight white teeth, and lips full when not pressed together. She recalled the night in the garden when he had told her the Silkie's tale. She gazed into his eyes, translucent gray and fringed with dark lashes. And beautifully clear! At this moment, for this time, he allowed his silver eyes to be unveiled of the misty fog—a barrier that had been present at their wedding and had remained to this moment. Twas vanished. She swallowed to catch her breath, averting her eyes and grasping her sling to her breast.

"Lochlan and De Ros insisted I throw pebbles before the stone is tossed. They said the next Laird of Rose cannot have an addled brain." She mimicked the words, pretending to toss pebbles into the air and to duck out of the way. "Tis a warning."

"I will be sure to remember," Braeson said.

As she turned toward the stream, he grasped her

hand.

"Nay!" she protested.

"I will have your hand."

Was he beginning to scowl again?

"Or your weapons." His eyes narrowed as he nodded toward her sling.

"Nay, not my weapons." She quickly slid her sling into the fold of her dress. "Tis my protection."

"Your protection surrounds you." Braeson waved his hand in the direction of the camp and his men. He glared at the dead grouse at their feet. "Jack finds the food. Tis his job to feed us." He ran his eyes over her body. Was he looking for her other weapons?

Bonnie tugged her hand free and knelt at the stream. She poured water over her face and neck. It trickled onto her clothes. She wished to remove her boots but that would reveal the two knives. Brianna had slipped one into her boot just before she entered the library to exchange vows with this man who now stood over her, glaring. Lochlan had slipped her the other after he had helped her onto her mare.

She immersed her hands into the clear, cool water waving them back and forth. She closed her eyes and inhaled the fresh morning air.

"Let us wade," Braeson suggested.

But when she looked at him, his eyes lifted from her boots slowly. The gleam of a challenge, that same look he had held just before he released her plaid some days ago and landed her in the pond, glimmered in his eyes. "Come, I will help tug your boots off."

"Nay." Her protest was louder than she wanted but she was determined to keep her sling and knives. She would not be fooled into thinking she was safe with Braeson and his men.

He reached for one boot but she stepped away from him, ran a distance and then knelt at the stream again. When she looked back, he was leaning against a rock ledge, arms folded across his chest, scowling at her. Again.

Bonnie threw a final handful of water over her hair and used the end of her cape to brush the droplets from her face. She stood and looked to where the hidden bird whistled. Its trill indicated that it was close and she searched the trees for it.

Suddenly, the covey of grouse fluttered from the tree and an arrow shot by her head. A horse and rider galloped through the stone alley way and sped toward her. Again, the strange bird whistled and another arrow flew by her. Fear choked her, tugging her forward, making her run. All logical thoughts disappeared and she ran through the grass, through the stream, scanning for a place to hide. She heard footsteps behind her and attempted to weave her way in various directions to avoid capture. As she lifted her head, she found herself running toward the edge of the cliff. Where was the rider? Who was behind her? Hands grabbed at her waist and twirled her around. She struggled against her captor, pummeling him in the chest and face.

"Cease!" Braeson commanded.

Bonnie came face to face with Braeson's steel gray eyes. One hand held her firmly to his side. The other hand reached into his boot and pulled out a long dagger. Just as Braeson tumbled with her over the cliff's edge he threw it. The rider's howl of pain splintered the air as she wrapped her arms and legs around Braeson, closing her eyes tightly and steeling herself for the inevitable landing on the ragged rocks below.

Instead, they fell onto a gently sloping hill of moss, and tumbled over and over until they slammed into the trunk of a large tree.

Braeson lay atop her, still and breathing heavily. He moaned and then silence ensued. He was alive but was he conscious? The dear man had just saved her from harm. She blinked twice and shook her head, bewildered that she would attach such a thought— dear—to Braeson. It was he that had snatched her from Rose Castle. Yet it was he who had just snatched her from the sharp tip of an arrow. The arrow the rider had shot would surely have hit her, had Braeson not flung them over the cliff.

She begrudgingly acknowledged that he had taken the full impact of the fall. As they had plunged toward the bottom of the drop, Braeson had spun them around so that it was his body that had slammed into the moss covered ground. Thank God there were no jutting stones on the slope. Over and under, over and under they had tumbled until their shoulders had crashed into the spruce.

Now Braeson lay still, his full weight on her. His arms still encircled her waist and his face had found a comfortable spot against her neck. She felt his breath shudder against her and it sent shivers through her body. He moaned again and she turned her head to his face. How badly was he injured? She gently pushed her hands through his black hair. The leather band that held it at his neck had come loose and his hair fell over her hands, thick and wavy. No cuts or open wounds on his head. Her hands explored his neck, muscled and strong, and then travelled over each shoulder. They were wide, solid shoulders and seemed intact, unharmed from the fall.

She could not squeeze her hands between their bodies. Bodies that seemed seamless, almost as one. Thus, she could not determine if he was injured on his chest. She continued her examination along his upper back and down toward his waist, caressing toward the sides of his hips. She could feel no blood or moisture. She stopped, hesitant. Should she continue her exploration over his buttocks? Her heart fluttered faster and she was almost relieved when she realized she could not reach down any further. She ran her hand over his upper arms and was thankful to feel that all was still intact. No bones jutted from the strong, muscled arms.

"You must run toward those who will protect you."

Bonnie gasped, startled, by Braeson's whispered words. "You speak."

"The day of the attack, you were running away from Rose Castle." He released a loud breath as if it took effort for him to say these words.

"You are injured?" she inquired.

"You ran away from me just now. Why?"

Bonnie closed her eyes. She remembered a time—long ago—when she was commanded to run.

"The first time I ran, I was but three years and lived with Ina. Our cottage was far from the MacEwen Castle. One night we saw the sky ablaze." She turned her face away from Braeson, and looked into the boughs of the spruce tree, remembering. "Ina said, 'Run, run! Away with ye, into the woods and only return when the dawn draws nigh'. Ina shoved my seal blanket into my hands and I ran and hid under the skin, below the boughs of a tree, much like this one. I waited. When I returned the next morn, there was Ina lying in the embers of our cottage, close to death." She turned her head to Braeson. "Ina's words are in my head. 'Run, run, away!' Tis why, when there is danger, I run."

The branches above them allowed for just a breath of space for Braeson to raise his head to look at her. His eyes were of the same colour as the snow in early spring. Throughout the winter, the snow collected the wonders of the Highlands. By spring, it was a lovely pale gray mingling with pebbles and leaves, twigs and dirt, flowing into streams and coaxing life back to the land. Oh, how she loved to sit on the hill beyond the castle and watch the snow sparkle and shine in the spring's warming sun. Melting, into its warmth. When Braeson rested his forehead on hers, she simply melted into him.

"Run, run to me, Bonnie. Run, run to me." His mouth touched her lips like a soft spring breeze. A velvety caress that flittered across her lower lip and then to the top. An infusion of warmth spread out from her stomach and her heart pulsed in her ears. How could she feel so safe in this man's embrace when he had taken her from her home? Braeson lifted his mouth and rested his forehead again on hers.

Scowling! The man was—"Scowling!" she hissed.

His eyes flashed open and he lifted his head slightly.

"You scowl! You do not like to . . ." She could not bring herself to say the word.

"Kiss you? Aye, I like it. I will try again and focus on not scowling." His lips were on hers again, his mouth open, smothering her with heat and desire. He trailed a path of kisses along her jawline and down her neck, then lifted his face to hers again. "Do I scowl now?" he whispered.

She studied his face, staring into his eyes that seemed almost colourless in the shadows of the spruce boughs. "You are attempting to hide it but you still scowl behind your eyes." She struggled to roll him off of her but he tightened his arms, still holding her waist.

"Cease," he muttered. His face lowered to the crook of her neck.

Bonnie turned her head away and stared through the boughs of the spruce. Tears welled in her eyes. She had kissed a few lads over the years but she could not recall any of them scowling at her. Those kisses had been pleasant, but she could not describe Braeson's kisses as pleasant. Nay. His kisses were delightful and beckoned her to want more of them. How could she want to kiss him more when all he did was scowl at her?

"Bonnie?" he whispered.

His breath caressed her neck and sent shivers into

her breast. She felt his body tense and his breathing was laboured. She would not look at him.

"Bonnie. I scowl because I am wounded at my shoulder."

She turned her head to him and met that familiar gleam of amusement, as when he had challenged her at the pond and more recently with her boots. "Tis truth?"

In one motion, Braeson rolled from her, through the branches of the spruce and lay on his back peering up at the sky. He winced and touched the front of his shoulder, looking at the blood that stained his hand. He released a low groan. "Tis truth," he echoed.

Bonnie crawled from their hiding place and knelt beside him. She had cared for the ponies at the keep and knew that blood could signal injuries from thorns to rock scrapes and could lead to infection. She pushed his hands away and studied the stain of blood on his shirt. It was the size of a horse's hoof and growing.

He grasped her wrists as she attempted to rip the material. "Bonnie. Jack will tend to the scrape."

Again, she pushed his hands away and tore the material. "Jack cooks the food and also attends to the scrapes?" The wound oozed blood, yet it was but a small one, easily mended. "I do not see or hear Jack."

Braeson looked up to the top of the cliff edge, worry

lines creasing his forehead. "Neither do I hear the strange bird call."

Bonnie also listened for the peculiar trill. The sudden attack must have scared the bird away. She ripped a strip of cloth from her underclothes and patted the wound. Braeson flinched.

"A wee tip of an arrow has lodged beneath your skin. Aye, tis the size of the nail on your thumb." She applied the cloth to the wound again to stench the blood flow. "I only need to cut the top layer of skin and the tip can be lifted. Tis a knife I need."

Braeson raised his eyebrows and nodded his head toward the top of the cliff ledge. "My weapon lies above, Bonnie. My knife is embedded in a scoundrel."

They stared at each other for a time. His eyes the palest of gray revealing a mixture of discomfort and amusement. "If you soon do not divulge where your knives are, I may bleed to death."

She continued to stare at him through slivered eyes. Finally she relented and pulled a knife from her boot.

"It pleases me that you chose not to become a widow so soon." He tried to smile. "There is alcohol in this flask that hangs across my shoulders."

Bonnie cleaned the knife with the alcohol and carefully cut the thin sheath of skin. She flicked the small arrow tip and it flew into the moss beside her. Setting her knife on the ground, she reached into the pouch that hung across her shoulders.

"Lady Brianna sent along a few vials of healing remedies." She pulled two containers from the pouch and lifted the lids. "We use these medicinals with our ponies to aid in healing."

The aroma from each container wafted into the air.

Braeson rose, sitting upright, back straight. "I am not Tokie," he growled. "Neither salt nor vinegar will touch this wound." He reached for the flask of alcohol and poured the liquid over his injury. Again, he winced.

Bonnie cast her eyes down to hide the humour behind her action. Mayhap it was unkind of her to offer the salt and vinegar when she had more suitable remedies in her pouch. But she was not pleased that her knife was revealed. She had seen his suspicious eyes flit to her other boot, searching for a second knife nestled within.

"My knife!"

Together they snatched for her knife but Braeson swept it from the ground and slipped it into his boot.

"Nay!" She scowled attempting to grab hold of his boot. "I will have my knife."

Braeson caught her hand and scowled back. "You do not need it. Your protection surrounds you. Look!"

His wolfhound came bounding through a grove of trees. It stopped before Bonnie and stuck its nose in her face, sniffing.

"Away with you!" She pulled her hand from Braeson's grasp and pushed at the large dog. "I'll not associate with one who wishes to kill mother cats." She shoved again.

Braeson clicked his tongue and the dog sat beside him, smelled his wound and then barked once.

"Well done, Colosse." He scratched between the large dog's ears. The giant barked again. "Colasse is signaling to the rest of your protectors that he has found us. Come let us finish with this wound or Jack will scold us both for not covering it properly." Braeson moved closer to Bonnie, looking at her to complete the task.

She ripped another piece of cloth from her underclothes and moved closer to this man. His shirt had fallen away from his shoulders and a warm flush crawled up from her neck as she studied his chest. She felt his gaze on her face, a breath away from her, as she wound the strip of cloth under his arm and across his shoulder. She felt shy and awkward under his watchful gaze.

"Food, scrapes and Jack even scolds." She attempted to change the subject and divert him from watching her. "Who is this Jack who prepares food, looks after scrapes and even scolds? And why does he speak like a Scot?"

Braeson laughed. "Jack is Scottish, a Campbell."

Her stomach clenched. Hadn't she heard De Ros and Lochlan whisper about the Campbells long ago? She had been warned often to stay away from the Campbells and their land. For certain, the two clans, Rose and MacEwen, worked to avoid contact with the Campbell Keep.

"A Campbell!" She had not meant to sneer so. Mayhap she revealed too much.

Braeson quirked his brows. "Aye, my mother, Lady Annella, is a Campbell."

"A Campbell?" Egads! She did it again. Bonnie breathed deeply trying to steady her heartbeat.

"Aye, she was a Campbell," Braeson frowned at her. "She came to England to marry my father."

Bonnie wondered if De Ros and Lochlan knew of his mother's heritage. Hadn't she heard them whisper that it had been the Campbells that had burned the MacEwen Keep all those years ago when Ina had told her to *run, run away*? She shivered. Who was this man who was now her husband?

Braeson continued to frown and studied her with narrowed eyes.

She shivered again.

"My mother came to England to marry my father." He paused. "Maeve accompanied my mother, and Jack followed Maeve. He swore fealty to my father, to

Braemoore—six and twenty years ago."

"And you trust him?" The question was just a whisper.

Braeson threw back his head and laughed. "His loyalty is evident. I trust him with my life."

Bonnie could only stare, her mouth agape. She snapped it shut.

All at once, a group of men crashed through the trees.

*Run, run away with ye!* Ina's words warned. As Bonnie began to rise to her feet, to run, Braeson's warm arms embraced her.

"Shhh, be still Bonnie." He pulled her to his chest and caressed her cheek. "Look again." He pointed at the men. "Your protection."

*Chapter Thirteen*

Braeson studied the horses and their riders as they rode along a narrow path among the trees. He considered himself a lucky man to be leader of this troop, Braemoore's best.

Braeson's men had fared well in the short-lived battle. Jack reported that only one guard had been wounded. Bonnie's mare had shied when the assailants had crashed into the camp. The mare had kicked and the guard's arm had been broken. Jack had reset the bone and the arm now lay secured in a sling, across the man's chest. Bonnie's horse had run off and was yet to be found.

Braeson scanned the trees as the troop wound their way along the narrow path. Where would a frightened mare hide? He had trusted the dog to retrieve the mare and only hoped the pair would appear when Bonnie was not present. The combined clamour of Colosse barking and the mare protesting would raise Bonnie's hackles again.

Bonnie rode with Braeson on his horse. She, too, seemed to watch expectantly for the mare to appear. She sat upright attempting not to rest against him as they rode along. Yet her body swayed back from time to time, as though fighting the sleep that tempted her.

In consultation with Jack and Oliver, Braeson had decided they should not remain at the camp. Only a few supplies had been unpacked before the attack had occurred. Oliver and a guard had been sent on to scour the countryside and determine if an inn was available to them. By the time they had returned with news of an inn a few miles beyond, the bodies of the three dead men had been searched and buried.

Bonnie bobbed to the right and Braeson pulled her back to lean against him. She struggled for a moment and then slept.

He had studied her face as she tended to his wound. Exhaustion and fear were etched on her face. Dark circles were stamped under her eyes and her bruises, though fading, still painted tones of purple and yellow on her cheek. She needed a place where she could hide away for a time and sleep undisturbed. During the past three days, as she had slept close to the fire, she had tossed and turned under her seal skin. He had felt helpless to know what to do for this young woman who had been forced from her home and was being stolen away to England. Sleeping in a soft bed for the next several hours would provide her with renewed strength and stamina to complete this journey.

A sense of overwhelming relief had shot through Braeson when, under the spruce boughs, Bonnie had begun to examine his body gently, hesitantly. She moved, she breathed. He had rejoiced knowing she lived. He could not have borne the thought of sending a missive to Rose Castle announcing Bonnie's death . . . admitting that he had failed to protect her within the first three days of their journey.

Rather, it appeared that Bonnie had weathered the fall from the cliff well, only landing beneath him when they had crashed into the spruce. He was the one whose breath had been knocked from him—who had struggled to hold on to consciousness in those first few minutes while he lay atop her.

All those days ago, when he had watched Bonnie pet Tokie in the shed, as her hands had slid over the animal, calming it, a pang of jealousy had shot through him. Today, under the spruce, her hands had slid over him, through his hair, down his neck to his shoulders, and beyond. But her hands had not calmed him. Rather he had been aroused, enticed. If she had been able to squeeze her hands between their bodies, she would have learned just how much he enjoyed kissing her. Thank God, the wee tip of an arrow had caused enough pain to stop him from doing more than just lie there. She tasted sweet and her kisses were delightful. Braeson pulled Bonnie closer, relishing this opportunity to hold her near to him as she slept.

As Jack led the group to the top of a knoll, Braeson scanned the path below. A dim outline of an inn came into view. The small two story inn was nestled amongst a grove of tall trees, tucked away, almost hidden from view.

Oliver had already purchased the services of the inn master and his wife, and a room was being prepared for Bonnie. The shed at the back of the inn would house the horses and Braeson's men.

Except for the rotation of guards throughout the day and evening, most of the troop would remain hidden. Some guards, alert and watchful, would act as simple travellers. The company would continue on the morrow and travel by day now rather than by night. According to Jack, they were well away from Rose land, which meant that De Ros, Lochlan and Caol no longer shadowed them.

A skirmish to Braeson's right grew louder and louder. Jack raised his arm to halt the group. His men turned as one to surround Bonnie and Braeson, hands ready at their swords, only to see Bonnie's mare crash through the bushes with Colasse nipping at its heels. Birds cawing, Colasse barking and the mare whinnying brought Bonnie upright, awakened to the commotion around her.

She turned toward her horse, clicking her tongue in a rhythmic pattern. Daisy charged toward her and then stopped abruptly when Bonnie raised her arms.

"Come, Daisy," encouraged Bonnie. The frightened mare continued to whinny and moved closer to Bonnie and Braeson. It quieted as Bonnie touched its muzzle, bending towards it and speaking unintelligible words. She eyed Colasse who stood by the mare wagging his tail.

"And you, you wild beastie, will walk on this side." She pointed to the spot on the other side of Braeson's horse. "For shame! You will not make a friend of the mare or me with such a din." The dog pulled back its ears, dropped its tail and slunk to the spot to which Bonnie had pointed.

Braeson frowned. Obviously Bonnie did not recognize that even Colasse was part of her protection. The dog had brought the mare to her and yet she reprimanded it, rather than acknowledge the dog as her aid, her help.

Having finished scolding the dog and calming her mare, Bonnie slumped back against Braeson. She wiped her brow and closed her eyes.

"What is it, Bonnie?" Braeson questioned.

"I think I could eat a horse." She frowned at Colasse

as it slunk along beside the charger. "Or mayhap a dog. I am verra, verra famished."

It was true. They had not eaten for several hours now. The morning hour of breaking their fast had come and gone in all of the commotion.

"Look yonder," Braeson directed. "A meal and a warm bed await you."

The troop snaked its way in and out of trees along the secluded path that led to the inn's shed. Braeson helped Bonnie from the horse and passed the reins to a guard. He stood for a moment, watching the horses and his men disappear into the shed. He scanned the area. All appeared calm.

Braeson noted that Bonnie was exhausted, shaking from lack of sleep and food. She needed rest after the long night's ride and the unpleasant surprises the morning had brought. He placed her hand gently into the crook of his arm to steady her as they walked along the side of the shed toward the entrance to the inn.

Without warning, a bulky arm snaked around Braeson neck. Something sharp was thrust against his back. He struggled against his attacker and feared for Bonnie's life. Her hand had slipped from him. Where was she?

"I swore someday I would kill you," a voice growled in his ear. As the snarling adversary swung Braeson around, gripping his shirt front, the metallic clash of swords drawn from scabbards exploded in the air. Jack and Oliver stood on either side of this enemy, swords held at his neck.

"Release him, you fool," sneered Jack as a shower of pebbles rained upon them and a stone pummelled into the assailant's head.

Braeson stepped away from the adversary's slackened grip and watched as the man's eyes widened in surprise. Then he grimaced in pain, fell to his knees and slumped to the ground unconscious . . . or was he dead?

Braeson swung around to see Bonnie standing a distance from him holding her sling limp in her hand, staring.

Anger shot through him. "Jack, Oliver," he commanded. "Drag this scourge to the shed and guard him with your lives."

He then marched toward Bonnie, fury oozing from his gut. Who did this chit think *she* was? *He* did not require *her* protection! Bloody hell! *She* required *his* protection. Did she not have enough sense to call for help rather than draw her sling and engage the enemy? The very enemy that wanted her dead.

Braeson bolted toward her, ready to shake her and lock her in the room for the day. As he neared, she took a step backward, then swayed, her eyes rolling upward. As she collapsed toward the ground, he scooped her up into his arms, and hugged her to him.

Braeson closed his eyes for a brief moment as all anger drained from him. He took a deep breath and smiled at her still form. She was a beautiful, brave woman.

And an excellent shot.

## Chapter Fourteen

"Shut your jaw," Jack roared at the prisoner, just as Braeson entered the shed.

Braeson stood in the shadows by the wooden doors, while Jack loomed over the assailant and smacked his face with the back of his hand. The stranger attempted to retaliate but the ropes around his wrists and waist held him secure to the far corner of the shed against the rungs of a stall.

"Bloody hell," Jack sneered. "'Tis a fool."

The stranger reared up and spit. The gob landing on Jack's forehead. "You speak like a Scot but dress like an English," the stranger sneered. "Traitor."

Jack lunged and grasped the man by his shirt front, smacked him again and then threw him onto the shed floor where he lay flat on his face. Two of Braeson's men hauled Jack from the man.

"Jack?" Braeson eyed his lead guardsman and then locked his gaze on the stranger.

Jack shrugged free from his guards and came to stand beside Braeson. "Our Lady?" he questioned in a low voice. "How does she fare?"

"My Lady is well fed and now sleeps in a soft bed," Braeson stated as he continued to observe the stranger. "Two guards at her window and her locked door." His gaze slid back to Jack. He noted Jack's pallor where his face should have been flushed from exertion. Even his white beard shook revealing his angst. The guardsman's eyes darted from Braeson to the prisoner. It was rare to see his lead guardsman agitated when dealing with a captive.

"Speak, Jack," Braeson commanded in a low voice.

Jack pushed his hand through his gray hair. "Tis his plaid. I have not laid my eyes on those colours for these many years. But a man does no forget the images of when he was a lad."

Braeson frowned at Jack and nodded slightly to urge him to continue.

"He wears the Campbell plaid," Jack spewed under his breath.

Braeson's gaze returned to the stranger. He had little knowledge of clan symbols, though he was somewhat familiar with the De Ros and the MacEwen plaids. He had noticed that Bonnie wore the De Ros plaid with an ivy design fashioned along its border. That was unique to her plaid. Neither his mother,

Jack, nor Auld Maeve wore any semblance of the Campbell plaid. Indeed, his mother spoke naught of her Campbell roots. Braeson's vague knowledge of clan life came to him from Auld Maeve who had whispered stories of clan folklore to him as a boy at bedtime.

"Tis a Campbell to be sure, yet I know not this donkey's arse from Adam," whispered Jack. "He's a fool spewing shite since he has awakened." Jack bent his head toward Braeson and whispered, "Neither have I revealed my recognition of his plaid."

Braeson stepped out of the shadows and into the middle of the shed several lengths from the prisoner. Perchance he should heed Bonnie's warning. Was the Campbell clan responsible for the threat that hovered over her? Yet the messages nailed to the trees that were shown to him in De Ros' library suggested Norse origins, not Scottish. If so, why did the Campbells want Bonnie dead? What role did she or the Campbells play in this treacherous midnight escape from Scotland to safety?

The stranger rolled over and struggled to sit up, finally leaning his head against the bottom of the stall post. Silence filled the shed as the belligerent man glared at Braeson. He was a big, bulky man. The blood that smeared his mouth and the bruises on the left side of his face indicated that a struggle had ensued to secure him.

Braeson narrowed his eyes as he studied the man's clothes and then his face again. A sense of familiarity wavered about Braeson, yet he was unable to understand it.

Danger surrounded this journey. The plot to steal Bonnie away from Rose Castle disguised as a bride was unravelling. Bonnie had been discovered on the cliff, and now here. Oliver was a master tracker and had reported that there was not a trail or sign of additional assailants after the attack on the cliff. Yet Braeson now stared the enemy in the face. The first captive to be taken alive.

Braeson held no allegiance to the Campbell name. His Campbell grandfather had severed any ties of loyalty that day long ago in Braemoore's library when he had struck his mother. Braeson would wring every piece of information from this man before he ended his life.

"You wish to kill me," Braeson stated. To his ears, his words sounded almost courteous, as though he appreciated this man's attempt to murder. His father had taught him this ploy. The appearance of a temperate persona, bordering on the mundane, to draw the fly into the web.

The stranger fixed his eyes on Braeson. Then he threw back his head and laughed. The laughter rose to hysteria and echoed from the low wooden rafters and off the stone walls of the shed.

Braeson took a single step toward the brutish thug, drew a knife from his boot, deliberate and unhurried. He tapped the blade once to the palm of his hand. Out of the corner of his eye, he saw Jack mimic the same casual motion. Then each man in the shed followed, one by one according to rank until the final knife was drawn. The ritual had the desired effect. The defiant laughter stopped. The web tightened.

Braeson recalled the first time he had joined in this knife-drawing ritual. From an early age, he was allowed to ride throughout Braemoore with his father and his men on the direct order that he must remain on his horse even if the others dismounted. If trouble ensued, Braeson might get away and even attempt to seek help.

That spring, he had turned thirteen and was riding with his father and a few men to investigate sheep thievery amongst the crofters at the south edge of Braemoore. They had ridden most of the morning and had just travelled through a narrow grove of trees when they encountered a brutish man hiding under a rock ledge. The man refused to provide his name or his destination. Braeson's father had dismounted, drawn out his knife, deliberate and unhurried, and stared at the stranger. Jack, the lead guardsman, had followed. Then, one by one, according to rank, each man dismounted and drew his knife. No one moved or spoke. It was as if they were waiting, expectantly. Braeson had realized in that moment, they were waiting for him. His heart leapt into his throat. He dismounted, walked to the space beside his father and drew his knife.

Frightened, the thug had revealed the whole story. Indeed, he had stolen the sheep to sell at a neighboring market. His father's men had escorted the thief to the port where he was placed on a working ship and indentured to pay off the debt.

"Pardon, my Lord," the prisoner now spoke soberly. "I mistook you for another."

Braeson's knife sliced through the air. The man's head flinched as the blade met its mark in the stall post a finger's width from his left ear.

"His name," demanded Braeson.

"It matters not, my Lord," replied the man.

"A man's blood was almost spilled," stated Braeson. "The name, I'll have."

"Mayhap, my Lord, you wish to know *my* name?" offered the man.

"Bloody hell," Jack hissed, as his knife flew through the air and embedded in the rail above the man's head.

The stranger's eyes widened. "Are you familiar with the MacEwen Keep, my Lord?" Panic wavered through the man's voice.

"Nay."

"Then, it matters not the person," squeaked the man.

Oliver's knife slashed through the left sleeve of the man's shirt and fastened it to the wooden post.

"Lochlan MacEwen," roared the man. He pulled his legs in to his body. His shirt ripped as he crossed his arms at his chest. "You have a similar look as Lochlan MacEwen around the eyes. Thus, I mistook you for the same."

Braeson stared at the man. Campbell? MacEwen? Was the danger surrounding Bonnie entwined with Lochlan MacEwen or the Campbells? Braeson felt his throat tighten. A sheen of sweat dampened his brow. Perchance it was he being caught in a web. A web of lies and deceit.

Had De Ros and Lochlan, even Caol, deceived him? Was there more to this race from the Highlands than they chose to reveal? Yet there appeared to be no guile in the library conversation. Indeed, all three men seemed ignorant of the meaning of the messages knifed on the trees. Each man appeared sincere in his quest to bring Bonnie to safety. The cryptic messages spoke of a treasure. Was that not the pearl necklace? When Lochlan threw the necklace at Braeson, he knew they had challenged his integrity. Would he take the necklace, the woman and run? Even in Braeson's surprise of recognizing the necklace and wanting it, his honour forbade him to succumb to this temptation to accept the rope of pearls. Bonnie was a human being worthy of more than the price of the necklace. If he had accepted the necklace, would they have allowed Bonnie to journey with him to England?

Was it a ruse? Had not Auld Maeve whispered about the treachery amongst the clans of the Highlands? Who was Bonnie, his bride, his wife? Perchance she was a MacEwen? Was Lochlan protecting his daughter in the guise of a foundling? Yet Brianna had explained that the mark of the MacEwen was reflected in the eyes. If she spoke the truth, Bonnie could not be a MacEwen. Bonnie's eyes matched the changing hues of her hair—cinnamon, russet, copper—with golden sparks that flickered like a fire according to her mood. Nay, it was Brianna and Lochlan who exhibited the MacEwen lineage. Pale grey eyes, oft times translucent, framed with black lashes.

Braeson slid his gaze to the captive. The man sat unmoving and silent on the dirt floor, his eyes riveted on Braeson.

"I know not of highland rivalry," Braeson stated. "What feud lies between the Campbells and MacEwens that cause you to attempt murder?"

The shed grew quiet. Braeson saw the man frown and turn his attention to young Williem, his third guard, who was readying to throw his knife.

"Seventeen years ago, a battle between the two clans ensued. Two men were killed," the man growled. "I avenge my father's death. Twas Lochlan MacEwen who killed him."

For how long Braeson studied the man he did not know. A horse whinnied, a foot shuffled. In time, the shadows crept closer around them as the sun's rays shifted beyond the single window in the shed. Braeson stood before a desperate man—a bitter man, a misguided man. But not an evil man. Like the sheep thief, years ago, this man, too, with some persuasion, told his story, his intent. The horsemen that crashed through the rock alley this morning and attempted to end Bonnie's life were evil. Stealing sheep, avenging a father, did not necessarily condemn a man to death. He sensed this prisoner was not connected to the evil men from the morning. Was this prisoner part of a second mystery? If so, what was he to do with him?

Braeson's aim was to take Bonnie to safety and banish threats along the way. If he released this man would he proclaim Bonnie's location? Yet the prisoner knew not of Bonnie's predicament. Were Braeson and Bonnie not simply a man and wife travelling to his home and her new home?

"Your name?" Braeson demanded.

The man's eyes shifted to young Williem who still

gripped his knife. "Iain Campbell." He bowed his head slightly.

"Your purpose for the morrow?" Braeson demanded.

"I travel from Edinburgh where I have been for a fortnight. I am expected at the Campbell Keep, my home."

Again a sense of familiarity wafted around Braeson. "You travel alone," Braeson stated.

"I am but a long day's ride from Campbell land," said the man. He stared at Braeson as if waiting for his next inquiry. "I sent my men on to allow myself the final day to ride alone and think." The man raised his shoulders slightly.

"Your men?" Braeson questioned. Who was this man to label others *his men*? Why did Braeson feel that the web was tightening around him?

"I am the Campbell Laird." The man raised his chin.

"Your sire's name?" The question flew from Braeson's mouth before he could stop it. If this man were the Campbell Laird there was a good chance that . . . Braeson took a deep breath stealing himself for the answer.

The man stared defiantly at Braeson. Silence wrapped itself around the group of men. Williem's knife shattered the stillness as the man yelped and drew his leg away from the blade that pierced the post beside him. "Angus Campbell twas my sire," he bellowed.

Braeson took a step backward as if the words the man roared struck him hard in the face. His stomach clenched. A sheen of moisture swathed his face. The man who had struck his mother, Annella, those many years ago and almost brought about her demise had been Angus Campbell! His maternal grandfather! No wonder he had sensed a degree of familiarity in this man. Indeed, the man was kin to his mother, her people, her clan. Braeson was staring at the clan leader, the Laird.

The Campbell Laird again laughed, allowing it to rise to hysteria. Then it came to a pronounced and terse stop. "You look like you have just seen a ghost, my Lord," the captive sneered. He stared at Braeson for a moment. "And so you have, for tis truth, I be the lad from long ago who accompanied my father, your grandfather, to England to meet you."

Braeson's heart slammed into his ribs. Blood pounded at his ears. Indeed, he was staring at his grandfather's son. His mother's brother. The boy, from long ago—*whose name Braeson had long forgotten*—and with whom he had played briefly before his mother had been struck.

"Tis truth," the Laird continued. "For you are the lad from long ago that my sire described as the boy with *eyes as pale as a silver moon.*"

A bitter, stinging taste flowed slowly into Braeson's mouth and his throat tightened. He turned to Jack. "Keep him bound." Then, he exited the shed.

## *Chapter Fifteen*

*"Run, run away and don't come back until dawn,"* cried Ina.

*"Run, Bonnie!" yelled Brianna.*

*"Run, Bonnie!" yelled De Ros.*

*"Run, Bonnie," yelled Caol.*

*Why did they all stand and yell at her? Why did they not come to her and help her?*

"Bonnie."

*Was it Lochlan? She was sure it was his voice.*

"Bonnie."

*Aye. Twas Lochlan. He looked at her with those eyes.*

*"Lochlan." She hugged him. "Help me. I must hide."*

"Bonnie!"

*Why was Lochlan shaking her?*

"Bonnie!"

Bonnie's eyes focused on the person sitting on the edge of her bed. A set of piercing pale, gray eyes stared back at her.

"Lochlan?" she whispered.

The figure rose from the side of her cot and pushed back the cloth draped at the window. The early evening light eased into the small room and fully nudged her awake.

"Bonnie? It is I. Braeson."

She stared back at Braeson who stood by the small window. A sense of despair wrapped itself around her, but she took a deep breath, trying to calm her beating heart and attempting to will it away. How much of the dream had been true? As she struggled through the nightmare, had she actually hugged Braeson believing he was Lochlan?

"Your eyes were open and glaring at me but still you were lost in a dream."

It was the same dream fabricated from her harrowing experiences over the past days. As Braeson advanced toward her, she pulled the bed covers up to her chin. She wore only a white chemise and shivered as he sat on the low wooden stool next to her small cot. She had no words to explain the terror of her dream and stared, speechless, at Braeson as he studied her with a hard, long look.

"You've slept for several hours. You look much improved." Braeson's lips turned up in what appeared to be an attempt to smile but his face was filled with worry and fatigue. "The mistress of the inn readies to serve dinner in the hall below."

Silence filled the small room as they continued to study each other. Bonnie should prepare for dinner but she could hardly remove herself from the bed with Braeson watching her. She pulled her arms to her breast. Her chemise was made of soft fine wool and revealed more of her than she was willing to display.

"Your scrapes and bruises are fading." He nodded toward her. "Yet I did not know that you were also injured along your shoulder."

She shifted her gaze and realized that her chemise had slipped low revealing her left shoulder and upper arm. Braeson hooked his finger around the delicate material, sliding her chemise back into place. Heat travelled into her face and low into her belly as his hand skimmed along her upper arm.

Braeson frowned. "Are there other contusions that need tending?"

"Nay!" She had noticed a purple and yellow bruise on her left hip earlier when she had bathed but was not about to have him inspect it.

Braeson rested his elbows on his knees and rubbed his face with his hands. His hair fell forward, damp and glistening with a few drops of water. A hint of familiar perfume wafted toward her and she chuckled in an attempt to divert the conversation from herself.

"You bathed?" she asked.

He pointed to the small metal tub behind a screen. "While you slept."

She did not think Braeson could easily have washed in that small tub. Her breath caught, captured by images of her husband standing in the pond with water sluicing down his strong body the day of the fire.

She grinned and took a deep breath "I think you found my soap."

"Aye, with a bucket of water poured over my head, I took hold of the nearest soap." His scowl lessened. "My hair smelled of roses before I realized. The rest of me smells like pine."

She saw the twinkle in his eye as he moved closer. "I can bathe again if the smell is bothering you." He began to lift his shirt.

"Nay!" she squeaked and shifted a bit closer to the opposite edge of the cot. She'd be on the floor if she was forced to shift any more. But she did appreciate his attempt to bring levity to this harrowing day. She smiled and watched as his frown completely disappeared. "Davyd did that once too."

"Davyd?" Braeson leaned in closer.

"Davyd is De Ros' and Brianna's child from their union. You did not meet him as he had already left to travel to MacEwen lands prior to your arrival," Bonnie explained.

"Aye, I recall Caol speaking of a younger brother," Braeson said.

Bonnie nodded and continued her story. "The first spring Davyd travelled with Lochlan to the MacEwen lands to work, along the way he bathed with Brianna's special rose-scented soap." Her smile grew to a giggle as she continued. "He was teased by the men and on his return he forbade Brianna to ever send her rose-scented soap with him again."

She enjoyed watching Braeson's grin grow into a wide smile. For certain, twas a rare sight to see Braeson smile when he was near her.

"What did Lady Brianna have to say to her son?"

Bonnie tried to make her voice sound like Brianna's. "My son, I thought you smarter! I thought that you might have found a fair lass to gift it to.'" She leaned toward Braeson to emphasize the final words. "Davyd turned verra red that day."

Braeson threw back his head and laughed. "And you are gifting your rose-smelling soap to me, this fair lad?" He placed his hand on his chest. "A wedding gift." That twinkle in his eyes grew.

"Nay!" She shifted further away and found herself tumbling onto the wooden floor. She grabbed the bed covers to her and glared up at him. Braeson stood and walked around the cot. Grasping her hand, he pulled her to her feet before she could protest. The bed covers lay pooled on the floor. Their grasped hands tightened as they each took a step closer. The combination of rose and pine wafted around her and a sense of joy tingled at her breast. He was going to kiss her.

"We will remain at the inn for this night and then continue our journey on the morrow." He took another step toward her as she rose on her tip toes preparing to meet his lips. For a moment, he studied her face. "Ready yourself for dinner. The mistress waits." He gave a slight bow, turned and walked from the room.

Disappointment washed over Bonnie as she sunk onto the edge of the cot and stared at the wooden floor for a time. Her long sleep in a comfortable bed had refreshed her and cheered her spirits. She had enjoyed laughing with Braeson. Comfort and peace had embraced her and made her feel as if she were at home laughing with her family.

She raised her fist and pounded it on her lap. She was *not* at home and Braeson was *not* her family and she had let her guard down! She had been sure he was going to kiss her and she, the silly lass that she was, had actually moved closer to Earl English in anticipation. She pounded her fist again, determined to be more attentive to her reactions to her husband, handsome though he was. From now on, she would keep her distance from this scoundrel who had snatched her from her real home to steal her away to

England.

Bonnie stood determined to rid herself of the disappointment that still lingered. Surveying the room, she recognized that the inn's mistress had been busy this day. She had washed the two travelling gowns that Lady Brianna had packed. Each hung over the screen in the corner to dry.

Bonnie searched through her bag and pulled her final gown from it—the green gown she had worn on the eve Braeson had arrived. Had Brianna chosen it with deliberate intent? It was a gown worn for celebration, and certainly not for travel. She even wondered about the soap Brianna had sent for her journey. There was more to the story than the short silly tale she had shared with Braeson. Later, after Davyd had stormed away embarrassed and angry, Brianna had told her that she had sent the soap along with Davyd to remind him of his home.

Lady Brianna made many scented soaps. Each spring, she set out to find the wild roses that grew amongst the rocks. She prepared the oils and mixture and spent several days making her rose-scented soap. It was made for special occasions and given as gifts. Her soap was an act of love, imparted to those she cared for deeply. Most of the crofters at Rose Keep had received her soap, many times.

Earlier when Bonnie had pulled the soap out to

bathe, she knew immediately it was a gift of love from Brianna. Now, she lifted the soap from the tub's ledge and turned it several times. The rose fragrance mingled with another subtle aroma in the room—the fragrance of pine, of Braeson. At Rose Castle, the wild roses that sprouted amongst the rocks mingled with the pine trees that grew tall above them. Brianna would say that each plant needed the other to grow and to thrive. Did Bonnie need Braeson to survive, to thrive?

She breathed in the soap's wonderful fragrance. Home! Bonnie felt her throat tighten and tears teased her eyes. She quickly donned the gown and her slippers, arranged her braid and exited the room, leaving her thoughts of soap, of roses and pine trees behind.

As she descended the inn's steps, Bonnie felt a quiver in her stomach and shyness washed over her, yet she was unable to divert her eyes from Braeson. He leaned against the stone wall at the bottom of the stairs, staring back at her. The quiver rose to her breast.

Braeson took her hand and placed it through his arm, escorting her along a quiet hallway that led into a small dining area. As she peered into the silent room, a thunderous noise exploded. Bonnie would have stumbled back if Braeson's hand at her waist had not stayed her. Men—Braeson's men—were shouting. Their hands pounded on the tables and feet stomped on the wooden floor. They laughed loudly and a few sent lewd comments and gestures their way.

"Oh, my Lady." The mistress of the inn curtsied before her. Pulling her hands tightly to her breast, she grinned at Bonnie, revealing several empty spaces where teeth should have been. "Oh, my Lady," she began again. "The lead guard whispered that you and your man have just married." She frowned and shook her head. "And without a celebration." Her grin returned, radiating a warmth reminiscent of Bonnie's home and her people.

This kind woman had helped Bonnie this morn after she had fainted. When Bonnie had awakened, the lady was in the room. She had chatted with her non-stop while Bonnie had broken her fast. Then the woman had helped her to bathe and tucked the covers around her before she had fallen into a fitful sleep of strange dreams.

"Come, my Lady, my Lord, we have prepared a fine meal." The mistress curtsied again and led them into the room as the men resumed their raucous behaviour.

The tables lined the perimeter of the quaint room on three sides, leaving the hearth open so all could enjoy the sparse fire burning there. Bonnie had counted at least twenty guards as they journeyed down the mountain but only about ten sat in the room. She wondered where the others might be.

Through the boisterous and wild noise, Braeson whispered in her ear, "I did not foresee such a wild and loud welcome."

Bonnie looked about the room at the men and the smiling inn keeper and his wife. She gazed into Braeson's eyes that were even paler in the low lights of the evening sunset. Rose and pine wafted around her, and Braeson smiled at her. His eyes seemed familiar in this strange little inn so far away from home, as if she had smiled into those eyes throughout her life time.

Braeson placed his hand atop her left hand and she looked at her wedding ring peeping through, engraved with ivy strands. She wondered about it all. So much she did not understand. Why did Brianna pack the soap? Why did the ring have the MacEwen emblem? Why did her people give her away and to an English? Or was it to a Campbell?

"They will not let us sit and eat until I kiss you." Braeson lips rose slightly. Bonnie was beginning to understand some of Braeson's facial expressions. In his attempt to smile, he endeavoured to hide his worry and fatigue.

Her stomach growled. Did the room spin a bit? Bonnie closed her eyes to steady herself. It was several hours since she had eaten and she was starving. Bonnie turned and narrowed her eyes at Braeson. She took a deep breath, leaned in and placed a chaste kiss on his full lips.

Braeson gave her a doubtful stare. "I do not think, my Lady, that your arduous display of love will allow us to eat." He looked to the noisy men and then slid his eyes back to her. "Let us eat."

As Braeson pulled her toward him, her hands landed flat against his hard chest. He clasped her at the waist and covered her mouth with his. Heat seeped into her lips and flowed through her body. She felt his tongue caress her bottom lip and she gasped as her mouth opened to welcome his embrace. She leaned into him as his lips fluttered up the side of her neck to her ear.

"Kiss you? Aye, I like it." His words echoed their earlier conversation below the cliff under the boughs of the spruce tree. His eyes shimmered with that familiar teasing gleam.

Silly lass, had she not just promised herself to be on her guard and her traitorous body was responding to him . . . again? She would commit to memory that mischievous twinkle that entered his eyes and be prepared for . . . next time.

As Braeson released her, she swayed. But this time it was not hunger for food that made her feel faint. He held her hand high as he turned and bowed to his men. They all looked at Bonnie and she curtsied. As Braeson escorted her to the middle table and pulled out her chair, the men quieted and the inn keeper and mistress began to serve the meal.

She placed her hand on her fluttering belly to still it.

"Hungry?" her new husband asked.

She gave a slight nod, knowing well that the flutter inside her had nothing to do with hunger for food.

She looked up to see Jack take the fare from the inn's mistress and place it at her table. The single platter was meant to be shared with Braeson. She looked at the fare served to the others and they, too, ate grouse with a mixture of vegetables and sauces. She frowned.

"A single dead grouse was found a top the cliff." Jack explained. He looked to Braeson and then again to Bonnie. "The men caught a few more. We thank our Lady for showing us a fine hunting spot."

Bonnie nodded. "Thank you," she said. These few words of thanks were the first that she had spoken to any of Braeson's men.

Jack gave a slight bow and retreated to the table next to the room's entrance. Bonnie watched him as she sampled her food. He stood while he ate, looking from time to time toward the door, always on guard, always watching, waiting.

She did not want to like any of these men who were celebrating this wedding. She had vowed to not speak to any of them, yet she had just thanked the man, Jack. Her protection. Is that not how Braeson had described them? This wild, hardy group reminded her much of the men at Rose Castle—brave and daring. Could she believe what Braeson had told her? These men were her protection, willing to lay down their lives for her. Did they not deserve her loyalty? Or, at least respect for what they were willing to do for her?

Just then the dog, Colasse, who sat at Jack's feet, stood and started to walk across the room to Braeson. Jack made a slight sound at the back of his throat and the dog returned to sit.

"I do not think that a beast who scares mother cats and nips at bawling horses should receive a treat," Braeson whispered in her ear.

Bonnie felt a slow blush rise up from her neck into her face and she turned to Braeson just in time to see him veil his teasing eyes.

"How do you enjoy your food?" he asked.

She had nibbled and sampled various parts of the meal on the shared platter but had been deterred by a rising sense of shame. She saw the open wound on the face of the guard they called young Williem. He had incurred it while in battle today with unknown enemies who had threatened her life. Yet Williem smiled and stuffed food into his mouth and laughed at the comments that echoed throughout the small stone room.

She saw the glances Braeson's men gave to him. Glances of pride and encouragement. There was no doubt in her mind that these men were dedicated to her husband and to his purpose.

She recalled Braeson's words from a few days ago, *Many have stepped in harm's way for your protection.* She did owe them a few words, words of respect and encouragement, rather than travelling in silence on this journey. It was not the fault of these men, or the dog, that she was forced out of her home. She vowed from now on she would give her anger to her unseen enemies if she ever met them.

"The Mistress has gone to much trouble preparing this fine meal," she said, glancing sideways at Braeson. "I must thank her well before we depart on the morrow." Now, she found herself eating heartily. Twas as good as the food from home.

A slow blush crept up her neck again when Braeson pulled his hand back from the trencher to allow her to finish the remaining fare. "I think I am more hungry than I thought." She gave him a lopsided grin and that gleaming twinkle appeared in his eyes again.

Braeson nodded toward the inn keeper who sat at the fireplace hearth. The man began to play the lyre. The guard, Oliver, joined him with a fiddle. The music drifted about the room surrounding them with soulful harmony. Then, the fiddle played a short tune. A flurry of notes that travelled up and down the scale in soft and gentle tones. Then, the lyre repeated the tune with similar tones and emphasis. The notes became faster and the tones louder. Bonnie imagined two butterflies fluttering across the meadow in a mating dance. The music rose to high tones of mounting exaltation and halted momentarily. There was silence in the room and then the music breathed and Bonnie's heart pounded so that it echoed in her ears.

She jumped when Braeson whispered, "We will not be allowed to leave this eve until we have performed our wedding dance."

His declaration only added to Bonnie's pounding heart and she found herself rising from her place with her hand in Braeson's as he led her to the floor. The din in the room mounted as the men shouted again, their hands pounding and feet stomping. Lewd remarks were halted by Jack with that strange sound from the back of his throat and some mumbled words about *our Lady*.

The room quieted. Only the lyre and the fiddle spoke

of majestic tales of grandeur and elegance as Braeson escorted her to the middle of the room. He held one hand to his side and the other he extended to her left hand, holding her at arm's length. He walked around the imaginary circle of the small room in rhythmic time to the instruments that strummed a marching, regal beat.

This was not a country reel that she had learned as a young girl. Nay. Caol had brought this dance to their Rose Castle from the courts of France. Braeson released her hand and stood gazing at her, waiting. That twinkle in his eyes had been replaced with a glint of challenge. Would she behave as the Lady that she was called to be, or would her response be sullen, ungrateful? This was her chance to demonstrate her gratitude to them. To thank these men for the grouse, the soft bed, even Williem's injured face.

Bonnie straightened her back, lifted her chin to Braeson and stepped into the dance. She flared her skirts and skipped gracefully around Braeson meeting him face to face and curtsied before him. When she looked up, he captured her gaze with a warm smile and did not release it for the duration of the performance. She felt the heat of a blush on her face. How many times had she tried to rid herself of this nervous response and keep her emotions hidden?

Staring into Braeson's silver eyes, a fluttery feeling

grew in her stomach and mimicked the dance of the butterflies the instruments had portrayed just a short time ago. She and Braeson twirled, stepped, and circled each other until the music slowed. Now, Braeson extended his left hand to her right, his other hand rested at her waist and they walked side by side for their final march around the imaginary circle.

Braeson's heat simmered through her body and her pulse pounded at her ears. He released her from his gaze as he bowed and her eyes slid to their hands. Her golden wedding band twinkled in the candle-lit room.

The room exploded into an uproar as the men returned to their pounding and shouting. Braeson bowed a final time to his men and placed Bonnie's hand into the crook of his arm, escorting her away from the small room and toward the stairs.

Her chest tightened and she snuck a glance toward Braeson, his eyes looking to the door at the top of the narrow stairway. She had just danced away from her wedding dinner. Was she now to experience her wedding night? She had demonstrated her gratitude to the men by dancing with their master. Was consummating the marriage expected of her to show her gratitude to Braeson? Twas not gratitude she wished to give if she were truthful with herself. She wished to give herself to him as his wife. She breathed deeply to calm herself and her growing eagerness for their wedding night.

As Bonnie stepped inside the open door, Braeson strode past and knelt at the fireplace to encourage the small fire that burned there. He stepped over to the window and flicked the curtains, looking into the darkness. Then, with a few strides he stood before her. There was no challenge just that tilted smile again that masked his fatigue and worry. He placed his hands on either side of her face and covered her mouth with his own. She moved into his arms as he pressed her back to the wall and ran his hands down her sides to her hips.

She flinched and he lifted his head.

"A hidden bruise?" he questioned.

She pushed against his chest but he did not budge and continued to hold her gaze.

"I think I should check it."

"Nay!" she protested and scurried around him to stand at the edge of her small cot.

He studied her for a time. Lingering over her face and her hips. Again he smiled. "We leave at first light. You require your sleep." With a slight bow, he turned and left the room.

Bonnie slumped on the edge of the cot, disappointment nudging her. The evening had been a lovely surprise – food, music, dance. But now, she was all alone in this small room with only confusing thoughts about this stranger that she had been forced to marry.

Twas something baffling about this new husband of hers. While they were racing away from her home and the mysteries in her life, for certain, Braeson Earl of Braemoore had mysteries of his own.

Why did her wedding ring have the MacEwen emblem engraved on it?

Why did Braeson's eyes hold a familiar resemblance to Lochlan and Brianna—pale grey eyes, oft times translucent, and framed with black lashes?

## Chapter Sixteen

The drink was angry and dark, burning as it sloshed down Braeson's throat and kicked hard each time it landed in his gut. He held the flask filled with liquor close to his chest where the pain lingered. The day's events swirled through his hazy thoughts, growing nebulous and vague as they mixed with the cruel drink. His eyes scanned the black night. No moon but a few stars lit the way, providing meagre slivers of light. The only shadows present were the ones that clouded his mind.

His horse stopped, no longer willing to follow the haphazard directions of his fickle master. Braeson slid off the horse, stumbled forward and brushed up against a trunk of an almost invisible tree. Using his hand, he guided himself down to sit at its base. He clutched the flask in one hand and tufts of grass with the other, hoping to cease the shifting of the ground under him and calm the rising nausea creeping relentlessly upward.

He must have dozed because when he opened his eyes Jack stood before him.

"You should be hugging your bride on this night rather than that wicked drink." Jack nodded at the leather flask that lay on the ground beside Braeson's outstretched legs. "You'll find more sparks in your marriage bed than in that firewater."

"My bride looks at me with frightened eyes." Braeson ran his fingers through his black hair and then dropped his hand to the ground. The earth below him no longer heaved but his gut tossed and turned like the gray waves that churned in the ocean just before a storm. He took a deep breath and willed the contents of his wedding supper to settle.

"The woman has hidden bruises, Jack, that she refuses to reveal. She requires an ointment to aid in healing." Braeson recalled the look of pain that fluttered across Bonnie's face when he hugged her. Fear and pain did not make good bed fellows. Nay, he'd have his wife come to him willingly. The consummation of their marriage vows would not take place on this dreary eve.

As Braeson stood up determined to find his horse, his stomach heaved and the contents of his wedding dinner landed at the foot of the tree. He clutched his stomach, closed his eyes and took a deep breath. His spinning head and foggy thoughts, along with the storm that churned inside him, stood in contrast to the calm, dull night that surrounded him.

Braeson glanced up to see Jack studying him.

"Aye, he couldna either." Jack shook his head several times. "Neither can you."

"Enlighten me Jack," Braeson growled. "Of whom do you speak?"

"I speak of your father, the third Earl of Braemoore." Jack continued. "He could not hold his liquor either. You are like him—a green lad when it comes to drink."

"Like *him*?" Braeson growled. "Like *him*?" He grabbed Jack's shirt front so that they stood nose to nose. "What do you know of my father?" He pushed Jack from him and turned away. The slow climb of heat crawling from his gut toward his throat had nothing to do with the liquor he had drunk. It was pure bitterness, resentment for the bloody lie he and his father had lived.

Braeson turned and started toward Jack. "Look at me. Do I wear the markings of the third Earl of Braemoore?" Again he grabbed Jack's shirt, shaking him now and bellowing in his face. "See my eyes, Jack. Do I wear the mark—any telling mark—of Timothy Lennox Moore the third?" He shoved Jack with force and coldly watched as his lead guardsman stumbled backward, flailing in an attempt to maintain his balance.

"I think not." Braeson seethed "We both heard it in the shed this morning and have seen it elsewhere. Now we must accept it." He pushed his face closer to Jack's. "How did Lady Brianna describe the mark—pale grey eyes? Yet my grandfather Campbell summed it up well. Indeed. Eyes as pale as a silver moon." Braeson could have sworn that his heart broke with this declaration. The man who had raised him was not his sire, his father. "Nay, I am no son to the Earl of Braemoore." Could it be possible that the whole world heard the bitter moan that he held tightly inside himself?

"You're a bloody fool," Jack sneered. "Tis a weary man I be, dealing with Lords and Lairds all this day."

Braeson staggered forward as the flat of Jack's hand slammed into the back of his head and the guard locked an arm around his neck. Braeson could muster no defense other than his flailing arms as Jack snared the back of his waist band and dragged him into the pond that lay before them. The frigid water washed over him as Jack held his head under the water for several seconds, then lifted him up by his hair and hauled him to his feet.

"You are the son of the third Earl of Braemoore, you fool." Jack gripped Braeson's shirt front, shaking him as if he were a spoiled child. "A man can plant his seed and sire many but a true father commits to his duty."

"Tell me true, Jack." Braeson spoke through the water that dripped from his hair and flowed down his face. "How did my father find me all those years past when I thought to be a sailor and stowed away?" His father and he had visited the port every time they travelled to London. At thirteen he had snuck from school and boarded a ship, believing himself ready to sail. "Answer me, Jack."

"You caused him trouble then and look at you now." Jack shoved Braeson and turned away.

"Face me, Jack. Look at me and tell me true," Braeson demanded. A gentle breeze fluttered round him, failing to lift the wet hair that stuck to his face. An owl hooted in the distance, a mournful sound.

Jack walked to Braeson. "All ship captains knew to look for a lad with eyes as pale as a silver moon."

Braeson snorted. "He knew."

"I know naught what your father knew. This is what I do know. Everytime I look at you, I see the markings of Moorey, the third Earl of Braemoore, your father. He raised you, taught you compassion and duty, pride of name, his name and your name, Timothy Lennox Moore." Jack looked away into the darkness. "Moorey shared you with his people which is reflected in the nekename they bestowed on you—Braeson, son of Braemoore." Jack turned and took a step closer to

Braeson. "His mark is branded on you, embedded deep on your heart, your mind, your life." He stared at Braeson for a time. "Complete," he stated.

Jack walked away into the darkness to return with the horses. "Many depend on you to take the lass to safety. Tis been too long since you slept, my Lord. Drink and lack of sleep do not mix well."

Braeson accepted the reins, swayed slightly and mounted. He followed Jack as they rode toward the small inn.

Two of his guards took the horses at his arrival. Braeson entered through the inn door. He climbed the stairs and nodded to the guard who sat outside his wife's small room.

The room was faintly lit by the fire that burned in the fireplace. Bonnie slept in the small bed. He peeled off his wet clothes and stood naked before the fire in hopes of driving the chill from his tired body. Arms extended, he leaned toward the fire and gripped the mantel.

*The boy with eyes as pale as a silver moon.* He took a deep breath and closed his eyes. He had remembered the words today in the shed when Iain Campbell had spoken. He had thought his Campbell grandfather only wished to strike his mother, all those years ago, but that was not so. His grandfather had cornered his mother and him in the library that day. He had ranted at her indiscretion which he said was written all over her son's face. All over the face of the boy with the *eyes as pale as a silver moon*. Earlier today, when he'd heard Iain Campbell say these words, the memory from long ago returned full force. His grandfather had attempted to strike him, but his mother had stood betwixt them. She had received the full blow of his grandfather's fist, causing her to stumble and hit her head on the wooden mantel.

Braeson rubbed his face and gripped the mantel again. The effects of the drink had lifted after the dunking in the pond, but his head still pounded. The picture of that explosive day, long past, was clear in his mind.

The boy Braeson had flung himself into a corner of the library, hugging his legs to his chest, still and silent, terrified of his grandfather's rejection and rage which he had not understood. He had remained hidden for a long time.

"Timothy." His father had entered the room. "Timothy."

Braeson had not stirred. Hadn't it been him, Braeson, who had caused his mother to fall? He looked at the blood that had found its way onto his shoes when he had run to the corner, terrified. Was she dead? Had he killed his mother?

"Timothy," his father had called again.

And then his father had stood before him.

"Timothy?" he questioned.

Braeson had been found. His body trembled as his eyes followed the line of his father's form from his black leather boots, over his trews, along his tall frame to his blond beard and...Braeson had stopped at his father's chin, unable to raise his eyes to his father's. Who could love him now? Did he not carry the marks of his mother's injury on his shoes, and on his hands when he had tried to wipe off the blood?

"Timothy?"

He had shut his eyes tight, defying the tears that had squeezed out.

A rustle, a breath across his face. "Son," his father whispered.

Slowly, he opened his eyes. His father knelt before him, studying him with eyes as dark as the night.

"Son," his father repeated, his eyes searching his face almost as if he were puzzled. Then his lips lifted in an attempt to smile. "Son. Thank God, you are safe."

Braeson had flung himself at his father. And Timothy Lennox Moore the third, his dear Papa, had wrapped his arms so tightly around him that even now, Braeson could still feel his touch, his mark, his branding. He had remained in his father's arms for the next two days until his mother had awakened.

Now, Braeson rubbed his hands over his face and

through his hair. He was tired, so weary, but the pain in his chest had lifted. Just a slight annoyance remained. He would speak to his mother upon his return to Braemoore.

Braeson, Timothy Lennox Mooore, the fourth Earl of Braemoore, turned to his sleeping wife who was curled up in the cot. He was sure there was enough room in the small bed for him, too. He lifted the covers and crawled in. Settled, resettled, then turned to Bonnie and wrapped himself around her and fell to sleep.

## Chapter Seventeen

Bonnie's nose was cold and she cuddled lower into the blankets of her bed. Moving closer to the heat emanating at her back, luscious warmth touched her cold toes beckoning her back to sleep. That warmth was most enticing. She rolled over and into it, finding a heated pillow covered in soft down. Warm wraps drew her closer and lulled her towards sleep.

Fragrances of rose and pine drifted around her and another odd scent. Stale alcohol? Bonnie's eyes snapped open and met the dull haze of predawn. The heat that felt so delicious was coming from someone who was in her bed. She ran her hand along a—she stopped and tried to clear her thoughts in these first moments of wakefulness. Aye, it was an upper leg, strong and muscled with a smattering of hair. Her hand caressed upward to a hip bone and stopped. She blinked several times, striving to leave her sleep behind.

"Just a wee bit to the left, wife."

Covers flew as Bonnie attempted to release herself from the tangle of wraps. The cold air hit her hard, as did the floor as she landed there on her bottom. She drew her seal skin blanket around her and rushed to the window.

Only then did she look back at the small cot. Tis what she thought! Naked! Not a scrap of clothing on him. Braeson rose from the bed, strode across the room, and lit the logs that had burned to naught in the fireplace. He turned to her. "The fire will take the spring chill from the room."

"Eek!" She turned back to the window as he reached for his trews and pulled them on.

"We depart at first light. Dress. Gather your belongings." She heard him move about the room, mayhap packing his travel bag. Then, the door closed behind him.

Bonnie waited for the low rumble of conversation in the hallway to disappear before she found the courage to move away from the window. She took a deep breath, but her heart continued to pound. She was grateful that the room was still dim and the fierce blush that reddened her cheeks had gone unnoticed.

What was it about the break of dawn?

Yesterday, it had been at the break of dawn that she had caressed Braeson under the boughs of the spruce? This morn the same had occurred. But this morn he had been naked. In her attempt to flee the bed, her hand had strayed to the left and caressed the most intimate part of his body.

Like yesterday, touching him stirred feelings of desire for her husband. She trembled and there was a pressure low in her stomach. Last eve, when Braeson had kissed her, similar feelings had arisen. She had been frightened, yet curious, at the same time.

"Make haste, lass," Bonnie mumbled. She did not want Braeson to catch her undressed upon his return. She folded her seal skin, placing it at the end of the cot and slipped behind the screen in the corner of the room. Peeking over the top, she let her nightgown fall to her feet. She poured water into the basin and sprinkled it over her face and neck. Even with the surprise of finding Earl English in her bed this morning, she felt herself refreshed from good sleep and good fare. After rinsing her mouth, she chewed on a sprig of wintergreen and donned her chemise and travelling gown. Then, she pulled a wooden stool before the fireplace to prepare her hair. Just as she lifted the brush, a slight bang at the door startled her.

Braeson entered fully clothed. The glow from the fire revealed a refreshed looking Earl English. The dark circles under his eyes had disappeared.

He smiled as he walked to her and leaned against

the mantel of the small fireplace. "You slept well?" he asked. "You were deep in sleep when I returned last eve. And a bit of space was available in the cot."

"Aye," she replied. "I slept and am refreshed." She feigned interest in a lock of hair, refusing to look in his eyes knowing that her tell-tale blush lingered.

"You were warm enough?"

Now her eyes flashed to his face. His silver eyes twinkled, crinkling at the edges.

She frowned. "Aye, the bed covers warmed me." She heard him chuckle as she continued to comb her hair before the warm fire.

Twas an untruth and they both recognized it. Had she not awakened this morn, cold and shivering? It was his warmth that she had sought and if she was honest with herself, she recalled turning to him often throughout the night for warmth. She quietly reprimanded herself under her breath. Even in her sleep, she had sought him.

"Jack has provided this salve." Braeson placed the small pewter container on the mantel. "He says to rub it on all your aches and contusions. It will aid in healing."

"I will continue to use my own concoctions." She nodded her head toward the container. "Give Jack my thanks."

Silence grew in the room. She avoided his eyes, his

stare, by sprinkling her hair with water to control the curls. Then, she wound it into a braid that fell down her back all the way to the stool she sat upon.

Braeson took a step closer to her and she paused in her morning ministrations. "You will apply Jack's ointment or I will do it for you."

Her eyes slid to his. Nay, she did not want him to see her tell-tale truths. Too many bruises and wounds were on her body. Between the attacks at Rose Castle and the tumble over the rock cliff, her body was sore and required ointments for healing. She did not doubt that he would be most willing to help her.

"Jack has journeyed and cared for many along our travels and this will bring immediate relief." Braeson grabbed the salve from the mantel and handed it to her.

"But—" she began.

He took another step toward her, salve in hand. "You must come to accept the kindness and the protection afforded you. When we married you became my Lady. You must now accept the notion of being served." He held out the salve, nodding toward it. "Begin with this."

Bonnie was used to caring for others, serving them as she worked alongside Lady Brianna at the keep. She travelled over Rose land to crofters, caring for the elderly and the sick. If she were at home, at this moment, she would be in the shed caring for the ponies.

She took a deep breath and accepted the ointment. "Aye."

Bonnie slid the container into the folds of her gown where she kept her leather sling. She frowned. Hadn't she placed the leather rope into this pocket last eve? She rose, searching for her sling in the few garments yet to be placed into her pack.

"I cannot find my sling!" With hands akimbo, she scanned the room and halted when she spied Braeson holding it high with one hand. The other arm leaned against the mantel.

"I hold it," he said.

"Where did you find it?" A few steps brought her standing before him. She reached for her sling, but he held it from her and slid it into his leather boot.

"Nay!" Bonnie protested. "Tis mine! A gift from Angus, our pony master!"

"Nay!" Braeson repeated using the same tone as she. "I will hold it for you until I see fit to release it into your care again."

Bonnie hands fisted and her chest tightened with anger. "Tis mine, I say, and part of my livelihood." As she reached for his boot he caught her hand, holding it fast. "Did I not fell a grouse for our dinner?" she demanded.

"It was not the time to fell a bird yester morn." Braeson gripped her wrist, stilling her. He bent his head closer to her face so that she could see his eyes. "The strange bird trill yester morn was a signal that the enemy was near. It was our desire to protect you between the rock walls." He raised his dark brows that were etched against his tanned skin, emphasizing the paleness of his eyes. "Not to have a flock of grouse flying to the trees, alerting the enemy to our position."

Bonnie drew in a quick breath and closed her eyes. The strange bird had been no bird after all. "You must reveal these things to me!" She took a step toward Braeson. "Aye, I can help!"

"Nay!" he continued. "You, my Lady, can trust your protection. When we arrive at our north England home, I want to be able to send a missive to De Ros stating you are alive. Did I not pledge my protection when I said my wedding vows?"

Bonnie dropped her eyes and when she pulled her hand, he released her. She hugged her body. The small fire in the fireplace had warmed the room, yet a chill ran through her. Could she trust him? Had he not said, *Run, run to me, Bonnie*? But taking her weapon only weakened her. Her eyes travelled to her boots that stood beside the door where she had removed them yesterday upon entering the room. She walked toward them.

His voice halted her. "Neither is the *second* knife in your boot."

The room grew colder. Her throat tightened. Fear. Had not De Ros and Lochlan taught her to sling and throw knives to provide her with protection? In fact, Lady Brianna and many other girls and women at Rose Keep could also throw knives. She felt bare, naked, just as Braeson had been in bed this morn, stripped of her armour. She would not cry and she blinked several times to ward off the tears before she turned to him. For the first time, she noticed her two knives nestled in pockets of the leather band he wore around his waist.

"But without my knife how could I have aided you yester morn?" She raised her hand to his shoulder, indicating the wound she had mended there.

Holding her gaze, slow and deliberate, Braeson drew a knife from each of his boots and held them up.

Bonnie narrowed her eyes. She had been fooled. He had forced her hand yesterday when she had pulled her knife from her boot. Assessing the situation, she should have known that he, too, had a second knife in his boot. One knife atop the cliff with the assailant and the second knife still tucked in his boot. Twas a typical strategy to carry a knife in each boot. Her raised hand fell to her side and she marched to the window and looked out at the rising light above the treetops.

He followed and came to a halt behind her. His breath rustled the top of her hair. "You can earn them back."

Bonnie twirled toward him and bumped against his chest. She could not step back or she would fall through the window. Placing his hands on either side of the window frame, he leaned into her. Cornered, she was forced to look at him.

"When you demonstrate your willingness to accept my protection. When you refrain from discrediting the efforts of my men." He breathed deeply and moved his head even closer. "When you accept your position as my Lady, then your weapons will be returned." He turned back to the room, scanning it. "Come, gather your possessions. The mistress has packed some fare that we will eat along the way." He exited the room, leaving the door ajar.

Bonnie pinched her lips together and waited until he had left, then screamed inside her mouth. Blowing out her breath, she pounded her fist on the window's ledge. "That, that, that—" She had a few words that she still wanted to say to her, her . . . husband. Bonnie grabbed her clothes and stuffed them into her bag. She rolled up the seal skin, shoved on her boots and ran down the stairs.

"Braeson!" She seethed under her breath. Lady Brianna would be most pleased to witness how she was striving to appear the Lady, and not bellowing like she so badly wanted to! She *would* have those weapons. She tramped through the inn door and out onto a stretch of sandy ground, bumping into a large man. As she stumbled backward, her bag and seal skin dropping to the ground, she drew in her breath and held it.

Before her stood a man wearing the Campbell colours. She would recognize that plaid anywhere. The verra symbol that she was warned to stay away from all of the seventeen years she had lived at Rose Castle. The man stared back at her.

"My pardon, mistress." He bowed then looked at her, as if waiting for her to reply.

Fear slithered around her throat and her breath shuddered from her. Her eyes searched for Braeson. She turned back and slammed into him as he walked out of the inn door.

"Bonnie?" Braeson caught her by the upper arms and held her at arm's length, studying her. "What is it?"

She fixed her eyes on Braeson. "A Campbell," Bonnie whispered through her tight throat. She nodded toward the man, and she watched as Braeson's silver gaze slid over her shoulder.

"Come, Bonnie." Braeson took her hand and pulled her forward. "Meet our guest. He has joined us on our journey to Braemoore."

With her other hand, Bonnie tried to release his grip. She dug her feet into the dirt as Braeson dragged her toward the man.

"Iain Campbell, meet Lady Bonnie Lennox Moore, previously Bonnie of Rose," Braeson said.

The man's mouth dropped open and he stared at Bonnie as if shocked.

"I have heard tales of you." The man's mouth changed into a sneer. "Brianna's Silkie!" He threw back his head and gave a boisterous laugh. His gaze then returned to her, a narrow-eyed stare that left her cold and trembling.

Braeson hands touched her waist as he placed Bonnie behind him. He took a single step toward this man called Campbell and drew a knife from his boot. He tapped the blade once to the palm of his hand. A rustle to her left, and she saw the guardsman, Jack, mimic the same casual drawing of his knife. Then, each of Braeson's men, one by one, did the same until the final knife was drawn. Her eyes dropped to Braeson's belt line to search for *her* knives but his cape hid them from view.

Campbell's grin faded away. "Pardon, my Lord." Again, he bowed to Bonnie. "Pardon, my Lady. Tis an honour to meet you."

Braeson pulled Bonnie to stand beside him. She

continued to tremble and he placed a hand at her waist.

She looked up at Braeson. His eyes, his clear eyes were filled with . . . she recalled how at their marriage ceremony she had thought them soulless. Now, she knew that was an untruth. In her anger, she had refused to acknowledge that what she had really seen in his beautiful eyes, twas the same as at this moment—compassion. Compassion for her, for the attack she endured, for the marriage she was forced to enter. Slowly, there appeared a subtle change in the way he gazed back at her, and she knew what she must do. Now, he was challenging her to be the Lady that their marriage vows had made her. Would she respond as the sullen chit, choosing to run in her fear and miss the opportunity to trust her husband and his men? Each held a knife steady, displaying they were there for her protection. Bonnie's hand trembled as she extended it to Iain Campbell, who placed a kiss on it. She pulled it back and wiped it on her dress.

"I understand that felicitations are in order, my Lady," stated Campbell. "Best wishes on your marriage to the Earl of Braemoore."

Campbell and Braeson both looked to Bonnie. Through her fear she uttered "Aye" and gave a slight curtsy to acknowledge his well wishes.

Campbell glanced at Braeson. "Me thinks it best to

journey alongside your men at the rear, my Lord?" Campbell questioned.

"Aye," agreed Braeson. He turned to Bonnie and took her hand, leading her to her mare. He assisted her as she mounted and handed her the reins. "Campbell is my relation. This is the reason he has joined us on this journey to Braemoore."

As Bonnie rode beside Braeson, she still trembled from the shock of Iain Campbell travelling with them. Why would he allow a sworn enemy of the De Ros and MacEwen clans to travel with them to his home? Which led her to another question. Why on earth would Lady Brianna agree to have her wed a Campbell? Well at least one half Campbell. For was that not what Braeson was—half Campbell?

All of her questions left her confused. This just added to her frustration for she realized she still had not retrieved any of her weapons.

# Chapter Eighteen

Braeson stripped and slipped into the cool water. The tranquil gurgle from the mountain spring emptying into the pool provided an excellent cover to any noise he made as he entered the water and swam close to his sleeping wife. His suspicions were confirmed. Along the left side of her body, from her shoulder to well past her knee, ran a trail of bruises, purple and blue.

Braemoore's troop had travelled at a steady clip this day and now were camped in a dale perfectly hidden behind a grass covered hill. Beyond the small valley, was this secluded nook where Braeson had discovered a small rock pool. He had allowed Bonnie some private time to cleanse and swim, and when he had returned from his sentinel post, just down the path, he had found her asleep.

He swam alongside the sleeping woman and studied her. Bonnie had climbed into a small rock nest carved into the edge of the pool. A spring, warmed by the late afternoon sun, overflowed into the nest. Garbed in her thin chemise, there she slept in the warm bath with one knee pulled up to her chest, the other leg stretched over the edge of the rock nest. She nestled her head against the soft, green moss growing along the far side. One arm was tucked into the warm spring water. The other rested along the edge.

As they had tumbled over the rock ledge yesterday, they had met an abrupt impact with the moss covered rocks below. As much as Braeson had tried to shield Bonnie from injury, the trail of bruises explained why she had winced the night before when he had kissed her in the small room at the inn. Today, he had noticed that as Bonnie rode astride her horse, she placed more weight on her right side to reduce the constant jarring to her left. While they must travel quickly to England, they would slow a bit to accommodate her injury.

Braeson dipped under the water and swam silently away. He pulled himself out of the water and gazed again at his sleeping wife. He would insist that she continue to apply Jack's ointments to her wounds. An evening breeze fluttered over his body and he pulled on his trews and shirt and pushed his feet into his boots to ward off the chill in the early spring air. He leaned against a large boulder and studied his bride.

Upon leaving the inn, he had ridden with Bonnie for

the first hour and then had left her to his guard, young Williem. He had purposefully avoided conversation with her for the remainder of this day. He had wanted to talk with her about Iain Campbell in private. Why was she so afraid of the Campbells? Secrets in the Highlands were abundant, it seemed. Perchance, she would share a few with him.

His wife stirred. Moving her head from the moss pillow, she peered up at the sky and then returned to slumber. She was lovely. When he had covertly inspected her in the pool, he had noticed more than the bruises. He marveled at her muscled long limbs which were a testament to her skills as a horse woman.

She stretched again and straightened a sleek leg so that it hovered above the rock nest. Her toes stretched outward displaying a slender ankle and shapely calf. Her skin appeared as if caressed by the sun but that was impossible since the winter had just passed. It carried a natural glow that matched the copper and golds of her hair and eyes. He wanted to run his hand along that calf much like she had caressed him under the boughs of the spruce. His heart quickened and his fingers tingled and warmed with the thought. But the lovely woman was injured and must be given time to heal.

The gentle wind wavered again, disturbing her braid

that floated atop the water. It lifted from the rock nest and then flopped down, splattering water drops on her face. Bonnie sat straight up, drawing both knees to her chest and ran her hands along her arms.

"The coming night brings a chill."

She turned her head sharply and glared at him.

"You must dry and don warm clothes."

Her eyes grew big and then began to narrow as he rose and took a couple steps toward her. Even from this distance, he could see the golden sparks shoot from her eyes.

"The ointment for your injuries is in your pack." He smiled as she looked down at the pattern of bruises that travelled along her left side. "I will gather the fare that has been prepared and return."

Braeson chuckled as he walked down the path to collect their evening meal. He would have enjoyed watching her rise out of the water, her white sleeveless chemise clinging to her wet body. He shook his head to calm himself. He must be patient. Had he not just asked her, demanded her, to accept his protection? Trust is what he wanted of her and perchance, unbeknownst to her, she had already displayed it when she had eyed Iain Campbell this morn.

Braeson had seen her charge through the inn door searching the small courtyard for him. In her frustration, Bonnie had walked right by him and then stopped in her tracks. Her anger had given way to sheer terror when she had spotted Iain Campbell. Her body had stiffened and then trembled. But in that moment he had heard her whisper his name, *Braeson.*

This was the first time Bonnie had looked to him for help. When Braeson had carried her away from the attack and up the steps of Rose Keep, she had called for Brianna and De Ros. When she had awakened from her sleep at the inn, she had called for Lochlan. But this morn, she had whispered his name, *Braeson.* She had also stayed close to him. He had felt the pressure of her body when she leaned into him in her attempts to shy away from Campbell, gripping his cape when he had placed her behind him. Braeson had wanted to sweep her into his arms, carry her away and calm her fears. Instead, he had challenged her to step into her role as his Lady. He did have to drag her obstinate body a few feet toward Campbell but in the end she had acknowledged herself as Lady Bonnie Lennox Moore, wife of the fourth Earl of Braemoore.

At Braeson's return, Bonnie wore dry clothes and sat on a small rock ledge. Her wet chemise lay flat on a rock absorbing the late day's cool sun rays and breezes that drifted amongst the boulders. He sat close beside her and placed a single cloth between them, and then opened the bundle of food. Oat cakes and two legs of meat spilled from it. Bonnie took up a cake with one hand and a leg of meat with the other. For a time, they ate silently. Their shoulders touched and legs pressed into each other as they reached for drinks and additional cakes.

"I wish you would share your secrets with me as easily as you share this food," Braeson said, nodding toward the fare.

Bonnie looked at him, wiping her mouth with the back of her hand. He was amazed at the amount of food his wife could eat. Just like at their wedding dinner the previous evening, she ate her portion and much of his.

She looked away, reddening and then turned her eyes to his. "Twas fine fare," she grinned. "You can share my portion on the morrow."

Chit. He would not be distracted from his purpose by her attempts at sauciness.

"I'd rather share some secrets," he repeated.

Her chin lifted and she looked sideways at him. "You already discovered one of my secrets." She ran her hand gingerly along her left arm and then countered, "Mayhap you can share with me one of your secrets?"

"Braeson is my nekename. Given to me by Braemoore's people early on, as a babe. At first some called me Braemooreson." He smiled as she wrinkled her nose at this strange moniker. "In time, it became

Braeson. My given name is Timothy Lennox Moore."

She stared at him with a blank look as if confused and then she closed her eyes. She had only known him as Braeson or the Earl of Braemoore as stated in their initial introduction days ago in the pony shed. She looked at him again and nodded. Perchance she had just recalled saying his real name in her wedding vows?

"I do not think that is much of a secret." She crossed her arms.

"Did you know?" Braeson questioned.

She shrugged, narrowing her eyes as she stared at him.

"Tis important to know whom you married." he nudged his shoulder against her. "Aye?"

She lifted her chin and turned her head away.

"Your turn," Braeson encouraged. "A secret, my Lady."

She drew a deep breath. Did she roll her eyes?

"I did not speak for many days after Brianna and Lochlan found me." She turned her gaze to him. Golden embers simmered low in her eyes. "I had just lost my Ina and was verra afraid." She crossed her arms and the familiar lift of her saucy chin appeared again. "Tis why I did not speak to you the first few days of our travels. I was afraid, for I did not know why Brianna would give me to a Campbell."

He nodded at her, surprised by her revelation. The belligerent chit was a scared young woman. "You seem like a brave woman to me. Even when you are silent." He nudged her elbow and her crossed arms fell into her lap. "You saved the mother cat."

She looked into the distant sunset. "Tis no good that babes would lose a mother."

Braeson believed there was more to her statement than just cats. He hoped that someday she would share her secret thoughts about her lost mother and father. Perchance someday, he would tell her that it was not the Campbell in him that she was given to, but the MacEwen. Yet that secret, too, could be discussed at another time. Right now, he must stay focused on his purpose.

Her gaze returned, challenging him. "Your turn."

"I know a fine young woman who slung a stone straight into the back of Iain Campbell's head and felled him."

Bonnie gasped and her eyes grew wide. "Nay." She protested.

So she did not recall. She had said not a word about the incident. In her stupor of hunger and fatigue her reality and dream world had melded together.

"Tis truth?" Her eyes were wide and the colour had drained from her face.

"Tis truth, Bonnie," Braeson confirmed. "You felled

him and then fainted straight away into my arms." Braeson smiled. "Aye, you are a fine shot."

"I was sure twas but a dream," she whispered. She was trembling and she wrung her hands tightly in her lap.

"Campbell knows not. His back was to you. Your secret is safe." Did he see a slight shift in her shoulders? A sense of relief that Campbell was ignorant of his assailant?

Bonnie leaned in to explain. "I was warned from a young lass to avoid all Campbells. De Ros and Lochlan made a determined effort to keep Brianna and me from them."

"For what reason did De Ros and Lochlan keep you protected from the Campbells?" Braeson kept his voice calm, conversational. This was the information he so desired. Would her words confirm the story that Iain Campbell told.

"I know but bits and pieces. The story has been kept close to De Ros' and Brianna's hearts." Bonnie explained. "The Campbells attacked the MacEwen Keep. A fire burnt the tower to the ground. The Laird, Fallon, was killed. Twas Lochlan's and Brianna's older brother." Bonnie took a deep breath. She looked down to her folded hands and then returned her serious golden gaze to Braeson. "Now Lochlan was the new Laird of the MacEwen clan. He fled with Brianna to

Rose lands and along that journey they found me amongst the burning embers of a little croft." Her gaze travelled to the setting sun again, as if she relived the memory of that day so long ago. "From that moment, I clung to Brianna. I would not speak, but I heard much."

Braeson recalled the conversation with Lady Brianna the day of Bonnie's attack. How frightened Bonnie must have been.

"When we arrived at Rose Castle, Lochlan and Brianna explained all to De Ros. Twas the Campbell Laird that killed Fallon MacEwen. But the Campbell Laird was also killed that night." Bonnie trembled. "To protect Brianna, Lochlan offered her to De Ros as his wife. Brianna knew naught of Lochlan's plan—to bring her to safety, to De Ros. She was most unhappy. Tis how Brianna married Justus de Ros." Bonnie took a deep breath and raised her eyebrows, leaning even closer to Braeson. "Tis why we are warned away from the Campbells. When two Lairds are killed in a battle, danger lurks." She frowned. "But I know naught why Campbell killed Fallon MacEwen. No one speaks of it."

Iain Campbell's story held true to Bonnie's tale of the MacEwen and Campbell battle. Yet Iain Campbell believed Lochlan had killed his father.

"Iain Campbell is my mother's younger brother. My uncle."

Bonnie's mouth fell open and her eyes widened with fright.

"It was happenstance that we both were at the inn. He was returning from Edinburgh. Iain Campbell thought I was someone else when he attacked me."

Braeson held her gaze, waiting, almost willing her to see what Campbell had seen. The breeze caressed the stray curls around her face. A shadow crept closer. An evening bird spoke and its mate replied.

As Bonnie leaned toward him her breath wafted across his face. She studied him, his eyes, his nose, his mouth and then her confused glance returned to his eyes. "Aye," she whispered.

Braeson smiled at her and pulled the end of her thick braid. "Tis your turn."

She drew back and crossed her arms. "Nay," she said. "Tis *your* turn."

He captured her gaze, frowning.

"I shared the secrets of the MacEwen and Campbell feud. Tis all I know of it." She counted on her fingers. "My injury, my silence, the feud. Tis thrice the secrets." She then looked at him sideways and continued to count on her other hand. "Your nekename, the lass that felled Campbell and . . . tis *your* turn," she stated firmly.

The way she spoke reminded him of an old nanny he had as a lad, very proper and unflinching in her thoughts. He really had no more secrets that he wished to share with her at this time. He was quite content that he had garnered information enough confirming the truth of Iain Campbell's story—two Lairds had been killed, a Campbell and a MacEwen.

Yet he would play this game of secrets to its conclusion. Braeson drew closer to Bonnie. His hands rested on the rock seat on either side of her and she pressed herself back against the rock wall. "I like to kiss you," he stated.

Golden sparks grew in her eyes. Did she know that her eyes revealed her own desire?

"Tis not a secret," she whispered. "You spoke of it under the spruce yester morn." She placed her hands flat against his chest and pushed.

He drew his face closer and studied her mouth that was slightly opened.

"I do not need to know any more secrets," she insisted, yet her hands travelled upward and rested on his shoulders.

"Tis only fair that I tell you another. Thrice for you and thrice for me," Braeson insisted.

She tilted her head a bit as if to consent to the deal, then dropped her eyes to his mouth, waiting.

"I want to kiss you," he whispered.

Her hands moved upward and entangled in his hair. He was sure that she pulled his head down to meet her lips. My God, her lips were warm and full and opened when he nudged them with his tongue. He pulled her to him and lifted her onto his lap. His arm travelled around the right side of her waist, drawing her supple curves against his chest. He willed his other hand to stay at her waist, careful to protect her injuries rather than journey upward to caress her . . .

"My Lord."

Braeson's eyes flew open and met the veiled lashes of his wife. She continued to kiss him oblivious to the interruption of the guard. He placed his hands on her forearms and set her away from him. Only then, did she open her eyes, disappointment sketched over her frowning face.

"Aye, Williem." Braeson watched as Bonnie's eyes registered the guard's presence. She scrambled off his knee and hurried to her drying chemise as if feigning interest in the piece of clothing.

Braeson turned his head toward the guard that stood just inside the small rock haven. "Williem, tell Jack I will join the men in a moment to discuss guard duty for this eve."

Williem gave a brief bow and left.

"Bonnie?"

She swung around to face him, holding the chemise to her chest as if to shield herself. "I do not think we should do that again." She swiped a loose tress behind her ear and then trailed the hand down to the base of her neck.

"I think it is too late, Bonnie, since now we both share the secret." Braeson smiled at his flustered wife. "This husband likes to kiss his wife. And this wife likes to kiss her husband. Aye?"

"Aye," Bonnie answered. "Nay!" she quickly corrected herself.

Braeson smiled at her as he watched a tell-tale blush redden her face.

"Our marriage happened only to take me from Scotland to safety, aye?"

"Aye," Braeson agreed. For now, it was one reason. Someday he would share with her additional reasons why he had married her.

"When we arrive at your home and I am safe, the marriage will be annulled," Bonnie explained. "You mustna kiss me again." She took a step backward and then began to fold the dry chemise.

"Bonnie," he whispered and took a few unhurried steps. He stopped a hand's width from her, waiting.

Her hands stilled and she raised her eyes to Braeson.

"You kissed me, wife."

She made to protest his declaration and then closed her eyes, releasing a slow breath.

Braeson scanned the small rock haven. "We will

sleep in this spot tonight. It will provide you with privacy."

"Nay!" Bonnie protested, her eyes wide as she stared at his mouth again.

"It is this spot or you can sleep around a smoldering campfire with Iain Campbell," Braeson stated.

"Nay!" Bonnie shook her head.

"Choose the spot, wife," Braeson commanded.

She scanned the rock haven for a moment and then turned back to him. "I will sleep here. It is safe and I need no guard." She crossed her arms and presented him with the familiar lift of her chit's chin.

"I will gather our belongings." He smiled and narrowed his eyes at her. "As long as you don't kiss me this eve, we should both be safe here." As he turned and left the clearing, he was sure he heard her mumble his name—his real name—under her breath.

Braeson gazed across the low burning fire at his sleeping wife. The light from a few stars and a moon that peeked through drifting clouds, showed her snuggled under her seal skin blanket, her face relaxed. Bonnie had not been able to convince him to leave her in this nook alone. He knew she would be comfortable here, away from Iain Campbell . . . even away from him. Yet Braeson, her guard, was determined he would bring her to his home alive, safe and thriving.

Bonnie's story of the two dead Lairds mirrored Iain Campbell's. Braeson rubbed his hands over his face, took a deep breath and lifted his gaze to the black night. The clouds were dispersing, the sky clearing, much like his secrets. Secrets of which he had not known.

He had thought his wife's secrets might be resolved as they journeyed along. He shook his head and his attempt to chuckle turned into a sneering snort. He calculated that his Campbell grandfather must have attacked the MacEwen Keep following his expulsion from Braemoore. Bonnie did not know the reason for the attack. Yet it was inferred in Iain Campbell's words— *the boy with eyes as a pale as a silver moon.* Lady Brianna had voiced it well. *Aye, a child of a MacEwen always takes on the MacEwen eyes. Tis the MacEwen mark.* He had not recognized his resemblance to Lady Brianna or Lochlan while at Rose Keep. His only excuse was that an auburn-haired woman had caught his eye. He was of MacEwen blood. It was written all over his face. His grandfather Campbell must have recognized Braeson's resemblance to the MacEwen clan, attacked Annella and then returned to Scotland to murder the MacEwen who had defiled his daughter. The calculations were exact. Twas seventeen years ago. He had been eight.

His father, Timothy Lennox Moore, was not his sire.

He knew naught who his sire was, perchance the dead Laird, Fallon. Or was it Lochlan MacEwen? Yet this he knew, that he had been born just short of nine months after his father and mother wed. She must have been with child, with him, even as she travelled to England to wed his father. He rubbed his chest and wondered if the break in his heart would be permanent.

A nighttime breeze lulled Braeson from his musings. He studied his sleeping wife. Last eve, he had found a place beside her in the small cot. Surely there was room now under the seal skin blanket for him as well to ward off the chill of the night air. He stirred the fire, rose and stood looking again at his wife. He did not believe that Iain Campbell had any connection to Bonnie's troubles. Her fear of the Campbells sprung from the stories—*bits and pieces* as Bonnie described them—that she had heard as a child.

Had it been happenstance that Iain Campbell and the Braemoore troop both arrived at the same inn? Early this morn, after Braeson had left the room to allow Bonnie to ready for the journey, he had met with Jack and Oliver to discuss Iain Campbell. Should they release him? Jack relayed that Campbell had requested to travel with them to Braemoore to visit his sister. Braeson had agreed. It would have been best to send Iain Campbell on his way, to his own lands, to lessen Bonnie's fear. Yet his gut told him to keep

Campbell close. The Campbells seemed a reckless breed. First his grandfather's attack on his mother, then Iain Campbell's attempt to murder him—or rather Lochlan MacEwen. It was difficult to surmise Iain Campbell's thoughts. Aye, best to keep him close.

Braeson lifted the seal skin gingerly and crawled beneath it. Annulment. He smiled and shook his head at the sky. Twas an idea from his wife's imagination. He had no intention of annulling this marriage. The idea left him with a sense of loss, a void. A *void too deep and too wide*. For now, his dreaming wife could believe that he married her only to bring her to safety. He would keep his reasons as to why he married her secret, close to his heart.

They lay under her seal skin fully clothed but still the early spring's night air nipped. He would gain a few hours of sleep and then take his turn at guard duty. He turned onto his side and Bonnie squirmed backward toward him, nestling into his heart. He placed his arm gently across his sleeping wife's waist, mindful of her bruises. She took a deep breath and slipped her hand into his.

Mysteries and secrets abounded.

## Chapter Nineteen

They had travelled through many days. The familiar, wild landforms of Bonnie's northern home—the jagged rocks, the pine trees grasping cliff edges, the stone forms and low bushes—bit by bit gave way to softer, rolling land with a greater variety of trees and vegetation.

The short time spent at the inn, with good sleep and fare, had soothed her and cleared away some of her many emotions—her fears, worries, and her anger. These emotions had intensified during the early days of the journey when they had travelled by night and slept by day. Bonnie recalled how Brianna oft had said, *A bushel of worry and a nighttime of darkness do not mix.* Aye, twas true. Much like the MacEwen and De Ros clans did not mix with the Campbell clan.

The mystery as to why she was forced to marry a Campbell still wrapped itself around her. It beat in rhythm to Daisy's steps as the mare trotted along the dirt path. Why, why, why had Brianna, De Ros and Lochlan given her to a Campbell? Bonnie could not fathom the reason. Yet the sunlight that caressed the growing buds on the trees and had embraced her over these many days encouraged within her a sense of hope. Hope for what? She knew naught.

She had witnessed Brianna's grief and Lochlan's resolve when she had stated her wedding vows. De Ros had stood with Brianna and Lochlan in the midst of that storm so many nights ago, stalwart, calm. And his hand had rested on Bonnie and Braeson's joined hands, along with the priest's, as the final wedding benediction had been given. She knew the people of Rose Castle, her people, would not bring her to harm. This realization had taken root and blossomed over these many days as they moved farther from her home. A growing awareness, a hope that she might trust their plan of having her marry a Campbell and find refuge in his home, had sprung within her. Yet something, a vague uneasy notion, still itched at the back of her thoughts and she could not quite grasp it.

Bonnie smiled. Her body was healing. When she looked at her reflection in the various ponds that they settled beside each eve, she saw the bruises on her face were diminishing. Still, when she rubbed her fingers along the bone above her right eye, a tender bump lay under the skin. The lacerations along her right arm and her thigh were only glaring red stripes which in time would fade. It was the trail of intense bruises along her left side that still required delicate care.

Braeson left her to care for her injuries as long as she applied Jack's ointment each morning. But she also relied on Brianna's concoctions to mend the wounds. After Braeson had learned of her hidden bruises, Bonnie noticed that the pace at which they travelled had slowed and they rested more often along the way. She still cushioned her left side as she rode astride the mare. At first, the muscles along her right side had ached due to the extra strain she demanded of them, but they, too, were strengthening and willing to take the brunt of this perilous ride to north England.

Bonnie lifted her eyes to the long single row of riders ahead of her. Presently, Braeson led the troop, but oft it might be Jack or Oliver. At times, she saw Oliver and Braeson ride off scouting the land to determine the least dangerous route, and reappear after many hours. It was the guard, young Williem, likely a few years younger than she, who now rode closest to her. At times, when she would look at Williem, she would see the longing in his face to ride alongside the three leaders. Bonnie had tried to engage him in conversation but Williem was a quiet man and encouraged silence, so their voices would not be carried along with the wind to alert the enemy. His eyes often darted from side to side as if he were scanning the landscape, readying for a sudden attack.

Bonnie studied Braeson. His back was straight as his hooded head bobbed with the familiar cadence of his horse. They all wore the same Braemoore dark brown hooded cape over their garments to blend in well with the spring landscape. Even Iain Campbell wore the Braemoore garment over his plaid. What he knew of this excursion to England she knew naught. She avoided him and he, as if sensing her discomfort, kept his distance.

Since Iain Campbell's appearance, the ritual of sleeping away from the men's fire in a hidden alcove had continued. She had not been able to persuade Braeson to allow her to sleep on her own. He always set a small fire in her chosen spot and either sat with her or slept alongside her. She would awaken in the darkness and feel his warmth next to her. Oft his hand would rest at her waist and she would feel his silent warm breath caress the top of her head. Other times, she would open her eyes and see him sitting across from her by the smoldering fire, staring into it.

Bonnie had heeded his words at the rock pool several days ago, Y*ou kissed me, wife.* Aye, and she had. She had pulled his lips down to hers. Twas true.

She had first kissed him in the garden many eves ago when he had shared his Silkie story. It was at that moment that she knew she desired his touch. Twas a new sensation for her after the many years living at Rose Castle and acknowledging the marriageable lads her age as mere brothers. Then along came a Campbell—and an English no less—who had caught her eye. Now, a low yearning in her stomach tingled whenever he was close.

Twas all too confusing to think about and she shook her head to rid herself of the thoughts. Since the rock pool, she had kept her distance from her husband, talking with him politely and clasping her hands in her lap if she thought they were itching to touch his broad shoulders again. Twas best and would make it much easier when the marriage was annulled upon their arrival in England.

The line of riders slowed and her horse followed as they veered off the path and trotted through a small meadow of low bushes and into a wooded area. Finally, they came to a small clearing with grass knee high. While the trees stood as sentinels on three sides of this clearing, a rock wall as high as two men rose up on the far side. A shallow ledge jutted out from it, providing cover and areas in which to sleep.

Atop the rock ledge stood Oliver, pouring water into his mouth from a leather pouch. As some riders neared the rock wall, Oliver jokingly squirted water at them and a low rumble of celebration erupted from the men. The day was strangely hot and Oliver's show of humour indicated that a pool of water lay above.

Bonnie dismounted and stood in the middle of the clearing, watching as some men pulled the saddles and blankets from the horses. Others led the horses to a narrow stream, encouraging the beasts to drink. Some men clambered up the rock ledge toward Oliver, readying for a swim.

Bonnie smiled, comforted by their actions, by the cooperation and teasing that existed amongst them. But her heart hurt and tears threatened to spill as she thought of her friends and family at Rose Castle and the similarities she saw between them and Braeson's men. So far away from those who loved her . . . so, so far.

"Halt," bellowed Oliver from his perch as his companions neared the water's edge.

All turned their heads to Oliver, standing akimbo, blocking the way of the men who were scrambling up to enjoy a swim in the cool water.

"Will you not let your Lady decide who will swim first?" Oliver said, bowing to her. "My Lady, excuse these ruffians, but do you not desire to partake of these cool waters first?"

Bonnie smiled at Oliver. "I will find my own corner,

Oliver." She watched as the men ascended to the top of the ledge.

"Halt," Oliver bellowed from his perch again.

The ruffians bumped into one another as they stared at Oliver.

"Who will guard our Lady?" Oliver demanded.

"Oliver," Jack bellowed. "Enough of this nonsense. Let them in."

Oliver did not have a chance to reply as a few of the men grabbed him and flung him out of sight of those who stood below. A splash and a deluge of water that poured over the ledge wall indicated that Oliver had found his mark!

Jack turned to her. "The lads need some fun, aye." He bowed slightly, then walked away following the path they had just ridden.

Bonnie raised her eyes to Braeson as he came and stood beside her.

"Jack will stand guard first," Braeson said. He smiled and lifted his hand to her face and ran a thumb along the path a single tear had trekked. "It was not Oliver's purpose to make you cry."

Bonnie rubbed her hands over her face, attempting to wipe away not only the tears but the sensation from Braeson's caress. "Tis foolishness," she replied. "I was thinking of home and the merriment we always had." Avoiding his intense gaze, she bent to pick up her pack, but Braeson swept it from the ground and placed it over his shoulder.

"Come," he said. He took her hand and led her toward the rock wall. Behind a low bush was a small rock alcove. They were both able to stand in it with a bit of room to spare above Braeson's head. The rock ledge jutted out far enough to provide cover for two people to sit or sleep. The opening would provide a clear escape for the smoke from a fire.

"Oliver and I found this spot earlier today. It suits our purposes well." Braeson placed her pack on the cave's dirt floor. "We are but a few days ride from Braemoore. Soon you will have a soft bed to lay your head on. If you gather your soap and clean garments, I'll take you to the water. There is another path, atop this ledge, that leads into a hidden shallow pool."

Yew bushes surrounded the secreted pool where the water reached to Bonnie's shoulders when her feet touched the bottom. She kicked her body in circles and moved her arms back and forth to hold herself above the water, bobbing leisurely. Colasse had been ordered to stay and guard her. He sat alongside the small pool, wagging his giant tail, saliva dripping from his mouth.

The men's voices that had raised a din in the waters just beyond the yew bushes began to fade and she knew that preparations for the evening meal would soon begin. She immersed herself fully in the cool waters, then reached for her soap that sat atop her clean dry garments. Its rose fragrance wafted around her as she scrubbed her body with it and washed her hair.

As Bonnie rose out of the water, brown-feathered birds in a tall tree above fluttered away, squawking. Even Colasse rose to his feet to study the flock, his nose twitching, eyes scanning. Sitting again on his haunches, the dog growled low in the back of his throat. Bonnie climbed from the pool and squeezed the water from her hair and her chemise. She squatted beside her dry garments, readying herself to remove the wet chemise and don a dry one, when Colasse's head snapped up.

A strange man stepped into the hidden nook. Bonnie's stomach tightened and her body froze, as she stared at the knife in the man's hand. Rising with a loud growl, the dog hurtled across the pool, knocked the startled man into the yew bushes and dug his teeth into the man's throat. Bonnie saw the knife flail over and around Colasse as a great howl arose from the dog's throat. She ran!

She ran from the pool, from the yew bushes, from her attacker, to the path that led back to the clearing where she knew men prepared for dinner and horses grazed freely. *Run, run to me, Bonnie. Run, run to me.* Braeson's words kept pace with her heart beat as she raced toward the camp. She looked for him as she turned each corner. He had said he was just down the path a wee bit, standing guard. Had he trusted the spot enough to leave her alone and allow her to make her way back to the camp?

Bonnie rounded a corner on the path and flung her arms out, sliding to a stop against a tree that grew at the edge of a shallow rock ledge. The pine needles and cones along the path had dug into her bare feet and she placed her forehead against the tree, eyes squeezed shut, striving to take in air. A rustling nearby startled her. She raised her head, her eyes widening as she stared at the scene below her.

Braeson struggled with another assailant, a large man, who stood behind him holding a knife to her husband's neck. Braeson reached back, grabbing the man by his head and toppled him over his shoulder to the ground. As the man slammed his feet against the rock floor, Braeson threw himself forward, kicking the sword from the man's hand. The weapon tumbled into the brush and a stillness fell over the scene as each men pulled a knife from a hidden spot.

Bonnie's heart crashed against her ribs as she watched the two men leaning in, knife in hand, circling, waiting, staring. As the large man lunged, swinging his knife, a rending of fabric sliced through the silence. Surely it was her husband's shirt that was torn. Had the assailant drawn blood? Her hand instinctively reached into her pocket for her sling. Empty! A low growl of frustration rose from her gut. Did a husband who had stolen her weapons even deserve his wife's help?

Through narrowed eyes, Bonnie shifted her gaze back to the struggle, at the grunts and moans rising from below. As Braeson stretched out his leg, toppling the man to the ground, he slammed a fist into the stranger's face. The only sound that rose from the scene was Braeson's heavy breathing as he bent over the man, who lay as still as death. As her husband placed his hand alongside the man's neck, the brigand rose up, grabbed Braeson's booted leg and felled him flat on his back, readying his knife high above Braeson's head.

Scanning the ground around her, Bonnie grasped some pebbles and dirt in her right hand and with the left, reached down for a palm-size stone on the ground beside her feet. She did not have her sling but she could still throw a stone. Mayhap not as far or as fast as with her sling, but she knew that her aim was excellent.

Bonnie rubbed the stone in her hand, feeling its jagged edges and weight and then let fly the fistful of gravel into the air. She raised the stone and flung it with all her strength toward the assailant who was thrusting his knife towards Braeson's chest.

# Chapter Twenty

Braeson plunged his knife through the assailant's clothes, ripping into the brigand's flesh below the rib cage. Shock gathered in the man's face and his knife dropped to the ground beside Braeson's head as blood oozed warm onto Braeson's hand from the wound. Braeson was always surprised what force was demanded to pierce a man's body. He stilled his knife, pausing, before he gave the final rend which would hurl his attacker to hell.

The man atop him mumbled words, and then drew a deep breath struggling to speak "My two companions and I seek the treasure and the la . . . la . . ."

A harsh shower of pebbles hurtled around them and a large jagged stone whizzed by Braeson's nose. It struck the dying man at his left temple. The villain flopped full onto Braeson's chest along with the rogue rock.

"Bloody hell," Braeson roared.

He shoved the man from him, vaulted to his feet and swung around to see Bonnie leaning on the side of a tree in her wet chemise, hugging her left arm close to her body. Braeson stormed through the copse of trees and climbed atop the rock ledge to where Bonnie stood. His concern for her safety battled with his anger toward her for tossing the stone rather than running to camp and seeking help.

Jack and Williem raced to them from the camp. Shouts from beyond the trees told Braeson that his men had spread across the encampment to seek out and fight the enemy that threatened.

Braeson glared at Bonnie who still leaned against the tree. Through his clenched jaw, he demanded, "What were you thinking Bonnie? You should not have stopped here but should have sought help at camp." He pushed her wet, unbound hair away from her face as droplets of water slid down her nose. He had a notion to haul her into camp and shake her until she understood that she need not defend him or his men but rather accept fully their protection.

Bonnie lifted a trembling right arm and pointed toward the hidden pool where she had been bathing. "A man. And the dog . . .

Williem rushed down the path to the hidden pool to where the man and the dog had fought.

Bonnie winced and massaged her left arm. Jack

threw his hooded cape around her wet form and Braeson tied it at her neck.

"Come lass," Jack said, eyeing the arm that Bonnie held tightly. "Let us return to camp and I'll check your arm."

Bonnie shook her head and attempted a smile. "I cannot Jack." She drew a deep breath. "My feet are pained from the pine cones."

Braeson swept her into his arms and carried her down the trail to their settlement. Men's voices, hurried and indistinct, travelled nearby, yet it was Bonnie's fragrance of roses that wafted around him and drew his attention, enticing him to pull her even closer against his chest. His heart beat quickened as her arm tightened around his neck. Imagining he could almost feel the satiny softness of her thighs through the thin layer of her chemise, his fingers tingled.

Inside their small rock alcove, he placed her onto her seal skin blanket and drew the hooded cape tightly around her. He watched his wife for a moment as Jack began to inspect her feet, then turned away, stepping out of the small alcove to stand against the rock wall, unseen.

Braeson drew a deep breath. She was safe in Jack's hands—cook, warrior, healer, loyal friend, elder. He gazed down at his hands. How was it that these hands wanted to wring his stubborn wife's neck, yet at the same time peel the wet chemise from her body and caress her until he knew every inch of her.

Colasse barked and Braeson turned toward the path from where he had just come. He fisted his hands several times to rid himself of his frustration. It didn't work. Finally, he pushed his hands through his hair, then let them fall to his sides as he walked toward the limping animal.

The dog had surface gashes over its torso and held a front leg high off the ground as it limped along. Braeson placed his hand on the dog's head as it settled by the main fire and closed its eyes. Its assailant had not fared as well. Dead. That made two men dead. Who they were and where they hailed from was a mystery.

Braeson gave the brave dog a final pat and rose. His eyes scanned the environment, studying the landscape. If only the stone had not hit the man, Braeson might have garnered additional information from him. The assailant had said, *My two companions and I seek the treasure and the . . . la.* Had he meant to say lady or lass? Braeson would never know.

He studied the parchment which Williem had found on the dead man's body by the hidden pool. The attackers had not had time to attach it to a tree. Both bodies had been searched, as they had done with the previous attackers. How many dead men did this make? Three at Rose Castle, three that De Ros and his men had confronted in the first days of this journey, three on the rock ledge and two this eve.

Three seemed to be a pattern amongst these assailants. Initially, De Ros had stated that at least a dozen men had hidden in the crags. If that were true, one man still was unaccounted for. One enemy who, perchance, schemed now to accost Bonnie and those who protected her.

His men were all accounted for. Oliver had organized them into pairs, positioned to stand guard around the camp.

What troubled Braeson more than a missing assailant was how Oliver and he had failed to detect the enemy prior to making camp here. Many days ago, they had identified the strange bird call of their assailants when on the rock ledge and had determined they must take cover. But this attack had been silent, without any warning.

Braeson turned to see Jack leave Bonnie's resting place. He stepped to the low burning fire with only wisps of smoke rising from a few heated stones and debris. He gathered pieces of meat, oatcakes and wine that he now took to his wife. He had words to say to her. The food might soothe the conversation.

Braeson carried the assortment of food into the

small alcove and sat beside Bonnie on her seal skin. He wished he could start a fire to chase away the chill in the night air but the camp had been tossed into darkness to prevent their enemy from sighting them. A short tallow sat along the far wall and cast a faint glimmer of light over Bonnie. Her feet had been attended to and she wore heavy woolen stockings to protect them from the dirt floor. She had donned dry clothes and her wet chemise lay on a flat rock near the entrance.

As had been the ritual over these many eves, Braeson placed the food between them and they ate in silence for a time, studying the shadows cast by the tallow. He wondered again if they should remain here for the night or move on while the darkness still afforded them protection.

"How goes Colasse?" Bonnie's voice broke into his meandering thoughts.

He turned to her. "He lives." Braeson studied her face where concern was etched around her eyes. He remained silent as she released a breath at the news.

The tallow's fire blazed gold in her eyes. "'Tis a brave cur. A man stepped from the yew bushes. The dog hurdled atop him." She fell silent, her eyes searching his for answers to her unspoken question.

"The two villains are dead," he said.

"'Tis truth?" she frowned.

"Tis truth, Bonnie."

She touched her hand to her head and breast and then back and forth to her shoulders, a solemn, sacred act. Unsure if the chill that was creeping in was from the night air, or from the knowledge that her blessing failed to redeem the two men whose souls now lingered in hell, Braeson pulled his cape tighter about himself.

Drawing a deep breath in an attempt to tamp down his ire, he began. "You gave your word, Bonnie." He rose and took a single stride to the opposite wall and leaned against it. He glared at her as she narrowed her eyes and pursed her lips, seemingly confused. "There would be no more stones flung at men."

"Tis no men. Aye?" Her eyes blazed bright as a fire, burning straight to his heart. "Savages! Beasts!"

Braeson rubbed his chest where his heart lay, soothing away the image of Bonnie lying injured, even worse—dead—because she did not follow his command. "You are not to toss stones," he growled. "Your aid is not required." He stared at her, watching as she drew her hands together and held them still on her lap. The fire in her eyes danced lower and left burning embers around the edges.

"Run, run straight away to camp, to the men, your protection," he ordered.

The embers tapered to sparks and he detected a delicate sag in her shoulders.

"Shriek all the way to camp to alert the men," he ordered. "It was the howl of Colasse that brought the men into the battle."

The sparks only smoldered now as she dropped her eyes to her tightly clasped hands.

"Shriek! We must know you live."

His lovely wife seemed to curl inward with her head down and her knees pulled closer to her breast like a crumbling piece of ash singed to naught. He closed his eyes and allowed his head to fall to his chest. He poked again at the lingering pain around his heart. She had lived through this harrowing experience and yet had he now not attempted to snuff out her will to thrive, to fight, with a few ill-begotten words? Words of anger, in a ludicrous attempt to regain control of her, nay, to gain control of the entire situation that caused them to race from Scotland toward safety.

How had he and Oliver miscalculated this location? They had scoured the land for several hours this noon to secure a safe respite. Had he not instructed Williem to ride beside Bonnie in silence in order to scan the landscape for enemies? How had he and his men not detected signs of them? Perchance they were fighting phantoms? Could phantoms be buried beneath rocks, cairns, that now rested on the cliff edges marking the assailants' entrance to hell?

Bonnie's skirts rustled. He raised his head to gaze

in amazement as she threw back her shoulders and lifted her head high. She stretched, bit by bit, from her coiled position, pushing heavily on her right arm to gain her balance. Her unbound hair danced around her in waves of golds and reds and her skirts unfurled about her legs, waving like banners to proclaim her ascent from the ashes where his words had tossed her. She rose upward to her full height, lifting her eyes— eyes that glowed like hot burnished copper—and seared him straight to his heart.

"You have found me lacking, my Lord." Her chin tilted higher. She looked at him down her straight, long nose, regal and elegant. "Tis good cause to sever this arrangement and annul the marriage when we arrive in England."

Braeson shifted from the rock wall and stood straight. "There will not be an annulment, Bonnie." His words were clear and firm. "The marriage will be consummated upon our arrival in England."

His wife nodded. "So be it." Her eyes blazed and shot warning fireballs at him. "I will have my weapons returned." She glared at him for a time.

How was she able to gaze at him down her nose, like a queen at her subject, even though she stood only to his shoulder?

"This wife will continue to provide her aid." She paused. "Her help, for her husband." Relying only on her right arm and hand, she twisted her luscious hair and coiled it around her head like a crown. She lifted her pack that carried Brianna's healing vials and walked to the entrance, slow and majestic. "I will tend to Colasse," she announced and stepped into the darkness.

Braeson slumped against the rock wall, rubbing his hands over his face. My God, she was splendid. Had she remained, he might have knelt at her feet, giving that brave woman all of the adoration that he held for her in his heart. He rubbed his chest again. The pain had lessened.

Braeson sat on his bed roll, leaning against the rock wall of the small alcove and studied the missives. Missives given to him by the Lairds, all those days ago in the Rose library when he had agreed to accept Bonnie as his wife. He compared them to the one found this day tucked in the garments of one of the dead men.

He lifted his head as a flash of lightning lit the rock chamber brighter than the meagre tallow sitting next to him. His wife stood at the entrance, then stepped inside as thunder bellowed and rattled. The violent weather and the threat of rain would cause them to rest at this camp this night. Bonnie remained motionless, studying the small alcove until her eyes came to him.

"How goes Colasse?" asked Braeson. Had he not known the beast, he might have believed the cur feigned injury. Several of his men had tended to the dog and he envied the attention Bonnie also provided to the animal. He coveted her hands running over him.

"Twill be fine. The gashes are shallow and the swelling in the leg begins to fade."

He had no doubt that Colasse would regain his strength. Even he had tended to the dog.

"I applied a mixture of Brianna's honey and berries. Tis a sweet beast."

He chuckled to himself. Damn dog had won her heart and was going to smell like a vial of perfume. He frowned, "You offered me but salt and vinegar." He rubbed his shoulder where the tip of the arrow had pierced, the wound now healed.

She dipped her head, placing her pack against the wall. She raised her eyes to him. "You are a brawny man, my Lord."

Was that a glint of humour in her eyes?

"Salt and vinegar works favourably on large beasts," she concluded.

They stared at each other for a time. Witnessing her return to this small alcove gave him hope she would extend mercy to him, forgiving him and his harsh words. The same mercy she had prayed for when she had made the sign of the cross for her assailants.

Braeson held out the parchments—his olive branch. "Would you be interested in studying these missives?" He leaned toward her, as his wife dropped her eyes to the parchments. Would she remain standing at the entrance all night? "I seek your aid," he said.

Bonnie took a tentative step deeper into the alcove. "Tis truth?" she questioned, eyebrows furrowed.

"Tis truth," he stated holding his breath as he held her gaze. He knew she questioned his sincerity by the way she tilted her head slightly to the right, appraising the situation. "These missives were nailed to trees after each attack—one at Ina's cottage and the other near to where you were attacked a few weeks past at Rose Castle." He held the third one higher. "This was found on one of the scoundrals this day."

Another step.

"How did you come by the first two?" she questioned.

"The Lairds." He continued to hold the parchments out to her. "Perchance my wife would like to study them and share her insight."

She took another step, a half-step.

"I would like your aid."

She stared at him. Would he ever win her, or had he done irreparable damage to this wavering relationship? "This husband would value his wife's aid, her help."

She took the remaining steps to stand over him, unmoving, staring at the missives. He watched her release a deep breath as if giving up the anger and frustration he had caused her. Then she slowly, hesitantly, sat next to him on her bedroll. He noticed that she winced and jerked as she settled herself beside him. The way she held her left arm to her chest indicated that further injury had occurred to her left side as she had run and thrown that damned stone.

"The Lairds believe they were left by the enemy to warn, to convey a message." He handed them to her and Bonnie remained silent for a time holding them in her right hand.

The tallow snapped and flickered, casting shadows along the walls and across the parchments, while lightning continued to fill the alcove. Thunder drove the horses closer to the overhanging rock. Snorting, they poked their muzzles into the chamber entrance.

"What might this symbol be?" She pointed to a line of many small circles. In the middle of this line was one larger circle. A poorly sketched weapon, perchance a dagger, was placed beside it.

"A treasure," he stated. "The missives appear to be written in a strange unfamiliar code."

"A treasure?" Bonnie brought the papers closer and frowned. "I havna been told of a treasure." She looked at Braeson. Her silent question hung in the air.

"Ina found you wrapped in your seal skin that long ago night," he began and watched as the fire in her eyes burned low and she looked away, always away into a long-ago memory, whenever her Ina was mentioned. "A necklace was also found hanging loosely around your neck. It is believed to be the treasure."

Bonnie's right hand flew to the base of her neck. "A necklace? I was not told of it."

He recalled the glimmering rope of pearls and the value it exuded. "The Lairds held it close to their hearts so that no one could speak of it. A way to protect you from harm."

"Where is the necklace now?" A light flush rose from her neck and the embers in her eyes snapped angrily as she turned back to the parchments, feigning interest.

"In a hidden chamber in De Ros' library." He lifted her chin, turning her face back to him. "There it remains. Its glory lost to the world."

She nodded and the accusation in her eyes—that he accepted the treasure, a payment, to bring her to safety—disappeared. "What does it look like," she leaned in closer to him.

"A pearl necklace of three, nay, four strands." He smiled as her eyes grew, filled with both amazement and surprise. "A large diamond sits majestically in its middle surrounded by the shimmering pearls."

"A diamond?" she whispered.

"Aye." His gaze dropped to her mouth where her lips formed a delicate circle when in awe. He remembered a similar pose when he had told her the story of the Silkie. That night in the garden seemed a life-time ago. Breathing in her rose fragrance, he gingerly pushed a strand of auburn hair from her shoulder. He could imagine the necklace placed around her lovely neck and the glimmering diamond accentuating her beauty. He felt the warmth of her burnished eyes on him and returned his gaze to them, only to see her draw back quickly and busy herself again with the study of the messages.

"Mayhap my mother had other bairns?"

Such a statement, the first in which Bonnie had directly mentioned her own mother, drew his attention away from her lovely face and to the parchment she clutched.

"This parchment was held by Ina," Bonnie said. "Twas singed by the fire, but look! Are these small, faded symbols of people?" She held the parchment closer to him and he studied it. "Look at this parchment that was found after the attack at Rose Keep." She pointed to similar distinct symbols. "Mayhap they represent bairns."

Braeson took the parchments from Bonnie and

studied them closely. He had not noticed the faded drawing on the first missive. Were these symbols an indication of Bonnie's connection to others? Others who were also haunted by abandonment and threats?

"It seems a possibility." He smiled at her, noticing the dark smudges under her eyes. She was exhausted. A day of riding, facing an assailant and being reprimanded by one's husband made for a tiring experience. "Tomorrow's light will allow for a clear scrutiny of these missives, aye?" Braeson tucked the parchments into his pack and turned to Bonnie.

She studied the bedrolls, frowning. "I do not think our beds are readied."

He had determined this placement while she tended to Colasse. She usually lay on her right side, likely to take the pressure from the left. But it also allowed her to turn away from him and tuck herself into the dark without scrutiny. But this eve, his bedroll sat on her right.

"Let me be your cushion this eve . . ." He nodded to her left side. "Take your rest from me. Aye? It will aid in your healing." Allowing the injured shoulder and arm to rest on him rather than on the hard ground or precariously along her side, would benefit the injury.

A slow blush appeared on her face, but it was her frown that suggested to him that he had not quite been forgiven for his earlier transgressions.

"Let me help you heal." He smiled and then repeated the words that she had stated earlier, "This husband will continue to provide aid." He paused. "For his wife."

Bonnie pursed her lips. "You mock me?" she questioned.

"Nay." He studied her frown, her lovely, luscious lips and the slow blush reddening her cheeks. "I admire you." *Adore you,* he wanted to say but was unsure of this growing admiration for a woman he hardly knew. The truth was he had never admired a woman like he did this fiery maid.

Bonnie stretched out on her bedroll that lay beside him and he drew her seal skin over them both. He propped himself on an elbow and leaned over her, drawing his finger under each of her eyes pretending to wipe away the dark smudges that revealed her exhaustion. Her hand grasped his wrist, holding it still.

"You are lovely, wife," he whispered as her arm slowly wrapped around his neck, her fingers leaving a tingling trail of caresses through his hair, drawing him even closer.

"Wives kiss husbands, aye?" She smiled.

"Wives forgive husbands," he answered.

Her soft lips opened under his and he slid his tongue along her lower lip and pressed his mouth along her velvety skin, trailing kisses along her neck to its base. Perchance the marriage would be consummated before their arrival in England. His hand trailed along her shoulder, sweeping downward and settling at her waist. Bonnie moaned as he pulled her closer and he was encouraged by her response until . . . she moaned again. Frowning, he opened his eyes and realized she was—

"Scowling?" he teased. "You scowl. You do not like my kisses." He attempted to feign insult but when she giggled he lifted his head.

"I would try again," she explained. "But I am hurt."

He smiled at the memory from days ago when he had scowled due to his own injury. "You mock me?" he taunted.

"Mayhap." This time, she did not attempt to hide the glint of humour in her eyes.

He released a low chuckle, eased down onto his bedroll and turned his head to her.

"Why did you throw the stone, Bonnie?" he questioned. "The man was already dead but for a twist of my knife."

"Tis my natural inclination to help. Brianna taught all of her children to help." She blinked. "Twas right to help you, my Lord, but I lacked the sling and threw the stone with all of my strength." She rubbed her arm. "I do not think the arm is broken but only bruised inside."

Braeson extinguished the tallow. But for the occasional lightning and the snorts of the horses, darkness and silence embraced the chamber. "Come Bonnie." He pulled her gently to him and she settled beside him, her shoulder and arm resting on his chest, her head tucked into his neck. She held her body tense against his, seemingly unable to relax in this novel situation. Perchance he could lull her into sleep.

"Tis your turn to share a secret, Bonnie," he whispered. "I shared the missives."

He felt her body vibrate with a chuckle. The tautness of her body slowly relaxed against him as she tapped a finger on his chest.

"I have but one to tell." Her face nestled closer to his neck as her energy seeped from her. "The ring given to me at our wedding holds the emblem of the MacEwen clan." Her words were wispy, indicating sleep was overtaking her. Finally, her body lulled toward him, dissolving into slumber.

Braeson lay awake for a long time following Bonnie's whispered proclamation. The ring had been given to him by his mother some years ago as she was organizing her jewellery. *To be used in your future*, she had declared.

But this secret was not the only scenario keeping him awake.

In the past nights while they slept by the fire, he had chosen to place his bedroll across from Bonnie, she on one side of the fire and he on the other. Her nearness had made him yearn to caress and touch her. But this eve, his lovely wife slept in his arms and his body lay ready.

Erect and ready to adore her.

# Chapter Twenty-One

"We will arrive this eve."

Bonnie turned and looked down, from where she sat on her horse, at Braeson who had spoken these words.

Bonnie closed her eyes remembering the confrontation with the assailants and the tumultuous storm that had left them wet and disgruntled. She turned from Braeson, looking out to where the men were preparing to eat and take a short respite. Braeson's words wrapped tightly around her chest, causing her to struggle for breath. Her stomach would not still. She felt as if the pebbles and dirt she always threw with her sling, rolled haphazardly inside her, making her anxious and unsure. What would happen when they arrived at Braemoore? Would the marriage be consummated this eve, or would she have time to settle? Would she meet Braeson's mother, Lady Annella, or might the Lady be away during this season? This final question was answered with

Braeson's next statement.

"You can expect to be pampered by my mother and Auld Maeve by this day's end," he said.

Braeson stood away from her, but she felt his eyes watching as she dismounted and her feet touched the ground. She scanned the area, looking out through the copse of trees searching for any possible assailants. All seemed undisturbed. Mayhap her enemies were but ghosts.

She opened her pack and withdrew the meagre lunch. When she looked again, Braeson, also, was scanning the landscape and the tall trees that guarded this resting place.

"They will pamper a stranger?" Bonnie questioned.

"They will pamper my wife," Braeson said.

A flutter danced in her stomach, a reminder of their marriage vows. Yet she frowned, skeptical of his statement.

"Do not fear, Bonnie. All will go well when we arrive at Braemoore." He paused, studying her with his silver eyes. "Our home."

When he smiled like that, it sent her heart a-flutter. Much had changed since that night under the rock alcove when Bonnie had confronted him, demanding her weapons, demanding her rightful place as his wife. She had silently forgiven him and his harsh words and demands. Her hope grew now for a marriage and for her future—her and Braeson's future. She took a single step toward him but then stopped. She must not.

"If only I might touch you for just a moment," Braeson whispered across the space in which they stood, staring at each other. "Yet I dare not. Your identity must remain a secret."

Twas true. She and Braeson dared not touch each other in the open. But the memories of the night under the rock alcove lingered and she desired his touch, again and again . . .

She had slept comfortably in Braeson's arms that night, in peace, accepting Braeson's olive branch and rejoicing in the new knowledge found in the missives. When she had awakened the next morning, his fingers were gently combing through her hair. The kisses they shared were a promise, an acknowledgement, of their mutual agreement for the marriage. Her wounded arm, now in a sling, had prevented them from exploring their maturing relationship further.

That morning, two morns past, a plan had also been put into place. It had Bonnie and the men assemble into two troops. They all wore the dark brown Braemoore cape ensuring the hood was pulled securely over their heads. Different horses had been assigned to her and a handful of men. Oliver led one troop and Braeson the other. Each group followed a different road toward Braemoore, staying to the shadows and away from the main paths.

In conferring with Jack and Oliver, Braeson hoped this formation would confound anyone who was watching them. Which group was Bonnie in? Which rider was Bonnie? Appearing the same and assigning riders to different horses, if there were an enemy watching, he might choose to follow Oliver's group. This plan also silently ensured that Braeson and Bonnie would not touch each other, as they rested, as they slept. She now ate with the men and slept near them to protect her identity. She did notice that Braeson, Jack and Williem had, for these two nights past, positioned themselves around her in this huddle of men while they slept. The troop slept for only a short time, enough to rest the horses, and then rose in the wee hours of the morn to push forward toward Braemoore.

Twas why Braeson stood a few strides from her now to give the impression that she was one of the men in the troop.

"Come, Bonnie, and join the others while you eat," Braeson said.

"Might I examine the parchments while I sit?" asked Bonnie. Since studying the missives, two nights past, Bonnie had wanted to hold them again—to attempt to decipher them, to grasp onto something of her lost lineage. The wet, rainy days had prevented her from exposing them to the weather, but this day, cloudy and dry, provided an ideal opportunity to examine them again.

Braeson looked up at the clear sky, then nodded toward his horse. "They are tucked deep inside my pack that hangs from my horse's left flank." He smiled and then turned to Jack to discuss the plans for this final day's journey.

From deep within Bonnie, a sense of joy bubbled up. So much had changed since she and Braeson had exchanged those harsh words. The following morning, she had found her weapons beside her pack. She had slid the knives into her boots and the leather sling, her constant companion, into the fold of her travel gown. Each weapon Braeson had seized from her, each harsh word he had spoken, had flayed a piece of her until the shreds were unrecognizable and tossed into the ashes. She had wondered who she was, losing herself under her husband's harsh words and demands.

Once when she was a girl, she had asked Brianna this question, *Who am I?*

*You are Bonnie of Rose,* Brianna had responded. *A brave lass. My help, my comfort.*

Twas the reason Bonnie had demanded the annulment from Braeson. He had not wanted her, *Bonnie of Rose,* helpful, brave, a comfort, friend and so much more. Nay, she was not helpless, a burden. She had claimed her courage amidst those ashes, knowing it also mingled with her anger. Her heart had beaten loudly at her ears, vibrating through her body as she had risen from the ashes, standing tall and facing Braeson, insisting that their marriage be annulled.

Bonnie was certain Braeson had trembled when she had demanded the annulment. Braeson's reply that the marriage would not be dissolved had provided her with the strength to state her conditions. She would be of help to Braeson and to the people of Braemoore, just as she had been at Rose Keep.

Braeson's acceptance of her terms for their marriage had been like a healing balm, like water that cleansed her wounds and enticed her to wade in deeper. And when he had offered the parchments to her, she had tentatively acknowledged them as an olive branch. She had thought that possibly their truce would be short lived, but nay, Braeson had, over the following days, encouraged her to be a part of Braemoore's troop. She knew she was ready to be his wife, his help, his comfort.

She felt like dancing and skipping in the wind as she approached Braeson's horse. Instead, Bonnie tugged her cape around her and walked calmly to conceal her identity. A long tress flew from beneath her hood and twirled in the wind. Capturing it, she folded it behind her ear.

She ran her hand along the horse's underbelly to calm the large beast and then tugged Braeson's pack open. Shoving her hand deep inside, she felt gingerly for the missives, her fingers rubbing along the edges of what felt like parchment. She reached deeper to grasp onto the bottom of the folded pages and pulled them upward. As she tugged, her finger latched onto a small cloth bag. It tumbled out of the pack and fell to the ground, spilling its contents at her feet.

Bonnie gasped and knelt by the object that had fallen from the bag. A necklace. Unbelieving, Bonnie stared for a time and slowly hooked a finger through the pearl rope, raising it to the light. A shimmering three strand necklace of luminescent pearls, lifted by the breeze, swayed and danced in an erratic pattern. Bonnie felt herself sway with the necklace, not mesmerized but rather struck faint by it. Nausea crept, bit by bit, into her stomach and she felt she might spew the contents of her morning meal.

This was the treasure. Her treasure. She recalled Braeson's words - *a pearl necklace of three strands. A diamond sits majestically in its middle surrounded by shimmering hues of pearls.* Where was the diamond? A small hole sat in the middle of the strand where the diamond should be. Bonnie rose, pulling her wounded arm from the sling and grabbed the remaining contents of Braeson's pack. Everything flew to the ground and scattered. The diamond was not there.

Bonnie stared again at the beautiful necklace that still dangled from her finger. She closed her eyes and attempted to breathe deeply. Why was it stuffed into Braeson's pack? Had not Braeson told her that it was safe in the library at Rose Castle? Her nausea subsided, replaced by a fire of anger in the pit of her stomach. The same fire that had burned when she attacked Braeson in the shed, believing him to be a reiver, a thief. So she had been right! Braeson *was* a thief, a fraud. He had accepted this necklace as his payment to take her to safety. He still held the diamond, her diamond! Twas not in a safe box in De Ros' library. The thief had lied to her, making her believe that he wanted the marriage. That he wanted her. He had only desired the necklace and its worth. She choked on a sob but refused to give in to the despair and hopelessness that wrestled for her heart. She stumbled away from the horse, grasping the necklace to her chest. Where was the lying deceiver who had made a fool of her?

"Bonnie."

She twisted around to face her enemy. Not the enemy that sought to steal her life from her, but this enemy, her husband who had stolen her necklace and had, at the same time, stolen her heart.

She noted that Jack stood beside Braeson and Williem also lingered near.

"Tis the thieving, lying reiver," she growled. Satisfaction wrapped itself tightly around her heart as Braeson jerked as if struck by her words. She was sure she heard their resounding thwack against his head.

"You lied," she sputtered. "You said it was in De Ros' library. But nay! Tis here!" She held the necklace high, then flung it, hitting Braeson with it alongside his ear. It slithered to his chest, then dropped to the ground. "Your treachery has been exposed," she spat the words at him. "I see that you've been paid in full for your kind gesture of escorting me from Scotland." She kicked dirt at the jewels and then pulled her sling from the folds of her skirt. "Let us agree that you have met the conditions laid out by the Lairds. I will not be needing any more help from you."

She turned and ran toward the horses. If she could just mount one quickly and get away she would determine her destination later. But her wounded arm slowed her as she clutched it to her chest to steady the aching pain that shot from it. She heard Braeson growl orders to his men and there was movement behind her. And then Iain Campbell loomed before her, blocking her pathway to the horses.

"Me thinks not, lass," he stated calmly, extending his arms on either side.

"The Campbells are murderers and liars!" she yelled. She pointed a finger at Iain Campbell. "Murderer!" Her eyes locked on Braeson condemning him. "Liar." She whipped her sling and hit her mark. Iain Campbell fell to the ground. She bolted up a series of rocks that formed a natural stairway and stopped a few feet from the top where Braeson now stood.

"Cease," he ordered. "I knew naught of the necklace. I did not place it in my pack."

"Reiver," she shouted. "I will not listen to your falsehoods. I will not be fooled again."

"It is the truth, Bonnie," Braeson extended an arm toward her. "Perchance the Lairds or Lady Brianna placed it in the pack, believing it safe there." He took a step down toward her. "I refused the offer, knowing it was your birthright."

She felt hot, damp, and was sure that the fire in her belly was burning her alive. The tears that she had earlier denied, now streamed down her face, blurring her vision, flowing into her mouth and dripping from her chin.

"Come, Bonnie. Your arm is still wounded and we can talk further as we eat."

Braeson's mouth continued to move but the words were garbled. Her brain addled. She could not remain here. As he took another tentative step towards her, she gripped her sling and slid down the rock stairs. At midpoint, she bounded toward a small opening in the trees and ran. She stumbled once and pressed her sore arm more tightly to her chest to ease it from the jarring and bumping. Her hood fell from her head and her hair, now loosened from its braid, flapped and waved in the wind, billowing across her face as if it, too, was protesting the injustice done. If she could just get to the boulder in the distance, she knew she could hide behind it, rest and consider her escape.

Bonnie did not hear the horse until it was upon her. She was grabbed by her hair, the assailant tugging her upward. Twisting and flailing, she came face to face with the rider who fell from his horse and grabbed her wounded arm, twisting it behind her. The pain seared through her, blurring her vision. She knew immediately this villain was not of Braemoore. Those who wished her dead had found her again! The knife that flashed before her face brought her surroundings into focus and she saw the cold eyes and predatory sneer of the man that gripped her arm. The assailant spun her around, snaking his arm about her neck. The sharp point of the knife was positioned at her throat.

Braeson! There he stood, several feet from her, still and watchful. His men stood scattered on either side of him. Colasse lay low to the ground, readying to leap.

"You wish to kill her?" To her ears, Braeson's words

sounded almost courteous, too cordial. She squeezed her eyes shut and felt tears escape and trickle down her face. Braeson's voice was mundane, dispassionate, as if he cared for her not at all and was in collusion with this evil man.

She heard the first knife hurtle by and spear into the tree to her left. Bonnie's eyes snapped open and she watched Braeson settle back into his stance. When her assailant pulled her a step back, she knew! She knew this predator worked alone and that the men of Braemoore, her protection, stood before her. Terror wrapped itself around her pounding heart and she dared not move as Jack's knife flew by her right ear and pierced the ground at her feet. As the villain took another step in retreat, she grasped his arm that was around her neck to maintain her balance.

"I'll take the treasure and then slit this sister's throat as is my appointment," her assailant snarled.

She held her breath as Williem's knife sliced through the air above their heads and found its mark with a resounding thunk. She was sure the knife had penetrated a tree some distance behind her. Another step back.

'You should have concern for your own throat . . ." Braeson, slow and deliberate, pulled the necklace from his cape and held it high in the air. The noon day light made it sparkle and various hues danced amongst the pearls. He nodded at the necklace. "If you even touch a hair on the woman's head."

"Such a lovely head she has. Twas a clever ploy to divide your men," he sneered. "But yester eve a lovelytress flew out from under this maid's hood."

The man's growl made Bonnie's stomach clench in terror. She had tried to be so careful, weaving her hair tightly to prevent it from falling loose and signaling her enemy.

"Indeed, a lovely colour of coppers and reds hailed her location." The villain took another step backward as Iain Campbell's knife hissed through the air and landed at the demon's feet.

Bonnie could only gasp in amazement, wondering why Iain Campbell would help in her rescue. A red bruise marked his forehead from the stone she had flung. Yet, he too stood with the men of Braemoore.

"The woman . . ." Braeson stared at the assailant for a time his words hanging still in the air. "For the treasure." Then, he pulled a second knife from his boot and lowered the necklace onto the blade, wrapping the beautiful pearls around it. The man gasped, likely believing Braeson might slice the valuable treasure into pieces.

The jewelled knife sailed through the air and speared into a tree close to the villain. Bonnie and the man stumbled backward again, her assailant tightening his grip and pushing the knife's entire edge against her neck.

Why had Braeson given over the necklace? Her eyes locked with her husband's.

"Now the woman." Braeson's hand extended outward toward the villain, toward Bonnie, indicating that she should be released to him.

"I canna give her up," the man announced. "She is the youngest of three sisters. And she will be the first one to die." He tightened his arm, like a noose, around her neck and she struggled to breath, to stay alert. If only she could reach her knives or her sling. "I am the last of her pursuers and I will not fail." The knife dug into her neck and he nodded toward the tree where the necklace dangled. "My reward awaits."

Silence hovered in the air. A bird spoke. The breeze trembled across her face as Bonnie stared at Braeson, amazed that he wanted her. He wanted her regardless of the necklace. How could she have been so daft to believe he hid the necklace? That he had spoken falsehoods. Everything he had done in this race from Scotland had benefitted her and kept her safe.

Bonnie scanned the line of men and the dog, her protection. Fingers flicked at knives and swords. But it was Braeson that drew her eyes. Beads of sweat broke out on her brow as she watched him bend to swipe a handful of pebbles and dirt from the ground, his eyes never leaving her face. She struggled for breath, her heart hammered too loudly in her ears as she recognized the warning. His warning! Her warning!

Braeson tossed the pebbles into the air and grabbed the hidden knife from the back of his belt so fast that she had but a moment to pull her head aside as he hurled it at them. The brigand's scream pierced the air and blood spewed about her. She stumbled backward with him, his arm still around her neck. The last she saw, as she toppled over the low bushes and crashed down the steep rocky crag, was Braeson rushing toward her and Colasse lunging over the cliff.

She and the dead man fell over each other as they slid down the jagged ridge, coming to a stop on a narrow ledge. She opened her eyes and stared into the battered, dead face of her assailant. Braeson's knife was embedded in the opening where the man's eye should have been. Braeson's words from two days past echoed in her head *Shriek! We must know you live.*

Fear rose up from her stomach. Fear never expressed when Ina's cottage had been burned. Fear held tight when her assailants had assaulted her at Rose Keep. This fear now spewed from her gut as she slapped and pushed herself away from the hideous sight. Shrieking, she tumbled over the narrow ledge and fell straight down into a fast moving river, swollen with the rain of the last two days.

Bonnie plunged deep into the cold waters, flailing her arm, kicking her feet in an attempt to rise to the surface. The deafening waters roared around her. Her hair clung to her face like a mask, blinding her. She rose above the currents once, gasping for breath, while the air slapped her face. Her heavy skirts and cape pulled her downward again into the black abyss where she spun in the frigid currents, thrashing in the gray waters.

Her wounded arm dragged alongside her, unable to move or support her in this battle for life. As she tumbled forward, her body bumped and scraped against rocks. God, God, her spirit cried. She wanted to live! She wanted to thank the Lairds and Brianna for their protection and love. She had not shown gratitude on that last night at Rose Keep, but had walked in a daze, and in her anger had not understood nor accepted her fate. Her life had been a gift. A gift of love. If only she would have another chance, another moment to express this.

As her foot knocked against the rocks on the shore, Bonnie attempted to reach out blindly, grabbing at something—anything! Suddenly her wrist was captured in a sharp, biting clamp. Something snagged her at her waist. She fought against this added weight but could not release herself from it. Down she spiralled. The river's foamy blanket embraced her, the rapids and the current lulled her, rocking her into a quiet sleep.

She slumbered toward the afterlife. Out of the gray waters, faces floated toward her—the Lairds, Brianna, other faces she knew naught. Confusion spiralled around her.

Then she looked up toward a pair of silver eyes, translucent gray, set in a face that smiled at her. She reached for the smile as the grays turned to pewter and darkness set in.

# Chapter Twenty-Two

Bonnie lay lifeless, breathless, dead, upon the hard, moss-covered rocks. As Braeson pulled her onto her side, water poured from her body and the dear woman gasped for breath. He closed his eyes for a moment. God, her rescue would haunt him for his lifetime. He had recognized the precise moment when she had stopped struggling in the wild river and had given herself over to death. It was as if the waters had lulled her into a trance, as she slumbered toward the afterlife.

Braeson and Colosse had followed Bonnie over the low hedge of bushes, scrambling after her to the ledge. But she had rolled away and down the steep incline into the roaring, cold river, her long and heavy skirts dragging her under. She had struck the rocks that stood sentinel along the shore of the wild water and protruded from its depths. While Colasse had grasped her flailing arm in his mouth, Braeson had clutched her around the waist, riding the reckless currents with her and finally hauling her to the shore.

Words were being spoken around Braeson, repeated and without clarity or meaning. A loud humming seemed to intensify in his head as his heart pounded and his blood coursed through him at a speed he had not experienced before. Water dripped from his body. A wind ruffled across his brow as he studied his wife, knowing that he must warm her.

Braeson stripped her of the wet and torn clothes and wondered how much a body could endure as he spied new lacerations and bruises on her. One gash across her shoulder demanded attention as blood spewed from it. Her left arm hung limp by her side.

"You cannot linger," Jack growled and shoved dry clothes into Braeson's hands. Braeson chose only to pull the gown over Bonnie's head and down her body. Then, he coiled her mass of wet hair into a long strand around her head. Jack tore the dry chemise and tied it around Bonnie's head, keeping her hair in place and providing more warmth.

"You must get the lass home," Jack stated. "My Maud and Lady Annella can apply their healing to her." Jack touched Bonnie's forehead and held her hand, staring intently at the still woman. "She breathes, but for how long, I cannot predict." He looked at Braeson with fear and worry on his weathered face that was rare for Jack. "You must not tarry." Jack fastened a strip of the chemise around Bonnie's shoulder to staunch the blood that seeped through the gown.

"Williem, bring the seal skin." Braeson's eyes did not leave his wife's face while he spoke to his guardsman. "It will keep her warm and protected as we race for home."

Braeson lifted Bonnie gingerly onto the skin and wrapped it around her body. A body that was bruised and wounded from the vicious attack and time in the water.

"My Lord. Dry clothes for you, too." Williem's face visibly paled as he looked at Bonnie. Frowning, Williem handed Braeson dry clothes. "Lady Annella and Maud would not be happy to receive two invalids."

Braeson stripped quickly and donned the dry clothes. He looked again to Jack who still knelt by Bonnie, silent and brooding. "It will be but an afternoon's ride. Search and bury the scum and then ride for Braemoore." He lifted Bonnie into his arms and carried her toward his horse that had been brought to him.

"Nay, lad." Jack rose and stepped toward Braeson. "You'll not be taking the lass and riding alone. William and the men will remain." Jack, too, stepped toward his horse.

"Nay," growled Williem. "I've ridden beside the Lady for many days and refuse to let her out of my sight until Braemoore."

Braeson remained silent as all his guardsmen stepped closer. He nodded to Jack and Williem as Iain Campbell pushed through the group of men.

"I will remain with your men and aid them here," Campbell said. He reached for Bonnie and held her as Braeson mounted his horse. "Godspeed, my sister's son," he whispered, lifting the still woman into Braeson's arms. "Godspeed."

Braeson nestled Bonnie across his lap holding her close as he, Jack and Williem spurred their horses toward Braemoore.

Holding Bonnie against his chest, Braeson rode hard along the narrow path toward Braemoore. If only the horse could grow wings and become Bonnie's Pegasus. She appeared a Silkie, wrapped in her large seal skin blanket and still as death. But she lived. She lived! The words beat in rhythm with his horse's pounding hooves and his heart. If he could get her home to Maud and Lady Annella and to their healing touch, Bonnie had a chance to live, to breathe, to love. Perchance love him.

The three horses neighed wildly as if in celebration as they galloped to the top of the hill, foam dripping from their mouths, their flanks glistening with sweat. The riders drew their mounts to a stop to catch their breath. Spread before them lay Braemoore, tucked into hills and dales, sparse and lush forests, bejeweled with spring colours of glimmering greens and golds and bathed with shimmering droplets of water from the recent rains. In the distance, Braeson could see the tips of the spirals that stood atop the two towers of the castle.

"Williem," Braeson commanded. "You will ride ahead. Prepare Lady Annella and Maud for our arrival. A bath is required, clean cloths and wraps, healing oils, all to be readied in my chambers." He lifted the flap that covered Bonnie's face, studying her. Her skin reflected a bluish hue, and as a breath shuddered from her still form, a tendril of doom crept from his belly toward his heart. Would she live? "Explain naught, but that your Master commands it. All is to be in place upon my arrival."

Williem tugged at the reins, readying his heels to dig into the horse's sides. He turned, sober-faced, toward Braeson. "I will ride like the demons themselves were chasing me." He bolted forward to his mark.

Braeson did not move as he stared after the rider disappearing into the distance. Jack stirred beside him, still brooding and silent. A sense of melancholy rolled over Braeson as he remembered the last time he had sat upon this same horse, this same hill, with the same man at his side, gazing upon Braemoore.

More than a year had passed since that day when he had been summoned home. Jack and Oliver had brought the missive to London. Together, they had raced through the days only to arrive at Braemoore to meet his mother standing at the top of the castle steps, waiting. He had rushed by her, to his father's chambers, to see a still, pale form lying on the bed.

The shadows had shifted throughout the day and the room had grown dark. Only when the candles had been lit had Braeson lifted his head to look into the eyes of his mother.

"I failed to bid him good-bye," Braeson had whispered. "I cannot imagine never to speak with him again.

"Nay, Timothy. All of his words, your words together, live within you. The conversation between you and your father has not ended. Listen well, you will hear him."

His mother had turned to the servants who had come to prepare his father's body. She had looked again at him. "We will hear him," his mother had concluded.

In the days that had followed his father's burial, he had heard his father's voice and sensed his spirit in the lives of Braemoore's thriving people, in the gusts of wind, and in the drops of rain upon the fertile land. His father's spirit had lived on.

Braeson took a deep breath and the scents of spring embraced him. Fields being prepared for seed and animals in pastures. New blossoms flourished and invited myriad creatures to commune with them, to thrive. He looked again at the still woman in his arms. She would live. She had to live, thrive, flourish. Is that not what she had accomplished thus far in her life? From the babe at Ina's cottage to the daughter of Rose Keep, she had thrived and flourished. He prayed that her life, her ability to live and thrive, would be found again, here, at Braemoore.

A sense of hope crept in and settled within him, nudging out the fear, the melancholia. Braeson dug his heels into the horse's sides, nodded to Jack and rode hard. Williem's words echoed in his head—*like the demons themselves were chasing him.*

A hidden path, once found in his boyhood, brought Braeson through a winding track around several lush woods and low hills, leading him onto a narrow pass and down into the valley below the castle. Jack pushed by him, the man and his horse galloping up the incline, the horse's sides heaving, the man yelling orders to the guards at the gates.

The portcullis had already been lifted and Braeson galloped into the courtyard a few moments after Jack.

In a single motion, he swung his leg over his horse and stood on the ground with Bonnie in his arms. People in the yard gathered closer, faces he knew. They whispered among themselves, wondering. He heard their favoured name, "Braeson". Yet he did not stop, only carried Bonnie up the stairs to the inner court where his mother waited.

"What do you carry, Timothy?" his mother questioned as he rushed by her and swiftly mounted the steps to the upper quarters that held his chambers.

The doors were open, awaiting his entry. His eyes barely glanced upon the sitting room but looked beyond to his bed chamber. The bath stood ready, the fire exuded warmth, cloths and oils stood upon the bureau. A small sewing kit rested upon a table beside the bed.

Auld Maeve stood at the window and turned to him. "Braeson?" she whispered as he laid Bonnie upon his bed.

Braeson drew away the flap that covered Bonnie's face and heard again his wife's wispy breathing. Her head fell sideways and she continued to sleep. As he pulled the strip of cloth from her hair, the tresses pulled from the coil and lay in red and gold waves around her head. Gingerly, he tugged the seal skin from her unconscious form. Her arms that were held at her chest fell lifeless onto the bed, slightly bent, fingers curled inward. The skirts of her gown lay around her knees and he noticed her feet were bare. Had he removed her boots? A blood stain oozed through the soiled gown at her shoulder.

He ran his fingers along her bruised jaw, and lingered at the faint line at her throat where the brigand had held the knife. He skimmed her lifeless arm and gently grasped her cold fingers. A death-filled paleness had replaced the bluish tinge?

"Tis a woman," gasped his mother.

"A Silkie," whispered Auld Maeve.

Braeson turned to the women who were closing in on Bonnie, readying to take charge.

"My wife," he stated.

# Chapter Twenty-Three

She opened her eyes and crawled through the throes of darkness to pewter, to gray, to dawn and finally to a green canopy that stretched above her. Where was she? She squeezed her eyes shut for a moment, searching for a memory. Her name? Who was she? She knew naught and fear skulked in, filling the empty hole where she struggled to remember.

Mayhap she was in a forest. Yet as her eyes focused, she became aware twas a cloth above her. She moved her hand across the ground beside her, realizing it was as soft as silk. Moss? Lifting her head a smitch, she saw a woman sitting in a chair staring at her. Fear tangled in her belly, terror that she did not understand. Words, seemingly familiar, roared and smashed together in her head. *Run, run away. Shriek so we know you live.*

Her scream pushed her to her feet. Her toes sunk into a plush, velvety moss. Through the dawn's light, she was sure there was a door across this enclosure. Why did she sense she should run and hide, mayhap fight? She knew . . . she knew . . . she must hie away from this dungeon, from her captors. Her eyes slid to movement at her side. The woman had risen from the chair and slowly extended a hand toward her.

"Lie down child," the woman said. "Rest."

Instead, she bolted for the door, tugged at it, and dashed into a hallway filled with daylight and warmth. The woman in the dungeon screamed. Nay, twas she that shrieked again as she ran along the hallway lined with tall windows. She rounded a corner. Flattening her back against the wall, she slithered past a small woman who reached for her. Screeching, she ran down a long staircase, stopping when she reached the bottom. She stared across a large space, with walls of stone that reached upward to a glass dome where light shone through. Several large wooden doors beckoned her, yet, uncertainty mounted. Which would provide her escape?

*Run, shriek, run, shriek!* The words pummelled and sparred forcing her to close her eyes and calm the dizziness that threatened to overtake her. She lifted a hand and held fast to the newel post. Nausea roiled in her belly and tears streamed down her face, tickling her mouth and dripping from her chin.

"Bonnie?"

Her name! Twas her name!

She twirled toward the voice, staring into silver eyes, and then was caught in the man's arms.

"Lochlan?" she whispered.

A blanket was gently placed around her shoulders as she collapsed down, down, down, through the grays and pewters, to darkness once more.

She was awake. Behind her closed eyes, she was awake. But she was too frightened, to open them. A sense of danger lurked near her but for all her efforts she could not remember why. Panic began to rise, coiling like a snake inside her, stirring her fear. She feigned sleep as she struggled to recall where she was. Who she was?

A vague memory drifted past—she in a dark room. She was sure it had been a dungeon. Yet behind her closed lids she sensed bright light and warmth. The hazy recollection floated closer and now a bit clearer. Stairs, and a man with . . . silver eyes.

Her thoughts muddled, she sensed she must flee from danger, from . . . aye, she remembered. She was inside a building. Twas a grand structure with high ceilings and glass windows. She was certain she was a captive and had run down a long hallway fleeing from. . .she knew naught. She took a deep breath to clear her thoughts. She was sure there was a hallway just outside of this dungeon.

A heavy weight held her ankles and feet. Mayhap she was shackled so she could not run from her enemy. Wiggling her feet a bit she tugged them and felt free but for her left arm that was bound to her breast. Twas strange that her arm was held captive to herself.

Words, garbled words, mixed with her confusion. *Run, shriek, run.* She had run. For certain, she knew that she had run beyond her dungeon. They had caught her. She would escape but not by running and shrieking. Rather, she needed a plan. For certain, she needed a weapon.

Bit by bit, Bonnie opened heavy eyelids to a room filled with sunlight. Above her was a green canopy. Turning her head slightly, she realized she lay in a bed and twas a dog, deep in sleep, that lay heavy on her feet. She rubbed her fingers along her body. She was dressed in a nightgown but she would need suitable clothes once she escaped from this prison. Surely there must be a forest beyond this structure. Once in the forest, she would snatch a crofter's garb from a drying rock. Then, she would . . . she knew naught what her plan was, except to flee from this dungeon.

Bonnie lifted her head just a smitch and froze. A woman, the dungeon guard, sat in a wooden chair beside her bed dozing. She needed a weapon to ward off that woman or anyone who stood in her way. Her gaze flitted around the room and there, on a small wooden table next to the bed lay two small daggers. Gingerly, she reached her hand to snatch one and hid it beneath the bed covers. She rubbed her hand over it and touched the blade lightly. Why did it feel familiar?

If only she could remember who she was and from whence she came?

A sigh like a soft warm breeze wafted around her. *You are Bonnie of Rose. A brave lass.*

She chuckled low. Twas true, twas true. She was Bonnie of Rose, the lass who could fling a stone and throw a knife, hitting her target, most times.

Caressing the knife and drawing deep breaths to steady her beating heart, she nudged away the fear that attempted to choke her. The dungeon guard still dozed. Tightening her grip on the knife, she rose swiftly and stood pointing the dagger at the sleeping woman.

"Braeson!" An unknown voice rang out. Two people rose from chairs before a hearth. Twas the man and the small woman she had encountered in the hallway in her dazed dash from this prison.

"Braeson?" Bonnie blinked to clarify her muddled thoughts. She was sure she had known a man called Braeson. Had he been an enemy or friend? She scanned his person from his head to his boots and then slid her eyes to his.

The man, Braeson, the man with silver eyes, took a single step toward her.

"Where am I?" Her voice trembled on the question.

"Braemoore." He took another slow step forward.

"I am a captive?" Her head spun with confusion.

"Nay, Bonnie. We are home."

Her eyes locked on his face. Dark circles lay below his eyes. "Home?" she whispered, frowning in confusion.

"Home." He replied as he reached out his hand to her and then to the small woman who stood beside him. "This is my mother, Lady Annella." He turned his head slightly and nodded at the woman, her dungeon guard, now awake. "And Maeve."

Bonnie looked at the knife in her trembling hand. A growing certainty told her that Braeson was a friend. The knife clattered to the floor and Bonnie rubbed her forehead, fighting nausea and dizziness. As she struggled to remain conscious amidst a spinning room, Braeson lifted her into his arms. His warmth dispersed some of her confusion.

"Braeson?" she questioned.

"Aye, Bonnie?"

"I am verra, verra hungry." Her eyes closed and she laid her head against his shoulder.

The woman, Maeve, brought a tray of freshly baked

bread and steaming soup. She placed it on Bonnie's lap and then stepped back. "Will heal what ails you," Maeve said. She stood and watched Bonnie for a short moment and then followed Lady Annella from the room.

The man, Braeson, stood silent, leaning a shoulder against the window sill, staring at the landscape beyond as Bonnie ate her food. She attempted to not devour it as she lifted the round wooden bowl to her lips and ripped pieces from the fresh bread. As the food warmed and filled her belly, she felt her fear driven from her. Even her trembling hands began to steady. She knew herself to be safe here in this room, in this bed, but she was unable to reason how she knew. She just knew the man who stared out the window was her friend.

"How long have I been at Braemoore?" she asked.

"Five days you have slept." He turned to her. "A wound at your shoulder became infected. A fever overtook you. You were fed a bit of broth each day." He turned again to the window and several silent minutes passed while Bonnie finished eating.

Five days had passed since . . . since when? She could not remember what had come before those five days. She squeezed her eyes shut for a time attempting to remember. Why did the man remain silent?

Bonnie lifted the tray from her lap, and attempted

to place it with its empty bowl and few crumbs on the stand beside her bed. But she felt weak and she dropped the items on the floor. The bowl tumbled across a plush carpet and then rolled onto a stretch of wooden floor boards. It twirled in a lone spot for a time, its clatter echoing from the ceiling beams.

It was when the man, Braeson, stooped to swipe it up that terrifying images slithered to her consciousness.

Pebbles!

She gasped, jarring herself upright, as she remembered a knife slicing her neck, warm blood raining on her face, rushing cold water . . . she remembered, she remembered!

Her eyes snapped back to Braeson.

Braeson! Her husband!

As Braeson slowly rose holding the bowl, remorse and guilt poured over her. The vivid memories grasped her tightly. She remembered! She remembered the accusations she had spewed at him. Words of hate and scorn. Heat climbed up her neck and into her face. She shook her head and squeezed her eyes tight unable to stop the barrage of her own words that swirled around her—reiver, liar, murderer.

Yet one image stood clear and true. Like a healing balm, it pushed through her muddled thoughts. Twas of Braeson bending low to the ground and swiping a handful of pebbles. After receiving her barrage of insults, Braeson had still trusted her and had followed through with her ploy, her warning, in his attempt to save her. He had flung the pebbles and she had ducked her head as Braeson's knife pierced her enemy.

She bowed her head and covered her face in shame. "Braeson," she whispered. "Braeson. I am sorry. I—"

"Bonnie," Her name on his lips was a soft caress across her heart.

She looked up as he stepped closer. "I remember." She clasped her hand over her mouth. Her heart beat fast and tears stung her eyes. "The words I said. I am sorry—"

Braeson perched on the side of her bed and pulled her hand into his. A fragrance of pine and musk enveloped her as he placed his fingers lightly on her lips halting her words. "Bonnie. It is not necessary to apologize. The journey—"

"Nay, Braeson." She drew her hand away, holding it in her lap. "I must speak. There are words that must be said." She gazed into his silver eyes watching as he nodded slightly to indicate his agreement. "Tis sorry I am. And, regret I hold for the accusations I spewed." She shuddered as the memories twisted around inside her. "Twas the necklace, I saw. I thought—" She shook her head struggling to express that which had confused her.

"When the Lairds offered your hand to me in marriage, they also gave me the necklace." Braeson took a deep breath. "I refused to take it. It is your birthright." He raised his brows and shrugged. "I believed it to be in the library at Rose Castle until it hit me in the face." He smiled and rubbed his hand alongside his cheek.

"I ask you to forget what I did, what I said, what I accused you of, and accept my apol—"

His fingers again touched her lips and halted her words. He caressed her face with the back of his hand, whispering words of encouragement and pulled her toward him so their foreheads touched.

Her worries fluttered away to be replaced by warmth—Braeson's warmth—that spread throughout her body, leaving her heart thumping and her hand tingling where she laid it on his shoulder.

"Bonnie," he whispered. "You are not responsible and require no forgiveness."

With each of his words and caresses, the heaviness that had attempted to choke her lost its grip.

He placed a loose strand of hair behind her ear, smiling at her. "In fact, be assured that your actions contributed to our safe arrival to Braemoore." He brushed his lips against hers sending a shiver to her heart. "My men believe you to be a brave woman."

He pulled her into his embrace and she rested her head on his shoulder, his strong arms wrapped around her. "Few husbands can say that his wife felled two men to save him."

As she nestled against Braeson, the beat of his heart and the soft caress of his hand on her back lulled her into a light sleep that was filled with terrorizing images of spiralling gray waters and the faces of Brianna and the Lairds. She abruptly awakened from this nightmare, still held by Braeson. He placed her against the pillows.

"What of the man who wished to kill me?" she said.

"Dead and sent to hell like those before him," growled Braeson. "He claimed to be the last of the brigands. Braemoore guards and people have been on alert. All is at peace."

Could she trust the peace here at Braemoore? There was a part of her heart that still churned with uncertainty.

"What of the Lairds and Brianna?" she asked. "Will they accept my apology as easily as you?"

Braeseon frowned. "But what apology must you give?"

"I refused to bid them farewell on the night of my departure." Bonnie trembled squeezing her eyes to block the tears. "I was so distraught to leave my home, my life, I failed to express my love for them . . ." Her words faltered as she hiccupped over a sob.

"Cease, Bonnie," he gently commanded. He lifted his hand to her face and brushed away her tears. "You have been a loving daughter. First to the woman, Ina, who cared for you from your first few days of life. Did you not run and hide as she commanded? Then, to Brianna and the Lairds whose daughter you were and still are. Did you not demonstrate your love by obeying their decision for you to marry and to find safety under my protection?" He drew her hands to his lips and kissed them. "Can love just simply disappear with a perceived snub or the death of a loving woman called Ina?"

"Nay," she whispered, trembling from his kisses, drawn into his pensive stare.

"However hard it was to do." He smiled again, moving closer to place his forearms on either side of her pillow. "You did marry and came away with me."

She studied his lips, brushing her hand through his wavy black hair, wishing he would kiss her.

"You came away with Earl English."

She snapped her eyes to his and felt a blush rising onto her cheeks. She was sure that she had not ever called him that name aloud.

"You mumbled it under your breath when you pulled your plaid from me, landing on your lovely bottom in the pond." Humour danced in his eyes and skipped across his words.

"I apolo—"

"Cease!" He growled. "You will give no more apologies."

Being close to him in these daylight hours, she was mesmerized by how the black of his eyes expanded with varying emotions and how a thin sliver of silver was now delegated to the edges.

"Aye, Master," she feigned agreement and he chuckled as he kissed her mouth briefly.

"You are brave and intelligent," he concluded. His thoughtful frown replaced his smile. "Now it is my turn to apologize." His pensive stare held her gaze for several seconds.

Sounds, smells, sights faded. Pine and musk encircled her. His breath fluttered along her face, lifting a loose tress above her eye. She drowned in the silver, translucent pools of his eyes. In these moments, she knew only Braeson and her arm snaked around his neck drawing him even closer to her.

"For I did not give you a proper marriage proposal," he murmured against her neck.

Her heart beat rapidly and she held her breath.

He lifted his head and thoughtfully looked at her. "I wish to offer you home and hearth, here at Braemoore. To be its Mistress and my Lady." He smiled. "Will you be my wife?"

Weeks ago—eons ago—she had stomped her foot and tried to scream her way out of this betrothal. Now, she wanted to only kick her legs and shout for joy. Braeson still wanted her. And, she wanted him.

"Aye," she whispered. "I will be your wife."

"Let me love you, "Braeson whispered.

Bonnie pulled him to her and his mouth lingered for a moment above her lips. He caressed them gently and she opened them to suckle on his lower lip. My God, he was wonderful. She wished he could pull her closer but her arm, still in the sling, cautioned them both to proceed carefully. He settled to kiss her, tracing a path of kisses along the side of her face, down her throat and lower to where her nightgown opened to reveal the top of her breasts. He pushed the material aside and—

"My Lord?"

Braeson groaned, as he raised his head in response to the sharp intrusive words. He pulled Bonnie's nightgown closer around her and took a deep breath.

"Maeve," he stated and then winked at Bonnie. "Are not servants to announce their presence rather than create a disturbance in their Master's presence?" Braeson emphasized the final word as if to send a silent message.

"I spoke twice. Aye?"

Although Bonnie could not yet see Maeve as she stood beyond at Braeson's back, she heard a smile in her words.

"Tis not I causing the disturbance, my Lord."

Bonnie heard a greater emphasis on the formal address. The gray-haired woman set a tray of items on a small table beside the bed and then seated herself upon the wooden chair.

"Now, tis my job to tend to your Silkie." The woman lifted her smiling eyes to Braeson. "Master."

Braeson rose, nodded to Bonnie and turned to the woman. "Thank you, Maeve." He walked from the room.

Bonnie watched Maeve prepare ointments to tend to her wounds. The woman moved briskly between the bedside table and a tall bureau from where she pulled cloths.

So this was Auld Maeve that Braeson had told her about. She was sure Braeson had said Maeve came from the Campbell Keep. A shiver skittered up her back. Would Braeson leave her alone with danger? He was her protection, was he not, proving his devotion at the cliff beside the wild river? And just now, when he asked her to be his wife. Bonnie jumped when Maeve's hand touched her forehead.

"You need not fear, Silkie." Maeve's voice was soothing. "The fever has broken. Tis good to see you in the land of the living."

Bonnie still felt heavy from her long, fitful sleep. Yet she sensed herself relax against her pillows and took a deep breath. "Why do you name me Silkie?"

Maeve stopped her ministrations and looked at Bonnie, frowning. "The Master rode like a demon into the courtyard, carrying his cargo wrapped in a seal skin. Tis the word throughout Braemoore that the Master brought home a Silkie and intends to make her his wife."

"I am nay a Silkie but a woman, Bonnie of Rose."

"Tis I who witnessed a woman slowly tumble from her seal skin, bruised and broken." She waved her hand toward the bed as she spoke. "Tis a story of a Silkie for sure. Aye."

Maeve slipped Bonnie's night clothes from her shoulder and began to unwrap the sling that held her arm tightly. Bonnie was surprised that the mild current of pain she now felt was due only to a sore shoulder and arm, rather than the usual sting of pain when someone called her Silkie. The nekename did not conjure hidden feelings of bitterness and resentment that had haunted her as far back as she could remember.

Braeson had described the name, Silkie, as a love term. Mayhap he was correct and somewhere as they raced away from Scotland, she accepted this part of herself. She a Silkie? She knew the stories told to her, how Ina discovered a bairn at her small croft door wrapped in a seal skin. Twas the same skin that Brianna wrapped her in to carry her to the Rose Keep. Maeve described a similar tale.

"Then mayhap I am a lost Silkie," Bonnie declared. Even though she smiled at Maeve, it was a smile for herself. For the first time in her life, she had just declared herself a Silkie and a lost one at that.

"Silkie, aye," replied Maeve. "Lost? Nay." The woman shook her head. "Some Silkies must journey a great distance to find home."

Again Maeve waved her hand, this time, toward her heart! "And love." She gently pushed Bonnie's wounded arm through the sleeve of the nightgown and then tied the ribband.

Images of an early spring garden floated into Bonnie's thoughts. The words from the story Braeson had told her so long ago, it seemed, now were echoing back. Braeson had said these verra words, Maeve's words. This Silkie had found love with Ina and at Rose Keep. Bonnie's heart beat quickened as she recalled Braeson's beautiful face mingling with the music and aromas of that garden story. When he had kissed her that eve while telling the story of the Silkie, a warmth so intense and unknown had engulfed her, frightened her. She had fled from him, upturning the bench they sat upon, and had run back to the safety of the great hall at Rose Keep.

Bonnie smiled at her silent thoughts—thoughts that would remain just that—silent. She had found love with Braeson.

"Hope," Maeve continued. "'Tis the call of love. Silkies hear it and find their way home." Maeve placed a cup filled with a liquid in Bonnie's hand and watched as she drank it. She pulled the covers up to Bonnie's chin. "'Twill make you sleep, lass."

The room darkened as Maeve pulled the window covers and then sat upon the straight-back wooden chair to keep vigil.

Bonnie's eyes slowly closed and she was lulled gently to rest by the potent liquid. Images danced before her closed eyes—Brianna, De Ros, Lochlan, Caol. She smiled when she saw Ina. Ina smiled back at her and then turned and walked away. Away, away, away . . .

Moments before her thoughts scattered into a restful sleep, Bonnie knew she would never tell Braeson her secret. She loved him. Loved him deeply. But to tell him so . . . it would mean she would have to leave him. Like she had to leave Ina and her family at Rose Keep. Nay, twould be her secret never to be spoken. Then, this Silkie could stay with Braeson forever.

## Chapter Twenty-Four

Braeson stood silent and still, on the walkway atop the castle draw bridge, watching the lone rider disappear into the horizon. The rider carried a missive to Edinburgh, where one of De Ros' guards would take it to its final destination, Rose Castle. It assured Bonnie's people that *their lass* was well. It also carried cryptic information about the final assault at the river cliff, the three sisters and the treasure. Braeson squinted and then closed his eyes as the rider vanished over a hill. He inhaled deeply in hopes of calming the sense of suspicion crawling up his spine. Was Bonnie safe? He wanted to believe so. The assailant had declared himself the final fiend before he tumbled to his death. The final demon sent to hell.

He took another deep breath and gripped the edge of the stone wall. Hiding in the shadows, the secrets surrounding his bride carried treachery and death as their companions. He had instructed Jack to alert the guardsmen of any suspicious behaviour. Until his wife's secrets were resolved, all of Braemoore would live in sustained vigilance.

For a sennight Bonnie had lain as still as death in his bed. Braeson had quickly put an end to any insistence from his mother and Maeve that Bonnie receive her own bed and chambers. By God, she was his! He had married her and he would keep vigil over her. By having her near him, Braeson was convinced he might will her back from the dead. Night after night, he had lain beside her, watching her breast slightly rise and fall. She lived because she breathed.

Attempting to conjure clarity to her secrets, Braeson had stared at Bonnie as she lay still as death. But the mystery that plagued him the most was, how Bonnie had managed to wrap herself around his heart and claim him as her own. It was clever how she had accomplished this. Braeson was hers!

Bonnie's allurement encompassed more than beauty. His heart belonged to a woman whose loveliness mixed naturally with her courage and physical skills and abilities. It was his wife's quick thinking that had somehow saved him from more than an assailant's knife or a Laird's sword. Bonnie had pulled him back from a deep despair that had landed on his shoulders after his father's death—a dark, murky place of pain and grief for a man who had left him far too soon. Over the past year, Braeson had striven to remember the lessons his father had taught him.

Jack was correct. His father's mark was branded on him. *Embedded deep on your heart, your mind, your life. Complete.* Sometime during Braeson's journey along that wretched Scottish path, he had recognized that his father's influence was a natural part of his existence, his thinking, his decisions, his role in life.

The banners waving from the gate masts snapped and drew Braeson from his brooding thoughts. Turning his head, he watched Bonnie and his mother, Annella, walk together inside the enclosed stone garden. The dog, Colosse, followed behind them, the brave traitorous beast. The hound had been found alongside the rushing river as still as his Mistress, wavering between life and death. He had been carried home across a guardsman's lap, and cleaned at Maeve's insistence. Then, Colasse had been placed over Bonnie's feet. They had warmed each other, in hopes of their resurrection.

On the second day after Bonnie's awakening, he had seen her touch the dog sleeping at her feet, seemingly dead. She had leaned over Colasse, whispering endearments and had run her hands soothingly over his body. An arrow of jealousy had shot through him to see the dog receiving her caresses.

The dog had awakened and chosen Bonnie rather than him to adore. Braeson smiled. The faithless, wonderful cur would always have an honoured place at Braemoore for helping to save its Mistress.

How many times had Bonnie walked the periphery of that garden or wandered with Braeson atop the walkway of the stone wall? Braeson had watched each day as her strength slowly returned and her golden colour brought life back to her face. Even the cloth sling that Maeve had insisted she wear was now gone. From time to time, Bonnie still cradled her arm, but more times he witnessed her exercising it. Day by day, coaxing its skill to return.

Braeson had noticed the leather sling hanging from the folds of Bonnie's gown, patiently waiting for its owner to fill it with stones and hoist it above her head. On the day she was carried to Braemoore, he had placed her sling and knives on the wooden table by her bed. He had reasoned if Bonnie could be surrounded by the familiar, she would return to life. She was recovering, bit by bit, and he knew her knives, which still remained on the bedside table, would soon find their place inside her boots.

The necklace, Bonnie's necklace, hung on a metal hook from the mantel of the fireplace in his chamber. Whether she knew it to be there, he knew naught. But there it hung, dancing subtly in the heat of the fire, calling to her through her illness and fever, calling to its Silkie. Was it happenstance or providence that the two halves of the same necklace were now both nestled under the same roof at Braemoore? Could he believe that Auld Maeve's fanciful story about a Silkie and her pearl necklaces actually was true? Incredible. Perchance each part of the necklace, each half, would meet tomorrow. Would Bonnie hear the necklace calling to her from the fireplace mantel and wear it at the celebration?

Braeson descended the stone steps and wound his way through the bailey. He stepped just inside the enclosed garden to watch his mother and Bonnie discuss the blooms and herbs.

The people of Braemoore had insisted that Braeson and Bonnie repeat their marriage vows before them. They would not rest until their son, Braemoore's son, married Bonnie in Braemoore's chapel. Bonnie had easily agreed with his people, his mother and Maeve. He had relented. *Even the sovereign court of England would demand proof of the marriage vows*, his mother had declared. Tomorrow, he and his bride would walk to the village church and again exchange vows. Tomorrow eve, he and his bride, at last, would consummate their marriage. He felt his body respond to the idea, imagining Bonnie next to him, caressing her, kissing her, exploring her secret places, feeling himself inside her and she caressing him, finally caressing him.

"Braeson," Bonnie's voice lured him from his fantasy as he walked toward the two woman. "We are finding lovely spring blooms for the morrow." Her eyes shone and she smiled when he lifted her hand to his lips and kissed it gently.

He touched his chest to ease the discomfort in his heart. He had been forthcoming, from the moment she awoke, in expressing his love for her. Yet Bonnie had not verbalized any such thoughts. Her actions, her smile, the way her eyes sparkled when she looked at him, told him she cared deeply for him. But when he held her in his arms and expressed his love, fear seemed to enter her eyes. At times, she shivered and quickly changed the subject. And here she was now, all but bursting to show him the flowers for tomorrow's celebration.

"If only Brianna, could see these lovely blooms." Bonnie held the pink roses to her nose and smelled deeply. "Oh, the lovely soap she could make with them."

"Brianna?" questioned his mother.

"Aye, Brianna." Bonnie smiled and touched a delicate petal.

His mother tipped the corners of her mouth, as though in an attempt to smile. "Timothy has told me very little about you."

Bonnie frowned as she glanced at Braeson, who stood silent beside her.

"It is Bonnie's story to tell," he stated.

"I am fascinated to know more," his mother insisted. "We were expecting many ponies to race to our castle door. But instead, we were blessed with you, Braemoore's bride." His mother's voice simmered to serious. "Who is Brianna?"

"I am Bonnie of Rose, raised by the Laird Justus De Ros and his wife Brianna MacEwen." Bonnie explained.

Braeson took a step back to watch, carefully, his mother's reaction to Bonnie's story. He knew Bonnie was not the only one with secrets. He had determined to speak with his mother about his paternal discoveries over the past weeks. Perchance the moment had arrived. Lady Annella's tight smile disappeared and Braeson was sure that his mother paled.

"MacEw—Ewen," Lady Annella stumbled over her words. "You are Brianna MacEwen's daughter?"

Braeson noticed her voice seemed to rise in timbre, panicked.

"But, De Ros is married to Mari, Mari..." His mother shook her head and waved her hand as if to remember. "Brianna MacEwen?" She repeated.

"Aye, De Ros' first wife, Mari, and young daughter died of the ague. Brianna is his second wife," Bonnie continued. "I was brought by Brianna and Lochlan—"

"Lochlan," his mother whispered.

"To Rose Castle when Brianna married De Ros."

"You are Brianna MacEwen's daughter?" His mother's voice rose with agitation. Was there fear in her eyes?

"If you know of the MacEwens, I canna be Brianna's daughter." Bonnie grinned. "Nay, Caol is De Ros' son from his first wife, Lady Mari."

"Caol?" his mother questioned.

"Aye, Caol. Brianna's oldest child, her step son. I am Brianna's and De Ros' second child, their foster daughter."

Braeson's mother released a breath that fluttered the loose strands from her coiled hair above her eyes.

"Only Davyd, their third child, is from De Ros and Brianna's union." Bonnie's grin widened. "Do you know of the MacEwens?"

Annella remained silent and Bonnie continued. "Davyd holds the mark of this clan, the MacEwen clan."

Braeson watched his mother's eyes grow bigger as Bonnie spoke. "Just like Brianna and her brother Lochlan, he has the MacEwen eyes. Silver gray, some say translucent, edged in thick dark lashes." She stopped for a moment and tilted her head. "How does De Ros describe these eyes?" She squinted and then her face opened into a wide smile, only to be clouded in confusion. Her glance darted to Braeson and she stared at him, open-mouthed. "As pale as a silver moon," she whispered.

Braeson recalled how he and his father used to race to the ocean shore to watch faraway storms roll in. They had sat atop their horses along the cliff edge as the clouds in the distance churned down to the sea and then rose, only to follow the patterned path downward again. Where they had sat, the air was still, silence prevailed, even the sea below had appeared frozen. The anticipation of the storm to come seemed to fill the air as if all, nature and man, had held their breath, waiting.

Braeson now felt as if he relived that moment, for it seemed that all noise and movement surrounding him stilled. He stared back at Bonnie and then, breathing deeply, looked at his mother. Her face was stark white and her dark eyes glistened. She held a hand high on her chest just below her throat, as if willing herself to breathe.

Braeson and his father had turned their horses and raced away from the cliff when the first streak of lightning had flashed far out across the water. The sky had rumbled and roared as the clouds rushed toward the land. Their goal had been to stay ahead of the rain and the storm.

Braeson silently chuckled and shook his head. He, his father and his mother had all stayed ahead of the storm, had they not? Living an idyllic life, like the calm before the storm. He could not recall once his parents ever addressing the invisible clouds that rolled in the distance of their existence, of his existence. The very man whom he had called father, was not his father. This dead man who had raised him, had he known? Had he lied to him? Who was his sire? Lochlan MacEwen? His murdered brother, Fallon? Along with Bonnie's assailants, the rolling clouds of his existence had chased him from the Scottish Highlands too.

"Braeson," whispered Bonnie. "Braeson." She shook her head and squeezed her eyes closed only to open them again to stare at him. Tears pooled in her eyes. "De Ros, Lochlan, Brianna. I do not think they gave me to . . . to a . . . Campbell or an English. I do not think they gave me away at all." Her glistening eyes darted to Annella. She placed her hand to her mouth, speechless. "They gave me to a MacEwen . . . you."

"Master!" a guardsman ran along the top of the castle wall. "A horse without a rider and a lone rider crest the yon hill."

Braeson raced to the stone steps and through the tunnel leading up to the top of the wall, shouting orders. He felt Bonnie at his heels. "Lower the gate!" he bellowed. "Posts."

Men and boys scurried around the courtyard and wall, taking up arms. Braeson peered out between the crenelated walls and saw a horse without a rider racing toward the castle. A horseman followed.

"Tis Tokie!" exclaimed Bonnie. "Tis Tokie." She laughed. "Listen."

The pony's bellow echoed across the valley below the castle. It was reminiscent of the day of the attack on Bonnie at Rose Keep. Tolkie had whinnied until Bonnie had been allowed to the shed to calm him. The pony was demanding an audience with her again.

The ground vibrated as over the crest several ponies trotted into the glen escorted by at least five riders. The horsemen wore dark capes that provided Braeson with little knowledge as to who commanded these ponies. Of course the ponies were from Rose Castle, but surely De Ros' men would have worn identifiable colours.

"Only the first pony and lone rider through to the inner court," commanded Braeson. "Bonnie, you will accompany my mother into the keep." He would take no chances. Bonnie would remain secure from these visitors until he knew their identities. He drew her elbow to him when she was about to protest. "Nay, wife. You'll hurry to the keep and only show yourself when a guardsman escorts you to me."

Braeson walked Bonnie down the steps and lifted a hand. Williem appeared, as if anticipating his thoughts. Braeson stood inside the tunnel doorway watching the women, with Williem, disappear through the garden gate and toward the steps leading to the keep.

A commotion at the gate caused Braeson to turn his head. Tokie came charging through, snorting and whinnying, dancing in circles. A guardsman flung a rope around the creature's neck and tethered it to a lone post beside the gate. The animal still flung its head, snorting and stomping, raising dust into the air. Braeson snatched a knife held at his belt. In his peripheral vision, he saw his guardsmen readying their swords. Oliver and Jack stood with knives in hand. Iain Campbell appeared and stood to the side, hand on the hilt of his sword.

The lone rider galloped into the yard. His cape flapped behind him, his hood lay crumpled on his shoulders. A plaid scarf was wrapped around his head, covering his face from the dust and grime of the journey. Only his eyes peered through a breach in the wrap

Eyes as pale as a silver moon. Surely, a tell-tale sign of who sat upon the horse.

"Who goes there!" demanded Braeson. Yet already he was slipping his knife into its sheath. He drew a deep breath and walked toward the rider.

"Lochlan MacEwen," replied the masked man. He grasped his head wrap, to widen the gap so that his eyes became more visible. Yet the cloth still held fast about his head and face. Lochlan dismounted, holding the reins tightly at the horse's head and laid a hand upon the animal's neck. "All riders are MacEwen men." Lochlan handed the reins to a guardsman at Braeson's direction. "We ask for food for this night. We can take shelter in the valley below."

Braeson stared at the man who stood before him. His throat tightened, preventing him from shouting, *Are you my sire?* His mother had whispered *Lochlan*, in a desperate plea, when Bonnie had relayed her family tale. The moniker, Falon, had gone unacknowledged by his mother.

Braeson felt his body shift. Higher went his head, straighter his back, a slight adjustment to his shoulders. He was the Master of Braemoore, the fourth Earl of Braemoore, Keeper of its people, a Steward to the Sovereign court of England. Son and namesake of Timothy Lennox Moore. He smiled. In this moment, he knew that he had turned his horse and raced back to the cliff edge to face the storm.

"Welcome to Braemoore," Braeson replied. He extended his arm to Lochlan in salutation. The older man nodded, grasping Braeson's arm in return. A shudder travelled up Braeson's arm. Was he touching his sire?

"The shed for the ponies is built and has been readied." Braeson gestured to the castle. "We will prepare a room for you and complete our transaction with Braemoore's steward."

Lochlan bowed slightly to Braeson. "The ponies are a gift, my Lord, in celebration of your marriage to our lass."

Braeson bristled. Lightning always flashed before the thunder rumbled. "Nay, a payment is not required for my wife." First the necklace and now the ponies. Did they believe he required an enticement to keep Bonnie? He calmed his voice, attempting to keep the roar of the thunder at bay. "The necklace was discovered in my pack." His gut clenched with the memory of the consequences of that discovery. "It is Bonnie's and in her possession. I ask for nothing."

"Aye, the necklace is Bonnie's." Lochlan paused. His dark eye brows lifted and were hidden for a moment behind the plaid. "We could not keep it, in good faith." He hesitated. When he continued, his voice was almost a whisper, its tenderness breaking the tension. "The ponies are her dowry, my Lord. Brianna hand-picked each one. It will add to my sister's broken-heart to lose her lass, then learn that the ponies are rejected."

Braeson stared for a moment at the cloaked man.

The gentle voice gave him guidance as to how to interpret the whispered words. Words spoken that were genuine and true. It was not a storm, but a quiet spring rain that washed over the land, gentle and warm. The ponies were not offered as an enticement or even as a test like the necklace had been all those days ago in De Ros' library. The ponies were a gift, a dowry, a celebratory act, made in good faith.

Braeson nodded in acceptance, then gestured toward the steps of the Keep. Bonnie stood at the top of the steps, hands clenched, waiting. Williem stood a few steps below, blocking her way. His mother had disappeared into the keep, likely preparing accommodations for their guests. "Bonnie will be delighted to see Tokie."

Lochlan turned toward the steps. "The lass is well?"

"Aye, she fares well," replied Braeson. "She has much she will want to tell you." He gestured toward the bawling pony. "Let us settle Tokie in the shed and then you can visit with Bonnie at the keep. My mother, Lady Annella, will insist on a meal for all your men and a chamber for you."

Lochlan remained silent as Braeson walked beside him toward the shrieking pony. It was difficult to read the man hidden behind the mask.

The pony refused any comfort and knocked a guardsman's hand away as it reared onto its back legs.

Lochlan grasped its rope from the post. "Wee beastie," he muttered and followed Braeson along a narrow path to a low-roofed, long wooden building.

Braeson stopped and studied the sky. Calm. An indecisive tinge of pink dusted the western horizon. Night was creeping in.

They entered the shed through a single door. Braeson directed Lochlan to place the unsettled pony in the first stall. He lifted oats into a small feed bin and returned to the centre of the shed to retrieve water from a barrel. When he turned around, Lochlan was pulling the plaid scarf from his head.

It was striking, the physical similarities he shared with this man. Braeson wondered why he had not noticed it while in Scotland. The sole purpose of the journey north had been to purchase ponies. Yet he had also been grieving for his father, inwardly reflecting and holding close the pain of the loss.

The two men stood a distance apart, facing each other. Silent. Braeson noticed that they shared an equal height and wide shoulders slimming to narrow hips. The same colour hair— dark, almost black— came down to Lochlan's shoulders and in the shadows of the barn a few gray strands might also be seen. Yet it was the eyes that caused Braeson to frown. Pale as a silver moon. Was he looking at his sire? Who was this man?

"Twould be for the best that I take my fare and sleep here this eve," stated Lochlan. "Tokie can be settled. The men and ponies will camp in the valley."

Braeson could not deny this request. A visitor would certainly be provided a bed in a guest chamber, but this guest, who shared a similar appearance to Braemoore's Master, would cause speculation and whispers. Best for Lochlan to sleep here under the canopy of darkness.

"We will be away before dawn to journey back to MacEwen land," Lochlan said.

Braeson knew that Bonnie would understand Lochlan's request due to her own words uttered just a time ago in the garden. *They gave me to a MacEwen.* The men who had travelled with Braeson to Rose Castle to purchase ponies were his kinsmen. A strong, loyal troop of Braemoore's best who had sworn their oath to protect the land, the people and to guard confidences. Braeson had not heard even a rumour in the wind that there were people on the Scottish Highlands who resembled him.

A sudden movement from the shadows beyond Lochlan startled the silence. A knife ripped from its sheath. A bulky arm reached out and grabbed Lochlan around the neck, twisting him and slamming his head against a shed post.

"I swore I'd kill you, if I ever happened upon you,"

Iain Campbell growled. "A life for a life." He gripped Lochlan's hair and pulled his head back, positioning his knife to slice through the older man's throat. "Your life for my Da's," he sneered.

Braeson drew his knife, as Lochlan flipped Iain Campbell head over heels and slammed him to the ground. Lochlan shoved his knee against Campbell's throat just as Braeson's knife pierced the shed floor close to Campbell's right ear.

Lochlan raised his eyes to Braeson. How Braeson knew the older man was requesting him to surrender control of Campbell to him, he knew naught. Yet there was a silent energy that passed between them—the son of Braemoore and the Laird of MacEwen Keep—that gave Braeson pause. He nodded his consent.

Lochlan sliced a knife through skin along Iain Campbell's arm to still him. He stared at Campbell for a time. "I should not be surprised that you are lurking in the shadows of Braemoore as you lurk in the shadows of our Highlands." Lochlan smacked the young Laird's face with the back of his hand as Campbell attempted to speak against the knee rammed into his throat. "Tis a coward's way, living in the shadows, in the dark. But now we meet face to face. You'll listen to my words."

The captured man struggled to gain freedom as Lochlan drew his knee from Campbell's throat.

"Listen well, cur pup," continued Lochlan now placing his hand at the man's throat. "A life for a life has been sacrificed. A Laird for a Laird. My brother, Fallon and your father, Angus." He paused, staring at the man and inhaled a deep breath. "Bitterness and resentment make for a vile potion, aye? You are proof of it. Too much time has passed to still be sitting in your own dung. The MacEwen clan rebuilt and pushed on through our loss. What of the Campbell Keep? Word on the mountain whispers that you are tearing down rather than building up a strong Campbell legacy. Choose!" Lochlan grasped Campbell's shirt and shook him. "Choose, before time passes you by. Will you follow your ill-begotten sire's malevolence, or accept the birthright that your people desire to give you."

Iain Campbell cursed as, in one motion, Lochlan dragged him up to stand before him. The men stood face to face. Lochlan shoved Campbell against the shed wall.

"A nod's as good as a wink to a blind ass." Lochlan pushed Campbell toward the door as Jack entered the shed. "Next time, I will kill you."

Braeson could not have Campbell wandering free throughout Braemoore. He could no longer be trusted. Braeson looked at Jack who stood silent, assessing the scene, frowning as Iain Campbell exited into the night.

"Jack, follow Campbell. He will leave Braemoore on the morrow. Between now and the morn, he should be watched. He'll not be part of the festivities."

Jack rubbed his white beard and turned toward the door. "Lords and Lairds, Lairds and Lords," he mumbled. "Does he need a dunkin' in a local stream, my Lord?"

Braeson narrowed his eyes. "A night in the dungeon will suffice, Jack. Only enough water to quench his thirst." He turned to Lochlan. The contentious scene he had just witnessed was a perfect link to ask Lochlan about his heritage, his sire.

"Lochlan! Lochlan!" Bonnie came running into the shed.

Williem trailed behind, flushed red with exertion. Braeson shook his head. It was obvious Bonnie had outrun the guard.

His wife flung herself into Lochlan's arms. "I knew twas you. I just knew it, as I stood and watched on the steps."

"Tis me, lass. Tis me." Lochlan hugged her close. "The last I saw, you were asleep in fits and starts alongside a warm fire on the mountain. How do you fare?"

"There is much to tell." Bonnie smiled, turning to Braeson. "And to hear."

Tokie started whinnying again, demanding Bonnie's

attention. She turned and hurried to the pony's stall murmuring unintelligible sounds.

Williem stepped forward, a grin spreading on his flushed face. "The men are assembling, Braeson. The festivities are to begin."

"Ah, the festivities." Perchance his opportunity to speak with Lochlan would have to wait. He turned to the older man. "Bonnie and I will marry on the morrow." He saw the confused gaze on Lochlan's face. "Bonnie will explain." Braeson bowed slightly. "Until then."

He walked to Bonnie and took her hand. Her warmth seeped into his heart and eased his confusion, his uncertainty about his sire.

Tokie snorted in protest.

"I'll see you on the morrow, my Silkie," he whispered into her shining eyes and went to join the men for his pre-nuptial festivities.

# Chapter Twenty-Five

The predawn grays teased the shadows, as Braeson leaned over his horse urging it onward to the castle. The prenuptial festivities had proceeded on through the wee hours of the night. He had just left the last of the cottages, completing the Braemoore custom that on the eve of his wedding a groom travelled from cottage to cottage to receive felicitations.

Braeson had lost count of the number of cottages he had visited. He had lost count of the number of men he had left behind at the cottages. Men who had made merry with too much drink. Strange that he could not tolerate strong liquor. He had toasted the festivities, feigned a sip of the liquor and galloped onward with his companions to the next cottage, congratulatory salutations following at his back. Had he learned this lack of taste from his father? Even though their physicality was different, were their mindsets and behaviour similar? He recalled Jack's words from all those days ago when he had pulled Braeson from the midnight water. *Your father's mark is seared on you.*

Braeson raced along a low ridge that looked over the valley. He hoped to speak with Lochlan in these early hours and continue the conversation of the night before. He wanted answers to his questions, to secrets that must come to light for his own peace of mind. Crossing behind the valley, he recognized movement amongst the MacEwen men that were camped there. They were readying for their return trip to Scotland. He urged his horse onward, determined to reach the castle and to stay Lochlan MacEwen's departure.

Braeson signaled from a distance for the castle gate to be lifted and only slowed his horse when he entered the courtyard. Passing the reins to a guardsman, he strode along the narrow pathway and into the pony shed, passed Tokie's stall and—

"Good God!" he roared.

The scene jarred his gut. For a man whose stomach was empty of strong drink, a wave of nausea blurred his vision for a moment. Why was his mother helping Lochlan MacEwen don his shirt? Why was she touching his face and pushing back his hair? Nay, she was caressing his face! And Lochlan was gazing at his mother with such devotion . . . These two people were supposed to be strangers, by God. Yet they were behaving like lovers!

As his mother swung around, startled by his intrusion, Braeson drew his sword. He rushed at the man who dared to look at his mother with such adoration.

"Timothy!" His mother panicked as she and Braeson stepped into the same pathway. She to protect the man Lochlan and he to skewer the man Lochlan.

His mother, though small, blocked his path and Braeson staggered back, dropping his sword to his side. His throat tightened, his breath caught, and he stared speechless at this woman, his mother, and at Lochlan. The man rubbed his hands over his face then turned and opened the wooden slats that covered the small shed window.

Beyond the pony shed, the meadow's jewelled greens sparkled with morning dew announcing that day's light had broken through the mists of the predawn gray. Braeson sneered at the scene. The dawn had also broken through his muddled thoughts and revealed the secrets of his own lineage. In the light of day, they stood before him. He shoved his sword into its scabbard and then slid his eyes to the woman who blocked his path.

"Mother?"

"Lochlan! Lochlan!" Bonnie bellowed as she rushed through the shed door. "I wanted to bid farewell before—"

Braeson extended his arms outward to block and silence his wife. She skidded to a halt beside him, both of her hands grasping his arm. Then, she leaned against it as if he were the support holding her up before this strange scene. Yet he was most certain it was Bonnie who was keeping him upright.

"Braeson?" she whispered on a breathless gasp.

"Mother?" Braeson repeated. "Explain your—"

"I will speak." Annella's firm words floated into the quiet shed. "I will speak. And you, my son of Braemoore, must listen."

His mother's eyes flittered to Bonnie and she looked back at Lochlan who remained like a statue, still gazing out the window. Then her eyes settled on her son, who now wondered if he really wanted to know the truth of his birth. Perchance continuing to live the idyllic life here at Braemoore was the better option.

"Ne're in my wildest dreams did I dare believe that the last hours would bring to us a memory so clear. I stand here still wondering if it is but a dream." Her voice was just above a whisper. It fluttered to Braeson on the breeze that entered through the window of the shed and flickered her golden hair that fell past her shoulders.

Braeson could not recall a time when he had ever seen his mother with her hair unadorned. It was not proper for a Lady to be undressed in public, as she was now, standing bare-footed in her grey woolen gown, shawl around her shoulders. He looked to where Lochlan stood and he spied her slippers against the wall.

"Mother, let us go to the keep and—"

"Nay," she stated. "Tis my moment to speak and I shall." She stared at Braeson, hands clutched before her. She held her small frame stoically. "I will share with you a story, my story, which I have held close to my heart forever." Her voice was soft now, a murmur, yet clear. "I give naught an excuse for all that happened. I give you only your truth, Timothy." She paused. "Truth."

Oh, how Braeson wanted to turn his horse away from this storm, from the lightning and thunder that was rolling in and about to strike, to roar, and bring the rain. Yet he could not. This was not the boyhood game he had played with his father. He had raced through the predawn light to this place, into the storm to learn the truth, his truth.

He drew a deep breath and waited for the rain to fall.

"My sire, Angus Campbell, was a cruel man," his mother began.

Braeson watched as a shadow of fear skittered across her face and she closed her eyes for a moment. When she opened them, she was again the brave, stoic woman that Braeson recognized and knew. From his earliest memories, his mother had always been a calm, uncomplaining woman who had served well his father and the people of Braemoore.

"You met him only once, Timothy. You will remember that he visited when you were eight years of age. Upon his arrival to Braemoore, within hours of meeting you, he waylaid us in the library, making harsh accusations. He was a physical man. Many lived in fear of his temper, even my mother, I recall. My sire attempted to strike you and I stepped into his path and received the blow in your stead. Your father, Moorey, would have killed him, I am told. In the end, Moorey forbade anyone in my family to return to Braemoore. He told my sire never to step into England again if he held dear his life. That is why you can understand my amazement when a fortnight past you returned to Braemoore with my brother, Iain.

A small sliver of regret slithered around Braeson. He should have left Iain Campbell in Scotland. The Campbells continued to wreak havoc at Braemoore.

"My sire's heart was hard and unbending. I, being his only daughter, he viewed as a pawn to be used to strengthen his power. My marriage to your father was negotiated in order to extend my father's influence into England—for trade, political favours and the power he so desired. He was a threat to my life and to any other who attempted to interfere. I was, against my will, packed and bound and brought to Braemoore at fifteen years of age to marry your father. I was terrified. Sick in mind and heart. Frightened in my soul of the unknown." She shook her head. "I never saw or heard from my father again until that fateful day eight years later."

Braeson recognized the signs and actions of one facing battle, of one who was striving to maintain control over mounting feelings of uncertainty and fear. His mother's calm composure was being challenged by her haunting story. She swallowed several times, taking deep breaths, fighting the terror of long past memories. Perchance his mother was the strongest warrior in Braemoore, as she now battled the tears that glistened in her eyes. Only one tear escaped and Braeson followed its path as it slid down her quivering face. It dropped from her chin and landed on her toe, which was peeking out from beneath her gown. When he returned his gaze to her face, the stoic warrior stood before him again.

"My new husband was also young," she continued. "Eighteen years, and as naïve as I was. Kind and true, as were his parents. I was amazed that a family could be dedicated to each other and their people without a vain motive. Even when I became sick after the wedding and was soon found to be pregnant, all kindness and patience was extended to me. I could not fulfill my role as the Mistress of the house. I did not recover to full health until after you were born. I believe my illness had much to do with my broken-heart. Grief for the one I left behind on the mountain."

Bonnie's tightening grasp on Braeson's arm made him turn to her. Her face was pale. He had wanted to speak privately with his mother about his discoveries before he shared his secrets with his wife. Now, he regretted the lost chance. Bonnie stood motionless, staring wide-eyed from Lochlan to Annella. Her ragged breath revealed her own swirling emotions about this unexpected account of his early years.

When Braeson looked again at his mother, she was staring away into a space in the shed as if remembering a long ago memory. He was uncertain whether he should prompt her to continue. She had accomplished enough in her battle for one day. This conversation could continue later. As he readied to suggest this idea, she turned again to him and lifted the corners of her mouth in an attempt to smile.

"I lay for days after you were born staring at my babe with the pale eyes. Moorey described your eyes *as pale as the silver moon.* I ne'er said a word to a soul that your eyes matched the eyes of the one I left behind, so far away, in Scotland." His mother's eyes widened. "Not even to Maeve, dear friend, for fear of retribution. My life was not worth much to me, but your life now was priceless. When I gained my strength, I rode out one day on my own, through the gate, over the bridge and tore across the valley. I entered the forest, fell to my knees, and wept and wept, thanking God in Heaven for giving you to me. You were like a healing balm that soothed my grief and gave me hope. Moorey found me there, asleep under a spruce. He took me back home and I became a dutiful wife and Mistress to Braemoore."

His mother lifted a corner of her shawl and wiped it across her face, much like a warrior after a battle, Braeson thought, cleaning off the stains of war.

"But enough of me," she concluded. "Moorey loved you from the moment he set his eyes upon you. All of Braemoore rejoiced over your birth. You, Timothy Lennox Moore, became Braemoore's son and soon you were Braeson to all.

A genuine smile lifted his mother's lips this time, spreading across her face in her recollection of life at Braemoore. Braeson knew that smile was always accompanied with a tilt of her head. As it did now.

"You were Moorey's and Moorey became yours. Your father and you had similar interests and tastes. How proud was your father to set his son upon a horse for the first time. Your physicality was evident and you thrived at Braemoore."

She continued to smile at him, chuckling low. He knew that she would throw in a slip of humor for him in hopes of making him smile too, to lighten this incredible tale for a moment.

"You were but three months old when your father sat you upon a horse for the first time. He had ridden into the courtyard and I was standing with you on the bottom step. Moorey bent down from his horse as if to whisper something to me." Her smile grew as she shook her head. "Instead, he lifted you from my arms. Moorey, I said, no, he is too small, too small. You cannot put a babe—"

Her smile faded. Her words trailed away. "I miss him . . . Moorey."

She dabbed at her eyes with her shawl. Those were the only words of grief for his father that Braeson had heard his mother utter. She had always held her emotions tightly to herself, like a stoic soldier should. After Moorey's death, she had carried on in a more hurried fashion as if striving to fill the loss with activity.

Here she stood before her son, unadorned and allowing him a glimpse into her wounded heart. He had been so immersed in his own grief for his father that he had failed to provide his mother with a measure of comfort.

"After I was struck by my sire, I am told that Moorey

sat beside my bed for two days, you upon his knee, willing me back to life. When I awoke, guilt overwhelmed me. Would my secret drive everyone from me?"

Braeson felt Bonnie move away from him, even before she dropped her hands from his arm and took a step back. When he looked at his wife a shadow of fear had settled on her face. It was similar to the shadow that had crossed his mother's face at the beginning of this tale. As he extended his arm to pull her to him, his mother's words interrupted his attempt.

"I tried to explain to Moorey the truth of your birth." Annella smiled. "I tried to tell Moorey why my sire was filled with such wrath. Moorey had been too kind and true to me, a woman who was living a lie beside him. On my final attempt to explain the truth, Moorey placed a finger over my lips. 'Nay, Annella, my love. All is well. Braeson is well. Braemoore is well. And, above all, you are well.' In that moment, I knew that my truth could destroy all that I loved—you, Braemoore, Moorey." She looked at Lochlan for a moment and then turned her gaze to Braeson again. "And all that I loved in Scotland. I tucked the truth away. From that day on, I gave to Moorey not only my devotion, but also my loyalty, my honour, all that was possible for me to give."

Braeson turned his gaze to Bonnie as she stirred beside him. She stood with her arms crossed tightly to her body as if preventing an escape of something that she held dear. His chest tightened and when he reached for her, to draw her into the protection of his arms, she took another step away from him.

"Braeson. You, Lochlan and Bonnie are the only people to hear my story, your story. Lochlan only became aware of your existence a few weeks past when you journeyed to Scotland to purchase the ponies. It is there your story began six and twenty years ago. For there, a young girl-woman, Annella Campbell, fell in love with a young boy-man, Lochlan MacEwen. My sire was opposed to anyone who showed interest in me. Lochlan and I kept our love hidden, wandering the valleys and crags of the mountain, dreaming of our life together." She looked at Braeson silently as if readying him for her final words, yet he already surmised what she would say. "A day before my sire forced me from my home in Scotland, Lochlan and I were married before an altar of an old stone kirk deserted years past. Before God in heaven and our ancestors past, we exchanged our vows. The ring that Bonnie wears on her finger is the same ring that Lochlan gave to me on our wedding day. The marriage was consummated. When I journeyed to England I was already married. I was already with child . . . with you."

## Chapter Twenty-Six

Bonnie gasped as Braeson turned abruptly from his mother and from her, and stormed from the shed. Even Tokie whinnied in reproach, as the door slammed and then rattled. She held her breath and stared at Lady Annella, who stood with her head bowed and hands clasped, and at Lochlan, motionless and silent. Then, she turned and ran after her husband, down the pathway and into the bailey. As she looked up determined to find him, a rider on a horse swooped down alongside her and grabbed her about the waist.

Bonnie struggled for a moment as the rider seated her upon the horse in front of him. Panic rose from her stomach into her throat. It was the same feeling that had overtaken her at Rose Keep and at the river's edge when she had been accosted by the evil men.

"Be still, Bonnie," the horseman whispered into her ear.

Braeson! The panic quickly subsided to be replaced

with frustration. She resented being snatched without her consent.

Braeson galloped through the gate and over the bridge. His arm tightened around her as he turned the horse into the strengthening wind. They raced across a flat span of terrain, the horse stretching its neck and lowering its head as Braeson gave it full lead to gallop down into a small vale and up onto a ridge of rock. They dashed through a span of trees and onto a great expanse of flat land. The vast region was dotted with dirt and tufts of grass that melted into a faraway horizon. Turning, they ascended a small hill and Braeson brought the horse to a sudden stop. Bonnie gasped at the scene before her. They rested at the edge of a cliff that stood high above the ocean. It reminded Bonnie of her Scottish home where, far above the rocky cliffs, Rose Keep stood like a sentinel against the elements that had battered it over the centuries. She gazed out across the ocean—the same ocean of her faraway home—and frowned at the rolling clouds that were steadily advancing to shore.

Braeson dismounted in one swift motion and then helped Bonnie from the horse. The feral look on his face dampened her own frustration at being snatched against her will. She dipped under the horse's head to distance herself from him. She could understand his anger and his shock after hearing the story of his lineage. She lifted her hand to caress the horse's mane and wondered how best to comfort Braeson.

"I became aware of my lineage a few weeks past," Braeson stated. "When I met Iain Campbell at the small inn, the truth of my heritage was revealed." He grasped her hand and now their entwined fingers rested as an arch over the horse's neck.

His words surprised Bonnie. She had thought his wild expression displayed his anger at the story Annella had shared. Yet he spoke calmly. When she peeked over the horse's neck, he still held a savage countenance. Something agitated him. If not his mother's story, then what?

"I had hoped to speak with Lochlan this morn, to flesh out the identity of my sire. Now, that too has been revealed," he concluded.

Twas a strange tone in his voice—almost mundane. It did not match the expression on his face. She pulled her hand away and scurried under the horse's neck to face Braeson.

"You are upset with this truth of your sire?" For certain, it was this fact that explained his anger.

"I am the son of Timothy Lennox Moore, Bonnie. Aye, Lochlan sired me. Yet my father's mark is seared so deeply upon me that I cannot be rattled by my paternity. I am not upset."

Mayhap the expression on his face was one of

frustration. But, if the truth had not upset him then what had. "Something angers you?" she questioned.

He stared at her for a time. The struggle to calm himself flashed in his eyes and flared at his nostrils. Then he tucked a strand of hair behind her ear. "As my mother shared her story, you stepped away from me, bit by bit." His final statement was filled with questions. "It was as if you were leaving me."

Panic rose from her stomach and a cold breeze wafted around her heart. "Nay. I am here and we will marry in a few hours, Braeson." She grasped his hand hoping to find warmth. "As we have promised." In the shed, she had thought him too focused on his mother's story, to have seen her own reaction to Annella's tale.

"Even as my mother spoke her truth, you pulled away from me, Bonnie." His breath caught on the last word leaving her confused. "You even refused the arm I extended to you as comfort. My mother's story is similar to your story, is it not?" Braeson stated. "You too were snatched from your home, forced to marry a stranger, one you did not love." She felt his hand twitch and then settle into a rhythmic caress as his thumb brushed along the palm of her hand.

"Nay, I did not marry a stranger. De Ros, Lochlan, Brianna gave me to . . . a MacEwen. They are MacEwens. For certain, not a stranger." She turned to the horse and caressed its neck. Bonnie wondered how she had not recognized Braeson for what he was, a MacEwen. Yet all those days ago at Rose Keep and all the happenings there, had frightened her and left her suspicious of anyone she did not know.

"My mother's story was alarming and it disturbed you. I saw it in the way you clasped your arms around you. Holding yourself so tightly. You looked scared. Curling inward as if you were hiding. What are you hiding from? Someone, something?" He stepped closer to her and frowned. "Do you hold a secret?"

Bonnie's startled gaze darted to Braeson. He raised his brow at her sudden reaction to his words. She recognized the cold that embraced her heart for what it was—fear. It was fear that she would be forced to reveal her own truth—that she loved him! She recalled the moment Lady Annella's words triggered her withdrawal—*I knew that my truth could destroy all that I loved . . . I tucked the truth away.*

Braeson was edging too close to her truth, her hidden truth. Bonnie needed to feign indifference and push him away . . . again. "Aye, your mother's story is frightening and aye, I reacted to . . . to . . ." She needed a distraction, something to turn him away from his intense focus on her. Even his silver eyes seemed to flash metallic. "Tis not Annella to blame for being forced from her home to marry a second husband and commit bigamy," soothed Bonnie. She breathed inwardly feeling rather cowardly for suggesting such an idea. Yet it was a diversion.

"There was naught bigamy," growled Braeson as he took another step closer to her. "Secret vows proclaimed before the dead makes naught a marriage."

Hastily, she made the sign of the cross and stared at Braeson, watching as his eyes narrowed in protest.

"The union was consummated on the mountain before our Lord," she exclaimed. "Tis a marriage!"

Braeson leaned closer and captured her against the horse's flank. "A bigamist? I think not." He nestled his lips against her neck. "An innocent girl whose sire, Angus Campbell, will be held accountable before *our Lord*." He mimicked her tone when he spoke the final words.

Bonnie was not deceived. Braeson's tension was palpable in the tautness of his body, a silent refusal to relax against her. She lightly massaged Braeson's back in hopes of chasing away his tension and this frightening conversation.

In a tone almost inaudible, he spoke. "What secret do you hold? Your silent protest of being forced into an unwanted marriage?" He stilled, only his breath gently tickled beneath her ear.

Oh, how wrong he was, and oh, how much she wanted this marriage. He was unrelenting and was pushing her toward forbidden ground. She did not want to talk about her feelings for this marriage. It pushed her too close to speaking words of truth, of love and blessings and her hopes for a forever happiness with him. These words were not necessary to be spoken aloud. Such words were sure to be a curse to force her, this Silkie, to leave, to run again from love. She had lost Ina and her people at Rose Castle whom she had dearly loved. She could not lose Braeson. But if she spoke about her love, somehow, as in her past, she would someday be forced to leave him.

"It matters not," Bonnie protested.

"It does matter. You must speak now before we exchange our vows," Braeson growled.

She shoved Braeson just enough to skitter around him and run along the cliff edge. She stopped and stared out at the sea. The storm was moving closer. Her skirts twirled about her ankles and her cape flapped in the wind. The gray sea appeared deadly calm in contrast to her own pounding heartbeat.

"A storm approaches," she said and turned toward the horse to race from the storm but Braeson blocked her way. "For certain, Maeve is waiting to tend to my bath and making preparations for our second marriage." She smirked in an attempt to be coy and to disguise the shadow of fear that was clamping down on her heart. Hearts could break. She knew this. She was sure hers would never mend if she had to leave him.

"I have only known my mother as a brave and quiet woman." Braeson's voice edged toward anger. "To witness her relive her story of that time, six and twenty years ago, wrenched my heart." He drew a deep breath and reached out tugging Bonnie closer to him, his hands on her elbows holding her in place. "The look of terror that crossed my mother's face as she spoke of her sire is unforgettable. She carried secrets that could not be shared for fear of repercussions." He stared at Bonnie, his eyes, icy grey, reflecting the coming storm. "Too much to lose. Too much to protect. A son, a husband, Braemoore and a young man-boy in Scotland." He ran the back of his fingers alongside her face, gently, soothingly, enticingly. "When I look at you and talk to you of my love, I see the same fear that crossed my mother's face just a short time ago." He leaned his face closer to her. "It was the same look of fear, of terror, that crossed your face as you stepped away from me in the shed."

The fear crushing her heart was no longer a shadow but a dangerous enemy. "I know naught of what you speak," she lied. She recalled the times over the past fortnight when Braeson expressed his love for her. She had pressed her mouth shut. Even bit her tongue once to prevent herself from speaking her own words of love to him. Aye, she loved him dearly. She pulled at his arm. "We must race back to Braemoore to outrun this storm." And to outrun the storm that was brewing within her.

He blocked her path and held her gently at her waist. "When I was a boy, my father and I would ride to this spot and watch the storm. At the first flash of lightning, we'd turn our horses and gallop toward Braemoore in our attempt to outrun the storm." Braeson turned then and stared out to sea, assessing the weather. "I have seen the fear in your eyes, Bonnie, when I speak of my love for you. It has me confused, this fear." He turned back to look at her. "It was only when I witnessed my mother's terrified expression and heard her story that my eyes were opened. What is your secret? What do you fear?"

Bonnie stumbled backward. Turning, she ran along a path away from the cliff. She would run back to Braemoore if that is what it took to avoid Braeson's questions. She could not tell Braeson her most treasured secret, her most treasured fear. She would lose again. Tears slid down her face and blurred her vision. Hair, tangled from the heightened winds, whipped around in her face and reflected the intense wretchedness that tore her breath away—wretchedness that she had known only twice before, when she had lost Ina and then, her people at Rose Keep.

Lightning lit the darkened sky. Hands captured her

at her waist and spun her around.

"Release me!" she demanded. Her feeble push showed that her energy was seeping away leaving only a desperate, broken heart. "Look yonder," she pleaded. "The storm is upon us."

"I will not release you," Braeson said. Gently he pushed the hair from her face, wiping the tears from her eyes with his thumb. "Bonnie," he whispered, "We cannot run from the storm. We are stronger when we face it together. How long will you keep a secret that terrifies you? Six years, six and twenty years?" He shook her gently and then pulled her to him, a breath away from his face. A drop of rain hit her nose and dripped off the end. It landed on her lip and trickled down her chin. Another and another dropped on her. She struggled again to get away and to run for the protection of a rock wall, but Braeson pulled her even closer.

The rain flattened her hair, drenching her garments. When the thunder rumbled, she watched as Braeson raised his face to the sky. The rain pebbled his beard with glistening water drops. Then he was kissing her, exerting pressure so that she opened her mouth to him. Tears and rain mingled with their lips. He kissed each eye and traced a line of light caresses along her cheekbone to her ear.

"I cannot bear to watch your pain when we talk of

our marriage, Bonnie. I feel it, deep and sharp, and I would take it from you if I could. Is it your lost heritage that haunts you, terrifies you? I reassure you again that we will strive to find your sisters and follow a path to your heritage. Already a missive has been sent to De Ros." He cupped her face between his hands. "I love you. Let us begin our marriage sharing joys and bearing our fears together."

His caresses warmed her and drew her closer into his safe embrace. Twas true, this is where she belonged, in the shelter of Braeson's arms, of his love. The fear began to uncoil around her heart. Together they were stronger to face the storm. They stood wrapped in each other's arms as the rain slackened, the winds subsided and then only the drips from the nearby rock ledge disturbed the silence. A light breeze danced around them. When she lifted her head to look into Braeson's eyes, she felt a lightness of heart and spirit. The fear had fled away with the storm.

"Braeson, those whom I have loved, I have always had to leave. Ina, Brianna, De Ros, Lochlan and Caol." She closed her eyes and remembered again their faces, the times past and then smiled. "This foolish Silkie feared to speak of love. If I kept my love for you a secret, then this time, mayhap I could stay at Braemoore forever, never to leave, always to love you." She watched as understanding dawned in Braeson's eyes. "Aye," she continued. "I was terrified, if I spoke the truth of my love, I'd be forced to lose everything— love, home, hearth and you." She brushed back his damp hair from his forehead and peered into his gray eyes, so clear and translucent with love for her. "But now I will speak my truth—our truth. Braeson, I love you."

Braeson pulled her closer. "My love, my Silkie. You have found your home, a safe haven. I have been waiting for you a lifetime."

The sound of galloping horses alerted them. They turned and saw two riders approach in the distance. One rode with his plaid scarf wrapped securely around his face.

"Lochlan," Bonnie whispered. She pulled Braeson to her, kissed him and then ran to the horses that had come to a stop near them.

Lochlan dismounted and embraced her. "We return to Scotland." He looked beyond her to where Braeson stood holding the reins of his horse. "I come to bid you farewell." He pulled a length of ripped plaid from the folds of his cape and walked with her to where Braeson stood. "We return to MacEwen Keep, Braeson. I've come to wish you both well."

Frowning, Braeson looked beyond Lochlan. "Iain Campbell is riding with you?"

"Lady Annella has reassured me that she has

spoken to him, and negotiated with him, last eve. There are enough MacEwen riders to keep Campbell on the narrow path as we return to the Highlands." Lochlan smirked. "But, me thinks that Jack persuaded him the most to see the error of his ways. Jack would not tell what he did but it seems that Campbell has seen the light. It is my hope that Campbell is not a blind ass any longer."

"We pray so, Lochlan." Again, Braeson looked at Campbell who sat on his horse a distance away. "Some of the Campbells are wiley characters, as you well know."

Lochlan's expression turned serious. "Surely the MacEwen men can influence him toward improved character as we ride north."

Lochlan held out the length of narrow plaid. It reminded Bonnie of a hair ornament that some of the women wore in the Highlands. "A gift," Lochlan said and lifted Bonnie's arm, nodding to Braeson to do the same. Wrapping the cloth around their wrists, he then made the sign of the cross above their joined hands. "Lady Annella will explain the story about this ribband."

Lochlan turned and walked to his horse. He looked back once, bowed his head slightly and gave a final farewell wave.

Braeson chuckled, drawing Bonnie from her sense

of awe at all that she had learned this day about Lochlan, Annella and Braemoore.

"I think, Braeson, that amazing things happen at Braemoore." Bonnie shook her head and smiled at Braeson as he leaned closer and kissed her.

"I was confused by your fear. I wondered, perchance, that you too had left another husband on the mountain," Braeson teased.

Bonnie giggled. "My Lord." she curtsied. "I also will soon have two husbands." She could not contain her laughter as she watched Braeson feign a sobering frown. "One I married at Rose Keep under protest and the other I will marry at noon willingly." She placed her hands around his shoulders and relished in the warmth of his low rumbled chuckle. "And they both look like you, my Lord."

Bonnie squealed joyfully when Braeson scooped her up, kissed her and placed her upon his horse.

They raced to Braemoore to ready for the noon nuptials.

## Chapter Twenty-Seven

Bonnie stepped from the large metal tub and reached for the cloth to dry herself. The warmth from the long and luxurious bath encircled her as she patted dry her limbs and torso, and wrapped the white towel around her head, tucking her damp hair under it. She looked for her nightgown, a beautiful silk garment that she had found in her pack a few days past, likely placed there by Brianna for such a night as this.

Laughter and music mingled with the nighttime sounds of faraway crickets and the cooing of doves that perched on the frames outside the windows. The celebration would continue into the wee hours of the night, Lady Annella had explained as she encouraged Bonnie to make her escape from the wedding festivities. Bonnie had been unable to find Braeson when she had looked for him before her departure to their chambers. He would likely be along soon, Annella had reassured her.

When Bonnie had entered Braeson's bed chamber, there was evidence that he had arrived before her. In front of the fireplace, two tubs had stood filled with water. Around one, splashes of water were scattered on the floor. A soap bar floated on the surface. Obviously, Braeson had made his escape from the festivities before her and had already bathed. Where was he, she wondered, as she scanned the screened area looking for her nightgown? Mayhap he was already in their new chambers awaiting her.

A few days past, the master chambers had been readied for Braeson and his bride. This room now was a side room off the master bed chamber. Its bed still remained yet it would be used only for bathing and other ministrations. Another quick glance, and then Bonnie remembered that she had placed the nightgown over a chair in the master bed chamber that morning as she readied for the day.

She reached for the seal skin blanket that lay across a bench and wrapped it around herself. She had hoped to greet Braeson in a lovely silk garment rather than her seal skin. Mayhap she could silently enter the master chamber and quickly don it.

She pulled the seal skin tighter around herself to capture the warmth from the bath and stepped around the tub. Her pearl necklace danced in the heat from the fireplace. When she had lain quietly recovering from her fever and bruises, she had watched the necklace dangling from a hook on the wooden mantel, its familiar presence soothing her. She had said naught a word about it, associating it with too much angst. But those days were now behind her.

This day had been wonderful. She had smiled throughout the ceremony, in part because she loved Braeson so and believed in their happy future. In part, because she remembered their first wedding and her state of mind that day. She chuckled and shook her head. Brianna, De Ros and Lochlan had taken quite a chance sending her to England with a MacEwen. She'd have to ask Brianna someday how long they had believed it would take before she realized they had married her to their 'own'—another MacEwen. Brianna's words floated to her, *Out of darkness comes many treasures, lass.* Twas true.

Bonnie looked again at the dangling necklace. Twas hers, her heritage. She gingerly lifted it from its hook and held it high. The translucent colours of pink and blue sparkled on the white pearls' surface. Bonnie studied her reflection in the mirror above the mantel as she placed the necklace around her neck. She brushed her hand along it, stopping where the diamond should have lain.

Braeson had described the beauty of the diamond.

It must have been lost on that day when the necklace had spilled from his leather sack and the final assailant had accosted her. Even without the diamond, the necklace was beautiful. Pearls and silk would be a perfect way to greet her husband on this special night. She felt her body warm and a nervous jitter ran up from her belly to her heart. Tonight, they would consummate their marriage.

Bonnie skirted around the screen toward the door to the master bed chamber when a noise, a murmur, drew her back and she scanned the room a final time. A bed drape moved slightly and then settled again. Frowning, Bonnie walked over to the bed and peeked around the drape.

Braeson!

He lay asleep on his back, head turned to the side. His black hair glistened, still damp from his bath. One arm was flung across his face and the other placed on his abdomen. She had seen him without clothes only once before at the Inn when they were still in Scotland. But she had hardly dared to look, those many days ago, being still consumed with her disbelief at being his wife.

But now, Bonnie stood and admired him. Long muscled limbs were covered by fine dark hair, similar to the hair on his chest that narrowed into a thin line past his belly button to—

She frowned. A white towel, similar to the one she wore on her head, lay crumpled over Braeson's midsection, partly on him and partly on the bed. Yet it still covered enough of him to cause her to take a deep breath and call on her patience.

Bonnie giggled, pulling the towel off her head, allowing her damp hair to fall around her shoulders. The night was still young and the revelry outside the window indicated that Braemoore's people were still in high spirits.

Braeson murmured and as he flung the arm off his face, a sparkling object spilled from his hand. His eyes opened instantly on Bonnie's gasp. His silver eyes stared at her and then scanned the room. She watched his consciousness grow as a slow smile widened his mouth and displayed his straight white teeth. He moved faster than the knife he had flung on the cliff days before to save her. He sat up, feet landing on the floor and pulled her to him. His hands found the opening in her seal skin blanket, brushing over her hips and then caressing her lower back and bottom.

"Bonnie." His face nestled into her arms that were grasping the seal blanket tightly around her. A warmth infused her body making her want to draw even closer to him. But, wrapping her arms around him would make her drop her blanket. Oh, how she wished she'd remembered the silk nightgown. Pearls and silk would make this moment perfect.

She smiled. "You sleep." Oh, how Earl English's roaming hands were causing her to tremble.

Braeson smiled back. "Not any more," he said, abruptly withdrawing his hands.

She gasped again, frowning, bereft of their absence. Reaching back, he lifted the sparkling object from the bed and then turned back to her, dangling it from his finger. He stared at it for a moment and then smiled at Bonnie again.

"The . . . the diamond?" She stumbled over her words. A single strand of pearls hung over his fingers and a diamond, the size of her thumbnail, dangled from its middle. She knew instantly it was the matching piece to the necklace she was wearing.

"You found it?" Bonnie questioned. "I did not see it when the contents of your pack were strewn over the ground." She touched the pearl strand and gingerly poked the diamond, making it spin.

"Twas never on the mountain, this part of the necklace," Braeson explained. "But safely tucked away in this castle's strongbox for many years."

Bonnie felt her stomach tighten, confused by Braeson's words.

"Many years ago, my father found it on the northeast shore of the expanse of sand we looked down upon this morn. He was riding his horse along the beach and spotted something sparkling in the sand." Braeson twirled the diamond gently, then looked back at Bonnie, smiling.

Bonnie found it hard to draw a breath with muddled thoughts swirling in her head.

"He tucked it into the strongbox and listened carefully over the years, hoping for a story or sign to direct him to its owner," Braeson explained. "My father thought there was likely a shipwreck and the necklace was lost at sea, only to come ashore with the tides."

"Strongbox?" Bonnie asked, breathlessly.

"The panel directly behind this bed board opens." Braeson nodded to the top of the bed. "Who would ever think of looking for a strongbox behind a bed board? Only my mother, father and I ever knew of the box."

Bonnie's heart beat too fast, making her catch her breath. She fought the tears that threatened to fall. Braeson had married her for the necklace! Not for herself, but for the baubles that dangled from his hand and on her neck. Taking a step backward, she pulled her blanket even closer. She stared at this man who sat on the edge of the bed, looking from her to the necklace as if choosing which he admired more. To rub salt and vinegar into her wound, Braeson sat there as nude as the day he was born, towel on the floor by his feet, incredibly handsome in form and face. She wanted to throw herself into his arms and beg him to love her! Not the necklace!

But she stood her ground and asked the question that needed to be spoken. "You will tell me why you married me," she stated calmly. "The truth. Only the truth must be spoken now."

Braeson squinted at her and his hand shot out quickly grasping her seal-skin and pulling her close again. "You of little faith," he muttered, holding the skin firmly in his grasp.

She watched as he closed his eyes and drew a deep breath. Suddenly, he stared at her again with eyes that battled between the anger of ice gray and something else. She frowned. What was that she saw in his eyes? Pain, like a hurting misty gray that rises on a foggy dawn.

"A wretched void grew inside me after my father's death. When I came to Scotland, I had pulled so inward that my existence was dark and gloomy. Despair reigned." He chuckled, low and deep, dispelling the pain. "Upon my arrival, a Scottish chit attempted to knock some sense into me. She had a saucy mouth. Still does." He smiled. "Her beauty and skill became like an ointment to my wound. Whenever I saw her, I could sense renewal, hope." His eyes reverted to icy gray as he continued. "The day your people offered your hand to me in marriage, I refused." He raised his brows as he watched her frown. "They threw your necklace in front of me, testing my integrity. And I threw it back refusing to be bought, or to buy you, a young, lovely woman. My departure being imminent, despair began to creep in. The light that you offered danced around me." His eyes softened. "Too wide and too deep," he murmured as his hand caressed the side of her face. "I could not leave without you, your joy of life, your love of family, your beauty and courage drew me to you. I took you and left your necklace on the mountain. You brought me back from the dead, to life, to this world where I have been called to love." His hands crept inside her blanket, again resting on her hips and pulling her closer. "I love you. My heart is yours if only you will, for once and for all, accept it."

Bonnie felt like dancing and spinning and flinging herself into Braeson arms. Her heart beat to his words—he loved her, not the necklace!

Braeson held the diamond out to her with a question still in his eyes. "The necklace has been tucked away awaiting this moment. You are its owner. Tis your birthright."

"I love you, Braeson and I promise I will spend all the days of my life showing you." She dropped her sealskin to her shoulders and he placed the strand around her neck, carefully inserting the diamond into its spot on the necklace.

"How could either of us know that the Silkie who lured me into telling her a fairy story would find me and bring me such joy?" Braeson wondered.

Bonnie smiled. Twas a question that they could spend the rest of their lives exploring. How could they be blessed with such joy?

Braeson's hands were caressing her again, over her back, her bottom, down the sides of her thighs, wooing her to join him on the bed. Bonnie remembered the silk garment. Silk, pearls and a diamond would make this moment perfect.

"Come, Braeson, let us go to the master chamber." She held the seal-skin tightly around her. "It has been prepared."

He tugged on her blanket, pulling it lower on her shoulders and placed a kiss between her breasts. "We will get to that chamber sooner or later on this night, my love." He chuckled as he lay back on the bed. "For now, come, my Bonnie Silkie, my beautiful Silkie." His hands reached for her. "And love with me."

Bonnie's hand caressed the necklace. She gazed into Braeson's smoky gray eyes that drew her into his heart, into his love. The seal-skin skimmed her body as it fell to the ground around her feet.

Silkie stepped closer to Braeson and lay herself upon him.

# *Epilogue*

**Three months later**, Scottish Highlands, MacEwen Keep

Lochlan stared at the wooden ceiling of his chamber. What had awakened him? He listened carefully. Twas early, but there seemed to be a clamour in the courtyard below. He rose from his bed and dressed quickly. He never liked to relax in bed when he awoke from his slumber. Lying awake and thinking, always took him back to that day of his clandestine wedding to Annella Campbell. After their loving, they had fallen asleep. When he awoke and found her gone, terror had gripped him. The grief and misery from that time so long ago, six and twenty years, still were unbearable. God, he missed her.

A sudden banging at his chamber door brought him from his musings.

The guard didn't wait for permission to enter.

"Lochlan!" The guardsman, who was also his nephew Davyd, hurried into the room, stopping abruptly when he saw Lochlan standing there, already dressed. "Iain Campbell is at the gate demanding entrance."

Twas always a name that startled Lochlan and brought him to attention. "Iain Campbell? Iain Campbell at our gate?" Lochlan was through the door before Davyd could answer. He took the stairs three at a time and entered the foyer of the keep.

"Are the archer's at the wall?" he questioned. "And why didn't someone wake me immediately upon Campbell's arrival?"

"The archers are at the wall and the guard at the gate reported that Campbell just rode out of the mist these last few minutes," Davyd explained. "He appears to be alone."

"Bloody hell he is! Tis probably a ruse to convince us he is alone," Lochlan scoffed. "Have you forgotten your upbringing, young Davyd? Never trust a Campbell. Likely he has men hiding in the mist or in the forest beyond." Lochlan stood still for a moment, shaking his head. Even though Iain Campbell had returned to Scotland peacefully with him and the MacEwen men, he simply could not bring himself to trust him.

Lochlan ran through the foyer and down the steps of the keep.

"Is the Campbell banner in sight?" Surely one of his guards had seen it waving above the mists. Twould be a sure sign that Campbells were hiding, readying for ambush.

"Nothing else is in sight. Only Iain Campbell sits on a horse before the gates waiting for entrance." Davyd was breathing heavily trying to keep pace with him.

Lochlan mounted the steps that led to the top of the castle wall. It stood higher than the gate's wall and allowed a clear view of the valley that lay in front of the castle. The mist still floated heavily across the land and little could be seen except for the rider who sat directly below Lochlan and Davyd. Lochlan stared at the man for a time, determining his course of action. For God's sake, did Iain Campbell think that a peaceful journey to Scotland meant a truce was established between the two clans? Twas an arrogant choice, to appear on MacEwen land uninvited.

"The archers are prepared to put their arrows to flight, Iain Campbell." Lochlan snorted, inwardly satisfied as Campbell, startled, snapped his head upward. "The warning was cast seventeen years past. A Campbell was never to show his face on MacEwen land." Lochlan raised his hand in signal for the first archer to shoot. The arrow landed to Campbell's right, disturbing his horse which took a few steps sideways.

"Bloody hell, Lochlan MacEwen. You will want to be

mindful of where those arrows alight, for I come in peace and I do not ride alone."

Before Lochlan could signal to the archers, another rider stepped out of the mist, pulled off his hood and peered up. Lochlan's heart slammed into his ribs and he bent over, gasping, with hands on his knees to steady his breathing.

Annella!

When he had bade her farewell three months past in England, there had been no promises spoken. She had been so well established as the Lady of Braemoore that he could not have asked her to return with him. It had broken his heart to leave her . . . again.

Iain Campbell's voice bellowed from below. "Lochlan MacEwen, tis your wedding day. Summon your priest, for today you will be given the hand of Lady Annella in marriage."

"Lochlan?" Young Davyd was studying him closely, while attempting to help him stand upright again.

Lochlan knew himself to be a strong, physical man, yet he willingly accepted Davyd's arm to pull him up and set him to stand against the wall. He peered out again. Was he still asleep? Was this only a dream? That recurring dream where Annella rode out of the mists and came to him.

Smiling, Annella peered up at Lochlan. "Tis I, Lochlan. I have finally arrived to MacEwen Castle."

And Lochlan smiled back at her like a silly, love-sick lad struck mute by her beautiful face.

"MacEwen, open the gate," demanded Iain Campbell. "The marriage will be done properly before a priest and witnesses."

"The gate will be opened, yet only Annella will enter. She has been my wife for all these six and twenty years, Iain Campbell. A priest is not required." No bloody way Iain Campbell would be allowed to step inside the castle wall. Lochlan scanned the valley but still the mists lingered, preventing him from determining if Campbell warriors hid beyond.

"Nay, that cannot be." Iain Campbell sat straight-backed, staring at the gate as he spoke, as if waiting stubbornly for entrance. "Annella has been Lady of Braemoore these past six and twenty years, married to her husband, Timothy Lennox Moore, and is mother to their son. What do you accuse her of, Lochlan MacEwen?"

Lochlan stretched his arms to hold onto the crenelated walls on either side of him and then stared up at the morning sky. Iain Campbell was a clever, wiley character determined to have his way. To make his union with Annella legitimate, Campbell was demanding that a wedding be done in public. To deny the nuptials before witnesses might prompt people to accuse Annella of . . . He shook his head to clear away the terrible thought.

Lochlan and Annella had dreamed of a community wedding all of those years ago. Yet Angus Campbell, Annella's father, had not considered Lochlan a suitable husband for Annella. They had been forced to wed secretly, naively believing that nothing could separate them. The terror and misery that had embraced Lochlan upon awakening all those years ago and finding Annella gone, had eventually evolved into a blanket of melancholia.

Lochlan had endeavoured to find Annella—had travelled into England and even onto the continent. He had hunted for her for years, yet had been unable to gather any clues as to where she had gone. Years later, only when Angus Campbell had attacked the MacEwen Keep, did Lochlan learn that Annella was still alive somewhere. Yet it was only when Annella's son, Braeson, had visited the Highlands in the early spring that he learned where Annella had been. Sheer joy had washed over him, finally after all these years, to learn she was safe.

"It only has to be a short ceremony, my Lord. Aye, with a blessing from the priest." The voice startled him from his thoughts. Jack, Braemoore's lead guardsman, rode out of the mist and settled his horse slightly behind Annella.

"Tis a chill within the early morning mist, my Lord.

Lady Annella and my Maeve are trembling from the cool air," Jack explained, as a fourth rider also appeared from the mist to align herself beside Jack. It was Maeve. It had been Jack and Maeve from whom Lochlan had sought for answers to Annella's disappearance. Yet Jack and Maeve had also mysteriously disappeared all those years ago.

Lochlan looked to the morning's sky and then out across the valley. The sun was breaking through the mist. The dotted heads of the purple thistles were raising their faces to the sun, seemingly rejoicing for this new day. He looked down at Annella, who still peered up at him, smiling. Much had broken through in these past few months. Precious secrets had been revealed. Lives had been changed.

Lochlan signaled to the guardsmen below to open the gate and allow all the wedding guests to enter. Then he rushed down the stairs to welcome his wife.

# Heart Keeper

Read on for a *sneak preview* of
**Book 2** of the

## Keeper Trilogy

# Chapter One

North of the Scottish Highlands, **1600 BC**

Twas no large bird flapping along the high cliff eating grubs and seeds from the stone wall. Twas no piece of ripped cloth from a sail that had caught on a sharp edge of the stone cliff and billowed in the wind.

Indeed! As he watched carefully, the far-away greyish spot was slowly descending the cliff. "Hmm."

Caol had spied it as he had climbed over the rail of the small ship which had carried them north of the Scottish coast to the Islands of Orkney. His eyes had not left the movement on the cliff wall even as he settled into the skiff and sat motionless while his travel companion, Iain Campbell, rowed it toward shore. He was relieved that Campbell had not spied the woman descending the cliff wall. The man's back was to her as he gripped the oars, propelling the rowboat through the choppy waters. In all honesty, he would have no explanation for Campbell, or any person, as to why that woman climbed cliff walls.

As Caol continued to watch her descent, he felt his ire rising. He had taken her at her word, two years past, when she had promised him that she would end this dangerous activity.

The skiff hit a sandbar close to the shore and both he and Campbell jumped into the water and dragged the boat to higher ground. They had travelled to this location to purchase ponies. Twas not a task that Caol had desired, but his father had demanded it of him and now here he was on the shores of Vali Island. The ship that dropped them off would sail again through these waters in a fortnight and return them to mainland Scotland.

Caol turned to his companion. "I would walk along this shore alone for a time before I begin my visit here." Twas somewhat of a lame excuse. But Caol wished to rid himself of Campbell before he ventured to that cliff to catch that woman in her foolishness and wring her neck. He noticed Campbell's frown but the man remained silent as Caol continued. "At the low bush yonder is a path. Twill lead you to the foot trail that brings you atop the cliff. Once there, you will see a croft of stone and peat and with a pointed roof. There live Alan and Ferna. Tell them I will be along shortly."

The frown did not leave Campbell's face as he lifted

his pack and turned toward the path. Caol held his breath as the man walked past the low bush and turned right onto the trail.

Caol turned in the opposite direction, settled his pack on the ground and gazed narrow-eyed at the expanse of beach that led to her. Twas a good distance, indeed. Then he ran, sucking in great breaths of air as he hoisted himself over large boulders that sat along the shore. He sped across the sands and pebbles and propelled himself through a waterfall that poured from a spring high along the cliff edge. He stopped to catch his breath and pulled the leather cape dripping with water from his shoulders and laid it on the ground. He turned to the sea, measuring the level of the tide waters. Still quite low, yet the waters covered the land path. Irritated, he shook his head and then waded into the heaving waves, to waist deep, and journeyed around a jutting rock bend. The shore beckoned him once again and he waded onto its solid ground. He bent over, hands on his knees, breathing deeply and striving to contain his anger.

"Hmm. I am a fool," he muttered. "A besotted fool." He stood upright, anger churning in his gut, as he watched her final descent of about a hundred feet to the ground below. She had tucked her skirt into her waistband and something stirred within him as he gazed upon her shapely legs. He nudged the stray thought away as he strode toward her. "Fool," he growled.

When her toes touched the sand, he grabbed her at the waist and twirled her round so that she stood with her back pinned against the cliff.

"Imbec—" Her whispered word slid across her tongue and ended in a surprised squeak. "Caol!" she breathed, dragging her skirt hem from her waistband and positioning it rightly.

"Sheridan." His hands skimmed up her arms and rested gently on either side of her neck. Her beautiful neck that felt slightly damp from exertion. He felt his anger replaced by fear, coiling in his belly. Fear that always gripped him when he thought of her falling from these high cliffs and finding her wounded on the ground. He could barely allow that other word to venture into his thought. But there it was. Dead. His dear friend, dead on the ground.

Caol gave her a slight shake and strove to take the tremble from his voice, "You promised, Sheridan. You gave your pledge to me—no more climbing cliffs."

She raised her hands quickly and gripped his wrists. Twas his turn to be startled as Sheridan narrowed her eyes, their golden flecks flashing, and stared back at him. She puffed out a breath, readying to speak, he thought. But instead, she scrambled around him, appearing distraught. Or, was that fear shimmering low in her eyes? Confused, he turned to her. "Sheridan?"

She stood looking at him, hands clasped against her abdomen. She rubbed a thumb across the knuckles of the other. "Caol De Ros," she began quietly. "I would ask that you do not speak to me of promises. You were to arrive here, to Vali Island, in the early summer." She raised her face upward to the cliff edge, scanning its horizon. Fear glimmered in her eyes and trembled at her lips.

"The ponies, all of them, were slaughtered." She wiped a hand across her eyes. "Although some also died. A sickness. It spread through the herd late winter, early spring—twas very wet and cold. I begged Vali the Younger to provide me more time. I might have been able to save more." Again she wiped her eyes and then shook her head. "Only two young females remain." She raised her clasped hands to her chest, staring into his eyes. "If only you'd come when you promised, you might have been able to help us. Given us some of your mother's wisdom. What does Lady Brianna do when her ponies fall sick?"

Before he could reply, she turned her face away and pulled her cape tightly about her. "Let us not speak of promises, Caol De Ros."

Now was not the time to explain to Sheridan his reasons for arriving to this Island so late in the summer. He would have to find a more appropriate time to share with her the happenings at Rose Castle. The early spring had brought enemy attacks on his family's land. He had remained to aid in its protection.

Caol reached out and touched her elbow. "Sheridan, I—

She spun toward him and took a single step. "Where were you? I waited so long." She scanned the top of the cliff again. "And could wait no longer. Tis the reason, I am climbing the cliff walls."

Her flashing eyes sobered as he quickly reached out to embrace her, holding her close, waiting for her taut body to loosen, for her fear—or was it anger?—to seep away. He vowed then that he would never challenge Sheridan on promises kept and promises broken.

"Caol?"

He smiled at the way his name skipped across her tongue. Twas melodic, a particular tone and cadence unique to her. "Aye, Sheridan."

"Vali the Younger. He is demanding that I wed him."

The jolt of anger that shot through Caol pushed Sheridan from him. He held her at arms-length, gripping her elbows to steady himself.

"He says I am to blame for the death of the ponies. That Alan and Ferna must pay recompense. Tis I, their daughter, that he wants. My talents and skills with the ponies. He says I can grow the herd back and help the island to prosper again." She tapped her fingers against her temple, shaking her head. "His mind has become imbecile."

Caol frowned at Sheridan's description. Imbecile? Feeble-minded? Nay. He thought not. He knew Vali well. The man had a reasonable and fair logic. Yet, Caol could not understand why Vali should blame Sheridan for the loss of the herd and demand that she marry him. God Almighty! There had to be more to this absurd story than what Sheridan described.

"Tis why I was descending the cliff. Vali vows that when he returns to the island on the morrow we will wed. He will not consider looking beyond this cliff. So, I will hide in a cave, over yonder." Sheridan took several steps along the shore and looked toward an unseen cave . . .

**Journey along with Sheridan and Caol as they continue to unravel the mystery of the three sisters and the treasure.**

## About the Author

Melanie Joye (Climenhage-Nopper) is an educator and writer with experience in elementary and post-Secondary education and holds a Master of Education in Literacy. She lives in Barrie, Ontario, Canada with her family. Melanie enjoys reading biography, history, romance and adventure—themes that are woven into the fabric of her stories. She loves to incorporate into her writings the natural environments where she has lived and which she has explored. In this series, the Keeper Trilogy, the setting is reflective of the Highlands of Haliburton, Ontario and Scotland. As you immerse yourself in these pages, you too will experience the adventure, soak up the rugged beauty and taste the dew of these ancient rocky lands.

Manufactured by Amazon.ca
Bolton, ON